UP IN SMOKE

A KING SERIES NOVEL

T.M. FRAZIER

TM FRAZIER

For everyone who thinks they can't.
You can.

UP IN SMOKE

A King Series Novel
By T.M. Frazier

Cover Photo: Wander Photography
Cover Design: T.M. Frazier
Model: Jacob Rodney

ISBN-13: 978-1985001206
ISBN-10: 1985001209

PROLOGUE

SMOKE

I deal in murder and mayhem.

Bullets and bravado.

Fear and faults.

I crush bones as well as spirits.

I plant seeds from which hatred and sorrow grow.

I'm a man among men, but I'm not really living.

I answer to no one.

I'm heartless. Soulless. Lawless.

Godless.

I'm what's left of humanity after it's burned. After good has succumbed to evil. When lies and lust roam free.

I'm what remains after the flames have been doused.

I'm Hell on Earth.

Brimstone and fire.

Embers and ashes.

I *am* motherfucking *Smoke.*

CHAPTER ONE

ONE YEAR AGO

SMOKE

Most folks turn out the lights before they go to bed, but not Morgan. For as long as I've known her, she's had this strange habit of keeping her lights on even when she isn't home. She even sleeps with her house lit up like it's her job to guide the god damned planes over to the airport.

That's how I know something's wrong.

Her house is dark.

Way too fucking dark.

Motherfucking shit.

I pull my gun and silently make my way to the front door. It's open. I lean against it with my shoulder and step inside. My boot slides over something slippery. An all too familiar smell singes my nose hairs.

I know the smell of death so well I can decipher the different stages of decay based solely on the stench lingering in the air. With one whiff, I know the death lingering inside is recent.

It's pitch black. I slide my hand against the wall and follow it until my fingertips hit the kitchen backsplash and I flip the light switch above it.

The house is bathed in bright white light. My eyes take a few seconds to adjust. The white shifts to red.

So. Much. Fucking. Red.

"Fuck," I holster my gun.

I've seen a lot of shit in my life. I've caused my fair fucking share of it, too. But nothing like this. There ain't an inch of the kitchen not freshly painted in red. It's smeared across the white tile floor as if someone crawled or was dragged from one side to the other. There's splatter marks on every wall. Every cabinet.

This wasn't just death. This wasn't just a kill. A hit.

This was pure fucking evil.

I round the center island, coming to a stop as my boot connects with a slender bare foot. There's no need for me to hurry over to her; it's not like there's any saving her now, but I shove my gun into the waistband of my jeans and race over to the other side of the island anyway. I crouch down over Morgan.

What's left of her. Every inch of her naked body is twisted and contorted. Her once blemish-free pale skin has been sliced and cut and opened at every angle exposing teeth and skull. Her dark hair is wet with her own blood.

My eyes travel down her battered body. "No," I shake my head in disbelief. "No!"

What's left of her once rounded stomach looks like something put through a meat grinder at the butcher shop. "God fucking damnit!"

I stand but I don't make it to the sink in time, emptying the contents of my stomach around the counter and onto the floor.

I've caused my share of death, but even my brutality has limits. I've never done something like this. Not to a woman at least. Not to an innocent, someone who didn't fucking deserve it. For the first time in my entire life the sight of death makes me physically fucking ill.

I steady myself with my hands on both sides of the sink. "Morgan," I whisper. "Fuck."

I crouch back down and attempt to cradle her in my arms but her body is so hacked up and bloodied I can't get a hold on her. Flesh flops from her bones, falling back to the floor.

"I'm so fucking sorry, kid. I'm so very fucking sorry."

I lie down next to her, getting as close as I can without touching her. My cheek is pressed to the floor. Morgan's still-warm blood clogs my ear, soaking through my clothes and skin. I'm surrounded by all that's left of her. I want it to sink into my bones and stay with me forever.

Morgan is dead. So is our unborn child.

And it's all my fucking fault.

CHAPTER TWO

PRESENT

FRANKIE

I'll be dead within a year.

Probably sooner.

I try not to dwell on the thought because it makes me crazy. Most days I'm seconds away from losing my shit and proclaiming the desk lamp as my new best friend/Queen of England. Being tired doesn't help. It's as if gravity is pulling down on me much harder these days. If I don't get a decent night's sleep soon I'm going to start hearing colors.

We all die after all. My death will just be a little sooner than most. Before the wrinkles have set in and old age has me repeating the same stories over and over again.

My eyelids are heavy. I'm fighting yet another battle in the continuing war against myself to stay awake. My elbow slides further and further off to the side of the desk, my chin propped in my hand.

A scratching sound at the window gives me a jolt. My

spine jumps. I'm jarred awake just before my forehead meets the keyboard.

Feeling under my desk I wrap my fingers around the knife taped underneath.

A shadow crosses the window and I pull my hand away from the blade and blow out a breath.

It's only Izzy, the fat white cat who visits me on a regular basis. She's preening on the other side of the high basement window, her collar scratching against the glass. I don't know who owns her. I only know her name is Izzy because it's written in large lettering on her pink sparkling name tag adorning her equally pink and sparkling collar.

It's just a fucking cat, Frankie.

I rub my eyes with the heels of my hands. My eyelids feel as if they are being weighed down by padlocks. I shake off the tired and the sudden panic and turn back to my work.

The lack of Z's isn't ideal, but so far, it's paid off. My latest project is worth every minute of sleeplessness and then some. If I were the bragging sort I'd call up everyone in my life and tell them about how I single-handedly…well, I guess it doesn't really matter because I *can't* tell anyone.

Plus, there's the little fact that I don't have anyone to tell.

"Izzy," I shout to the cat's shadow. "I'm doing a good thing. A really good thing." The fat cat darts away from the window with an exaggerated leap, most likely startled by a lizard in the grass. "Dick."

Great. Not only am I talking to a cat I don't even own, I'm offended by the fur-ball.

I spend way too much time alone.

Today and yesterday have blended together. I'm not sure where one started and the other ended. The basement has such little light sometimes it's hard to tell if it's day or night.

My phone buzzes on my lap, and I jump like I've been

kicked in the spine, knocking over a stack of paper coffee cups. "Fuck," I swear, looking down at the phone now laying on the ground with a crack across the screen. It's only the alarm.

I'm getting jumpier by the day, but it's not without reason. My work has come with a sacrifice of sorts. I've pissed off a lot of people. The kind most sane people wouldn't dare piss off. I've taken precautions but there might come a day when those precautions aren't enough.

Maybe one day I'll be finished with my work. Finished looking over my shoulder. Maybe, if I'm lucky, I'll even stave off that heart attack threatening to take me under with every startled jump and jolt—well before I've hit the quarter century mark.

Probably not.

I pick my phone up off the floor and swipe my thumb across the screen to kill the alarm. The time can't be right. Has it really been eight hours since I've so much as moved from my chair?

I push back the chair and stand, rolling my shoulders and neck. My back lets out a series of popping cracks that feel a lot better than they sound. My spine protests the shift in position, but I keep stretching, knowing the more I move the better it will feel. I bend at the waist and reach for the floor with my arms straight and my fingers out-stretched. Slowly I straighten, raising my arms, pointing my fingers toward the ceiling. I remain this way until my bones feel like they've shifted back to more of a normal position and aren't all crunched together somewhere in my lower back. A tingling feeling of relief buzzes through my aching muscles.

My legs are buzzing with that pins-and-needles feeling. I make sure to use the handrail as I ascend the stairs so I don't go flying backward since I can't feel my feet. The torturous static feeling thankfully lets up by the time I've reached the door at the top.

I cross through the living room and head for the kitchen. On the way, I stop in the hallway. I kiss the tips of my fingers and reach up to press them against the only picture hanging in the house. A picture of my mother. "Hey Mama," I say, smiling up at her. She had the same long dark hair as I do and the same unique yellow/orange eyes. The picture was taken around the time she died, when I was just a toddler. "I hope I'm making you proud, wherever you are."

My stomach growls, reminding me of where I was heading and I pad into the kitchen. When was the last time I'd eaten? Breakfast? Dinner last night? No, it was definitely breakfast. Breakfast *yesterday*. My stomach growls, louder this time.

"Yeah, yeah. I hear ya," I mutter.

The contents of the refrigerator are…well, there aren't any contents. Unless Google can show me how to make a meal from a half jar of pickles, two slices of cheese, and a six-pack of beer.

I lean on the counter and pull up the GrubTrain grocery delivery app. I order a few essentials, using the last forty dollars in my account.

I use the thirty minutes until the food arrives to go upstairs take a quick, much-needed shower and change into a baggy off the shoulder t-shirt with the logo of my favorite band, Veruca Salt, emblazoned across the front. The grey shorts I change into used to be sweatpants, but when they became frayed from stepping on the bottoms of the too-long legs, I took a pair of scissors to them and *boom*.

Sweat-shorts.

When I'm done, I head back downstairs and sort through the mail. My last name is Helburn, but all the mail comes in the alias name of Jackson. My father had changed it years ago. Insisted it was because of his work with the government.

It was years before I found out that was all a lie.

HE was a lie.

I swallow down the familiar anger rising in my throat. I don't have the time or energy to deal with memories of my father's actions or the mess he's made of our lives and the lives of countless others.

I chuck the junk mail in the trash and set off on the first of my several-times-a-day routine of checking the locks on all of the windows and doors. Flipping open the alarm panel I click in my code and make sure it's in working order.

Twice.

In the master bedroom, I step over my dad's clothes strewn about the floor, walking with purpose over to the window. I check the lock. It's intact. I head back out, shutting the door behind me quickly, releasing a breath I didn't realize I was holding.

Taking the steps two at a time, I head back down to the living room of the two-bedroom, three-level, dilapidated townhouse.

It looks the same as the day we first moved in four years ago. Empty nails from where the previous tenants hung decorations and pictures poke out from the drywall at various intervals. The only furniture, a ratty brown three cushion sofa in the living room—no television— and a couple of mismatched barstools tucked under the raised counter separating the small living room from the equally small kitchen.

The doorbell rings, and even though I was expecting it, I'm still cautious.

I'm *always* cautious.

Standing on my tip-toes I glance through the peephole. On the other end of the brass tunnel is Duke, wagging his eyebrows and contorting his lips around his teeth. I smile because it's impossible not to smile. Duke's carrying a grocery bag in each hand. He holds them up to the peep hole, grinning proudly like a hunter holding up his kills.

Unbolting all the locks on the door takes a while because there are eight of them.

Duke's megawatt smile greets me after I finally open the door.

"Hey," Duke says smoothly. "I saw your order come through, and I wanted to make sure I brought it to you *personally.*" His smile widens and it's is so damn bright it's like staring into the sun. His sandy blonde curls are being cruelly squished by a neon green GrubTrain baseball cap.

Duke raises the bags again, flexing his muscular biceps beneath his matching GrubTrain polo shirt. He winks when he catches me looking at his abs flexing under the fabric. My face warms. He leans in and gives me an awkward hug around the grocery bags. He smells good, like Irish soap.

"Hey, Duke," I say slowly, drawing out my words so he has no choice but to look at my lips. I bat my eyelashes and meet his hazel gaze. "Thanks for bringing those over so fast."

"Anything for you, ma'am," he says with a fake western style drawl.

"Ma'am? Hmmmm…I like the sound of that," I tease, biting my bottom lip.

Duke shifts from one foot to the other, and I realize he's shifting the bags to cover the growing bulge in his pants.

"Is your dad home today?" Duke asks, poking his head through the door and looking around.

"Working in the basement as usual," I say. "Also, ignoring me as usual." I stand to the side and let him in.

"*I* won't ignore you," Duke says suggestively, wagging his eyebrows on his way to the kitchen.

I chuckle and playfully swat at Duke's butt. I'm about to close the door, but I freeze as I'm hit by a hot tingling of awareness. It warms my chest and spreads through to my limbs. My pulse spikes. I slowly push the door back open half expecting to see someone standing on the other side.

There's no one there.

Duke is talking to me from the kitchen, but I'm not listening. Cautiously, I step out onto the little concrete pad of a porch and look around in every direction.

Nothing.

The gas station across the street has a few customers walking in and out. A few kids are playing catch in the empty lot next to the fence that separates it from the convenience store.

The choking feeling in my throat dissipates and I find my ability to swallow again.

Yup. I'm going crazy.

"Sarah? Where did you go?" Duke calls from the kitchen.

I step back inside and shut the door, locking all the bolts out of habit. "You and those damned locks. Your dad really is paranoid, huh?" Duke says, coming up behind me and lifting me off the ground. I kick my feet in the air and laugh. He carries me into the kitchen and sets me down on the center island. He turns his cap backward, takes a joint out of his back pocket. He lights it and takes a long pull.

"Your pops might be paranoid and ignore you all the time, but I think it's fucking awesome he lets you smoke weed in the house," Duke says on an exhale.

I shrug and take the joint from his fingers. Taking a long drag, I hold the smoke deep in my lungs before exhaling slowly. The pot does the trick and within a few seconds the tension eases, my shoulders drop.

"Even if he wasn't okay with it, I doubt he'd notice," I reply, sounding bitter.

"You alright, lady?" Duke asks, searching my eyes for clues.

"I'm fine. I just haven't been sleeping all that great," I admit. It's the shortest explanation of a much larger issue, but Duke and I don't have a big issue kind of relationship. We have a smoke a joint in the kitchen, make out until I send him home kind of relationship.

"Here," he says, pulling a plastic sandwich bag chock-full of joints from his back pocket. GrubTrain is only one of Duke's part-time jobs. A lesser paying one than his main job of weed dealer. He pulls two joints from the bag and places them in an empty coffee tin on the counter. "These are for later. It will help you sleep."

"What do I owe you?" I ask, leaning back on my hand and taking another hit.

"Oh, I can think of things. Actually, I can think of many *many* things." Duke drags his gaze over my body. He lifts his hand to his mouth and playfully bites down on his knuckles, making a growling sound I can't help but laugh at.

With a wink, he moves over to the bags and begins to take things out and put them away. Having been my grocery delivery boy for months now, he knows his way around the kitchen as well as I do. "The weed is on the house, of course," he says.

"Thanks," I say, and I mean it.

Duke's always nice to me. I mean, he's nice to a *lot* of girls, but he's genuine and that's why I've broken my rules and allowed him into my life.

Duke's *the* popular kid at school and a total man-whore. He's stuck his dick in most of the cheerleaders on the varsity and junior varsity cheerleading teams, but he doesn't lie about it, doesn't make them any false promises. Honesty, for me, is the greatest quality a person can possess. I value it above all else. Maybe, it's because I've been forced into dishonesty for most of my life. Maybe, it's because my father's entire life was a lie.

Duke must be reading my mind because he flashes me his Hollywood smile. "Have you heard?" He folds the paper bags and shoves them into the recycling bin. He then launches into an animated retelling of the 'most hilarious'—his words, not mine— dick and fart joke he heard in the weight room from some jock on the football team.

I take another hit from the joint and drop my shoulders. I tilt my head back and exhale toward the ceiling. The front of my brain feels fuzzy. A soft buzz travels to the rest of my body, continuing to dull the sharp edges surrounding me.

"You know, you don't act the same here with me, when we're alone, as you do in school," Duke mentions out of the blue. I'm blinking rapidly as I try to take in what he's saying. "Why is that? You walk around with your hair in your face, staring at the floor all day. You don't talk to anyone. You don't look at anyone. I bet you most of the kids in school couldn't point you out of a line up."

Bingo.

"Not even me," he continues. "You ignore me like you don't even know me. But we're…friends, right? Because here, with me, you're…"

"Normal?" I suggest. "At least, normal-ish?"

Duke shakes his head. "I wasn't going to say that."

Maybe, he wasn't going to use that exact word, but I sensed him searching his mental thesaurus for something comparable.

"Why? Why are you so different here than you are there?" He asks, with what sounds like genuine concern in his voice.

I crook my finger at him like I'm about to tell him all my secrets.

Duke leans in close. My lips are at his ear. "I'm Batman," I whisper.

Duke rolls his eyes and groans at my horrible joke. "Seriously, Sarah. You never come to the games. You don't hang out with anyone else but me outside of school, well, not that I know of anyway."

"Maybe, I'm giving you space," I suggest. It's a lie of course. One of a million I've told Duke over the last several months. "I don't think Missy or Misty or…Maci?" I grimace. "Would like it very much if they saw us together."

"Well, I happen to not give a shit what *Melanie* or anyone else thinks. I like you, Sarah." Duke pushes my knees apart and stands between them. "I like you a lot."

"Melanie," I nod and snap my fingers. "That's it. Melanie. I'll have to remember that one."

I pass him the joint. He takes a long hit, grabs the back of my neck with the hand holding the joint, using the other to press on my cheeks, parting my lips. He blows the smoke into my mouth, our lips only a breath apart. I inhale deeply.

Duke pulls back as I exhale. He presses the glowing end of the joint between his fingers, extinguishing the cherry, tucking it behind his ear.

"I think you like me, too." Duke says softly. He's kneading his fingers gently into my thighs, inching his hands further and further up my legs with each rotation of his skilled fingers.

"I do like you," I tell him. And in another life—no, if I were another person, I might give Duke a real shot.

But not in this life.

"So then, why do you pretend you don't know me?" Duke presses, pursing his lips.

So no one sees us together. So you don't become collateral damage if the shit hits the fan.

"I guess I don't like high school all that much. Plus, I like to keep to myself. That's all," I assure him.

Duke gives me a knowing look. He's not buying it. Not one bit.

I try again. "Or maybe," I sigh dramatically and let my shoulders fall. "I just don't want to be considered one of the many in the Duke Weathersby Harem."

"The what?" he asks with a laugh.

"The harem. The bevy of beauties that run after you, leaving puddles of drool in your wake. Don't pretend you don't know what I'm talking about, Duke Weathersby. I've heard that term a million times so I know you have, too."

"I might have heard it a time or two," Duke admits. A sly smile tugs at the corner of his mouth. He wraps his arms around my waist, pulling me to the edge of the counter. "I mean I guess it's good you don't talk to anyone else. That way, I get to keep you all to myself."

Duke leans in and presses his lips against mine. Our mouths meld and move together. It's an enjoyable kiss, it always is. I liken it to finishing a great book. A nice hot shower. Or finding a killer pair of jeans on the 50% off rack.

There's fireworks, but not the exploding colors, loud booms, fourth of July finale, kind. No, what we have is more of the waving-a-sparkler-around-in-the-front-yard kind. I like sparklers.

Sparklers are nice.

Plus, the chances of getting hurt or burned are low. And just like Duke—they're *safe*.

I return his kiss. My mouth opens to his when he parts my lips with his tongue. My nipples harden when he presses closer, and I can feel the heat of his skin through our shirts. I relax and push myself up against him, needing to feel his hard body against mine. Needing to be reminded that I'm human and that I'm alive and that someone else in this world knows it, too.

Duke Weathersby is the closest I've ever come to having a boyfriend, even though he isn't my boyfriend and never will be. Our pseudo-relationship consists of small talk, getting high, and making out. Which is basically a lot of over-the-clothes petting followed by me sending Duke home with a raging case of blue-balls.

Duke pulls back slightly, fingering the neckline of my shirt, brushing along my skin toward my exposed shoulder. His forehead is pressed against mine. "I think we should take this upstairs to your room. All these clothes are getting in the way," he whispers against my lips, tugging at the frayed end of my sweat-shorts. He rocks his erection between my legs.

I smile against his lips and lift my ass off the counter, shamelessly grinding myself against him.

Duke groans into my mouth and grabs my hips, rotating them, grinding me against the hardness jutting up against the zipper of his khakis.

I'm turned on. I am. I am female, after all, and Duke's stunningly attractive. As much as I know I'm not like other girls in school, I'm not immune to the charm, smile, or muscles of Duke Weathersby. I blame nature and pheromones. Birds and bees. You know, science-ey stuff and all that jazz.

A part of me would like nothing more than to let him drag me upstairs so he can have his wicked way with me.

A much bigger part of me just can't go there.

I'm a damn tease. I know it. Duke has got to know it, too. But he keeps coming back, and the truth is that's what I want. Him to come back. Company. Human contact.

My friendship with him was already breaking one of my

rules. Sex would be obliterating it and I'm not willing to take it that far. Not yet, anyway. Not while there's so much on the line.

I pull back. "I…I can't. My dad," I whisper, dragging my teeth along the skin of his neck— just below his ear—rejecting him while promising him the possibilities the future might hold.

"He never comes out of the basement," Duke reminds me, peppering kisses along my neck, trying to convince me with his lips. He moves to my clavicle, adding light biting and licking to the mix. I feel my muscles tensing. My desire building. My determination to keep this relationship PG-13 crumbles as he sucks my bottom lip into his mouth and traces it with his skilled tongue.

I must admit that the boy is gooooood. There's a reason why he has a harem. A well-deserved one at that.

"Let me make you come," Duke whispers, squeezing the tops of my thighs sending a jolt of happy pleasure between my legs.

I'm desperate. I'm needy. I'm high. I'm lonely.

So very fucking lonely.

I don't want to be. I just want to feel…something else. Something at all. Something that doesn't come with worry or hurt or panic.

"Okay," I hear myself say.

Duke makes a sound low in his throat. A little bit growl. A little bit groan. He snakes his hand up my shorts. The heat from his fingers alone is driving me to the edge. I've never let him touch me there before. I've never let ANYONE touch me there before. I'm both excited and nervous and totally reckless, wrapping my legs around his waist, urging him closer.

The tips of Duke's fingers brush across my throbbing folds

and achingly neglected flesh just as a loud crash echoes through the room.

"Where did that come from?" Duke whispers.

The basement.

It came from the basement.

CHAPTER THREE

FRANKIE

"Shit! Your dad!" Duke leaps away from me as if he's been stung by a bee.

I'm off the counter, ushering him to the door, while white hot fear burns inside my chest.

"Sorry, maybe some other time. I'm gonna go check on my dad."

"I…I guess I'll see you tomorrow at school," Duke says with obvious disappointment in his voice.

"Yeah. Tomorrow. School." I mumble, unbolting and unlatching the series of locks.

I get the door open in record time. Duke steps out onto the concrete porch, tapping away at his phone. I'm sure he's sending a text to the next—more willing—girl on his grocery delivery route. I honestly wish I could bring myself to care, but I've either pushed that part of me so far down I can't find it anymore, or I never had it to begin with.

I smile and try to remember to look disappointed when all I really want to do is scream at him to run for his life.

But I don't. I wait. I have to wait.

And it's *killing* me.

Duke shoves his phone into his pocket. He gives me one more killer smile before pecking me on the lips and reaching around to smack me on the ass. His gaze lingers on my body for a few seconds.

Just get in your fucking car already.

I wait patiently with what I hope looks like a smile on my face for him to walk backward down the steps with his eyes never leaving mine until he reaches the curb where his Prius is parked. It's wrapped in the same bright green GrubTrain logo as his hat and shirt. He turns his baseball cap back around before he gets in and starts the engine. He rolls the window down. "Bye, Sarah," he says with a wave.

The way *Sarah* rolls lazily off his perfect lips makes me almost wish it were my real name.

Before Duke's car turns the corner, I've got the security camera app on my phone up, and I'm looking at the black and white video feed from the basement. I notice immediately that one of my computer monitors is on the floor, the screen smashed. My chair is tipped over.

I'm trying to figure out if I should grab the emergency bag I've buried in the lot across the street, or just leave it and take the next bus out of Banyan Cay, when I see Izzy on my screen. The fat cat is taking a leisurely stroll across my keyboard in all her black and white fluffy glory.

She must have gotten in through the basement window somehow. I remind myself to check the lock and the alarm wiring.

I bend at the waist and rest my hands on my knees feeling a few years closer to that heart attack than ever before.

My ass hits concrete. I rest my head on my knees.

How much longer can I live like this?

Probably not much longer.

Several minutes pass before I feel steady enough to try standing. I get to my feet, and suddenly, I feel the same hot awareness I felt earlier. I snap my head up, and this time, I do spot someone who looks out of place.

There's a man across the street, partially concealed as he crouches on the other side of a big matte-black motorcycle. His sculpted and tattooed biceps flex as he works on something on the other side of the wide back tire.

As if he knows I'm looking at him, the man peers out from behind the tire. I'm caught. I don't run, but I can't look away either.

Everything about him is dark. From his shoulder length hair to his black clothes. His facial hair falls somewhere between scruff and beard, longer, shorter on the sides.

His eyebrows are knitted together in a sharp scowl. I realize it's not me he's looking at, it's his bike.

He's just a guy working on his bike. He's not here for you. Sleep, Frankie. You need some fucking sleep.

The stranger tosses down a wrench, it bounces around on the concrete. I can hear his growl of frustration all the way across the street. He pushes off his knees and stands.

Whoa.

He's large. Not just his body, but his presence. A soaring skyscraper casting an endless shadow. His stride is long and sure as he makes his way from his bike into the service station. Each step of his boots is a claim of ownership upon every crack in the asphalt. His tight black t-shirt hugs the rippling muscles of his chest and arms. His jeans hang low on his waist and show off the perfect high curve of his rounded ass. An unlit cigarette dangles carelessly from his lower lip.

I've never seen anyone like him before. Raw. Powerful. I can't stop watching him. Maybe it's because I'm still high, or maybe it's because Duke and I were just making out and I'm still primed with lust. Or because I just freaked out for the third time today. But this man is a walking billboard for both terror and lust. A human thunderstorm.

He's beautiful.

My father's words from years before ring in my ear. *Men are meant to hide from, Frankie. To fear. At best they are meant to manipulate. Be the manipulator, Frankie, not the manipulated. Run before you have to ask yourself if you should. Know what they want from the look in their eyes, not from the words coming out of their mouths.*

The man comes back out of the service station. He lifts one long leg and straddles his bike with ease. It thunders to life. I'm all the way across the street, but the vibrations reach out under the asphalt and touch me. I feel the rumble in my chest. Dirt is suspended in the air a good inch above the pavement as the ground underneath shakes.

He rolls his bike out of the parking lot and then turns down the road in the opposite direction without so much as a glance my way.

I'm disappointed

What did I expect from this momentary one-sided infatuation?

I rub my eyes and decide I'm one sleepless night away from creating false relationships with celebrities in my head. I can hear the news anchor now.

A young woman was arrested today at the home of Sam Hunt for breaking and entering. The woman was delusional, insisting that she was Sam's wife. She repeatedly shouted 'what about the babies' until police were finally able to apprehend the woman. Mr. Hunt, who has no children, confirmed for the record that he'd never met the woman, although he sincerely hopes she finds and receives the help she so obviously needs.

The roar of the motorcycle is an echo in the distance. I go back inside, engage all the locks, and now that I know it's safe, I head to the kitchen first to scarf down a protein bar.

When I'm finally fed I head to the basement to assess the damage. Luckily the monitor that fell is banged up but still works. I clean up the rest of the mess then locate Izzy who I shoo back out the window. I attempt to lock it, but the latch won't click shut. The glass above it is smashed.

But the alarm still didn't go off?

I check the wiring around the window and see that it's been chewed through. *Damn cat.* I splice the wire and twist the inner workings together. I nail a piece of wood over the window.

I light one of the joints Duke gave me and sit down at my computer. My fingers fly over the keyboard. I won't be able to sleep for a while so I might as well get some more work done.

After a few hours, my phone vibrates on my lap. The alarm. I'm proud of myself this time for not leaping in response. I turn everything off and head back upstairs. It's time to at least try and get some sleep. After all, I have school in the morning.

I sigh.

I might be a liar, but what I told Duke earlier is the truth. I don't like high school all that much.

Not now, and not when I graduated the first time.

Four years ago.

CHAPTER FOUR

SMOKE

Every morning, or afternoon, or whenever I wake the fuck up, the first thing I think about is the night my life went from being all about my work to being all about revenge.

Ain't no doubt in my mind that when my time comes and I'm delivered to Hell, the memory of finding Morgan dead in her house will be the one I'll relive over and over again on a never-ending loop.

Then again, maybe I'm already in hell.

That night changed me. Made me harder. Crueler. More unfeeling than ever.

Except anger. That I feel just fucking fine.

The blast of a car horn brings me back from the past. I'm grateful for the distraction until I glance in my rearview mirror at the little shit throwing his hands in the air like I'm somehow blocking him when I'm parked next to the curb and there isn't a single other car on the fucking road.

I hold my favorite finger out the window of the van. I ain't going nowhere.

The little shit shakes his head and maneuvers his little Mazda, turning the wheel hand-over-hand like he's driving a fucking big rig.

He pulls up beside me, blocking my view of the townhouse I've been watching for weeks, and rolls down his passenger window. He's yelling, but I don't hear his words 'cause I'm not fucking listening.

The fucker's gotta go.

I hold up my hand like I'm about to apologize but grab my gun from the console instead and prop it up against my open window.

I smirk.

That does the trick. One look is all it takes for the fucker to slam on the gas pedal, his little roller skate screeching against the pavement as he takes off.

I return my gun to the console and lean over, popping open the glove box. I feel around until I find what I'm looking for. I sit up, open the bottle, and toss back two pills, swallowing them down with a swig of whiskey from my flask.

Adderall.

It's needed, especially today. Watching this house for weeks isn't good for a mind that tends to go searching in the past when it isn't concentrating on the present. The Adderall helps me focus when I got too much time to think. Plus, it's a better high than coke and lasts a fuck of a lot longer.

The only thing keeping me here, in this van on the side of a nameless road in Banyan Cay, besides the steady diet of whiskey and amphetamines, of course, is revenge.

Frank Helburn is going to die by my hand.

As soon as I can fucking find him.

I've never spent a year looking for someone. Finding people, tracking, is what I'm paid a shit-ton of money to do. I can usually trace someone in hours, days at most.

Never an entire fucking year.

I may not have found Frank, but I've found the next best thing.

His daughter.

Frances Helburn, named after her sorry fuck of a father, Frank, is now going by Sarah Jackson.

She has a miserable excuse for a life. Seriously, the bitch barely leaves the house. From what I can see she doesn't have any friends, except of course for the curly haired motherfucker who barely looks old enough to shave. Although, Frances could be hiding a beard of her own for all I fucking know with that hair always in her face. I'm surprised she makes it to school every day without getting hit by a fucking car.

She spotted me across the street today. I felt her eyes on me. I pretended to be repairing something on my bike, when, in reality, I'd just ran from her house after breaking into the basement. I didn't make it one foot inside the little window before I was clawed at by some fat feline who jumped past me in the dark, knocking a bunch of shit over.

Fuck that cat.

I didn't have time to search for clues to where Frank could be hiding. Patience isn't my strong suit. Finding Frank Helburn is testing my very limits. I was growing restless again. I remind myself of the goal and how sweet spilling his blood will be.

And, for a moment or two, I'm at ease.

Well, at ease as I can be.

I crack my knuckles and then my neck. I pull out my phone and click on the file Griff sent me a few weeks back. There are only two pictures in the file and one is of Frank and his daughter. The picture itself is several years old at best and blurry as all hell. Frances has no discernable deformities from what I can tell, but again, the picture is so distorted I can't even make out if she's smiling or not. Just dark hair and weird yellow-gold colored eyes, which must be another testament to the quality of the picture.

I may have never seen her face but when I was across the street from her I felt her eyes watching me with interest, and when I saw her shoulders drop from the corner of my eye I knew she'd removed me off her list of possible threats. I smile.

Wrong move, kid.

The other picture is a grainy security footage still showing Frank Helburn leaving the bloody scene at Morgan's house and I feel the anger rising through my body settling in my throat where it's been strangling me since that fucking night.

The phone rings, and I cringe at the name on my screen. I answer without a greeting, but Griff is Griff and doesn't need one. He talks enough for the both of us.

"No sign of our boy Frank?" Griff asks, speaking fast as if someone pressed the fast forward button on his mouth. His voice is nasally. High pitched. Whiney. Every word he speaks sounds as if he's complaining even if he isn't. I look forward to when the job's done so I don't have to hear it on a daily fucking basis.

"None," I confirm. "Just the girl and occasionally some little delivery boy twat."

Griff makes a noise. Half sigh, half growl. "Well, Frank isn't as good at covering his tracks as he thinks he is because last night my nephew Leo picked up a trace of him deep in the dark corners of the web only few know how to get to. He's still hacking. Still doing jobs. Leo's tracking him now. He may not be there with his daughter, but we'll find him. Soon."

"I'll keep watching. If he comes here I'll know it," I tell Griff. It's true. No one has ever slipped by me and they never will. "But I think it's time to find out just how much Frank Helburn loves his daughter."

"I think you might be right," Griff agrees.

I look out the window at the dark townhouse. I press the speaker button.

"Take her." Griff's says. His voice deepens with the intensity of his words. His excitement is more controlled now. Darker. "Take Frank's daughter. I want to flush this fucker out. He took Morgan and your child from you and he stole millions from me. He deserves everything he has coming to him." He lets out a long breath directly into the phone causing static on the line. "He needs to pay." Another long exhale. "And then he needs to PAY."

I don't say anything, but I agree. Griff knows I agree.

"You're one tough man to get more than a word out of." Griff says, changing his tone from bitter to amused in single chuckle. "I like that about you."

I don't like anything about you.

"I hear you're back to a one-man team," Griff says, suddenly changing the subject.

I grit my teeth. This fucker sure knows how to piss me off. "None of your fucking business, Griff," I snap.

I look out the window for the millionth time. The townhouse is still dark.

"I'm just saying, you must have been mad as hell when Rage left your team." Griff continues, ignoring my warning. His mention of Rage's name makes me want to call the entire job off. "He must've not been as loyal as you thought."

Griff said HE. My anger fades. Griff apparently doesn't know who Rage is, never mind what SHE'S capable of.

I release my grip on the steering wheel. "We might have the same enemy, Griff, but make no mistake, that don't make us friends."

"Good, because I've seen first-hand what happens to your *friends*," He drawls.

I hang up and toss the phone onto the passenger seat. I slam my closed fist on the steering wheel.

If Griff was in front of me I'd strangle the life out of him right here and now.

The fucker thinks he's untouchable and to a certain extent he is. His organization has grown leaps and bounds over the last few years, but the guy is still a dick who likes to brag about his accomplishments, which gives his reign an expiration date. The best organization in the world can't protect a leader who continually runs his mouth all over the place.

Loose lips sink ships, but in my world, they'll also earn you a dirt nap.

Longevity comes with the ability to be silent. I give Griff one more year before someone's paying me to dig him a hole in the ground. Of all the people in the world he had to be the one to discover that Frank was the one responsible for the slaughter that took place at Morgan's house.

A light turns on inside the girl's bedroom, I watch as her shadow crosses over the window.

I don't know if it's my need for revenge or my conversation with Griff, but my patience is at an end. And so is this girl's freedom.

I'm not waiting anymore.

Frances Helburn is *mine.*

I'VE SWITCHED OUT CARS AND CLOTHES. I'M NOW SITTING IN front of the school watching as the students file in.

Frances is one of the last ones to enter.

She's wearing the same school uniform she wears every

day. Your basic plaid skirt, sweater, shirt combo. If the entire reason behind wearing school uniforms is to prevent indecent exposure then this school is succeeding because hers is three sizes too big and drapes over her body like a shapeless sack.

Even her socks are ridiculous. They're forest green and ride high on her legs, almost to her knees, although one keeps falling as she walks. The black top she's wearing under her sweater has a collar, but she walks with her shoulders hunched forward, hiding not just her face but any signs of having tits.

You can't hide from me, Frances. Not under all those baggy clothes. I see you. I see you, and I'm coming for you.

Frances stumbles on the sidewalk, dropping a book. She bends to pick it up, and I catch a glimpse of the bottom of perfectly rounded ass cheeks, which are barely covered by red panties.

Red, huh? Surprise, surprise.

I have a moment of imagining the things I could do to that ass when I remind myself of who it's attached to. Frances is awkward, and from what I can tell, she's all elbows and knees. Shapeless.

I don't give a fuck what color eyes or hair a woman has, but the women I like to fuck look like...well, women. Tits. Hips. Lips.

Today, Frances seems heavier than the rest of the girls piling into the front doors of the school. Not her body, she can't weigh more than a buck twenty, tops, but heavy like she's troubled.

It's not like it matters.

Not my fucking concern.

I'm about to pile on the trouble and for the first time in a long time I feel excited. Amped.

Ready.

Frances stops. Her eyes travel over her shoulder, scanning the parking lot until they land on me. She pauses and turns her head to the side. The bell rings, and she pushes open the doors, disappearing inside.

I gotta give this Frances chick credit. She's smart. Not smart enough to throw *me* off, but all the others Griff and I hired to find her father had failed to find her as well.

Now, I know why.

The others were all looking for Frances Helburn. A young woman in her early twenties. What they found instead was an eighteen-year-old catholic school girl named Sarah Jackson.

She was hiding in plain fucking sight. In high school of all places. Clever.

But not clever enough.

I open the car door in front of the school and step out into the blinding sunlight.

Her plan was decent, while it lasted, but that's all over now.

Frances Helburn is about to learn that she isn't nearly as smart as she thinks she is.

CHAPTER FIVE

SMOKE

The receptionist looks me up and down. She can't hide the surprise in her eyes as she takes in my tattoos and my police uniform. She stands from her chair behind her desk and brushes a strand of hair behind her ears. She sets her mouth into a polite yet worried smile.

"Can…can I help you, officer…?" she stutters, linking and unlinking her fingers together.

"Officer Wiggum," I finish for her, using an emotionless yet polite tone. I inwardly chuckle because no one ever seems to notice that when I impersonate a cop I use the name of a character from the fucking Simpsons. "And yes, as a matter of fact, you can, ma'am."

I hand her the phony paperwork and check my watch like this is the last thing I want to do be doing before my shift ends.

Her eyes go wide as she reads over the papers, her lips moving silently. She looks up to me and clears her throat which is now as red and splotchy as her face. "Just a…just a moment, officer," she excuses herself, scurrying away like a rodent being chased by a cat.

She's frazzled. I can't blame her. It's probably not every day a police officer comes in carrying a warrant to arrest one of their students.

A few minutes later, I'm standing in the middle of the principal's office waiting for the principal herself to bring Frances to me.

I glance up at the framed United States flag hanging above the desk and watch my reflection in the glass.

It's almost too fucking easy.

CHAPTER SIX

FRANKIE

Principal Gregory pokes her head inside my math class and clears her throat.

Mr. Timball stops his geometry lecture; his marker pauses against the dry erase board. He raises his eyebrows in a silent. *What do you want?*

"I need to see Sarah Jackson," she answers, scanning the rows of students until she finds me in the back. Her eyes lock on mine. "Now."

I feel every single set of eyes boring inquisitive holes into my skull as I slide out my chair and make my way to the front of the room. Thirty heads swivel around, gazes following me like some weird slow synchronized dance from an eighties music video.

"Grab your things," Principal Gregory says when she sees my hands are empty. I nod. Grabbing my things means that whatever she's calling me to her office for is going to take a while because I won't be back to class today, at least not this one.

A foreboding pricks at the back of my neck, and it's not from all the eyes watching my every move. It's the dread pitting in my stomach and a feeling like everything is about to change.

Again.

I gather my bag and my books and wrack my brain as to what school-related thing this could be about, but I come up empty.

I make my way to the front of the room for the second time. Only the tapping of a pencil against a desk and the popping of gum can be heard along with the echo of my shapeless black shoes against the linoleum.

Principal Gregory holds the door open, and I follow her silently to her office with my head down and my long hair draped around my face like a shield.

She allows me to go in first, and it's not until my knees have brushed one of the two chairs in front of her desk that I look up to see a police officer standing at the window with his broad back to me. Colorful tattoos take up every inch of space on his arms. His long dark hair is tied together at the nape of his neck under his hat. I feel like I know this man, somehow, or maybe it's just deja vu.

Regardless, I begin to relax. I have no business with the police. Not that they could possibly know of, anyway. Whatever the officer is here for is probably just a misunderstanding of some sort.

Maybe, it's about one of my neighbors. One side is a drug den, and the other side is occupied by a couple who fight all hours of the day and night and scream more than they talk. It's more likely that one killed the other and they're looking for witnesses than me being in any sort of trouble.

Or so I think.

"I'll leave you two alone to discuss this matter," Principal Gregory says, reminding me of her presence. "I'll be here to escort you out when you're ready." She flashes me a tight-lipped smile. An apology.

The officer waits until the door clicks shut to turn around to face me. I recognize him instantly as the man from the service station. Only now I can see his face more clearly. His dark gleaming eyes. The scar above his right eye. I'm intrigued by him the same way I was when I first spotted him.

The officer puts his hands on his belt and smirks. I return his smile, but drop it just as quickly when he speaks, his voice deep and raspy. "Hello, *Frankie.*"

My heart stops. My blood turns to ice. I can't swallow. I can't breathe.

He used my real name. He used my real fucking name.

I drop my books on the floor and dart back toward the door. I open my mouth to scream, but before a single sound escapes, he's on me, covering my mouth with a hand that's so large it covers most of my face. He pulls me back from the door, my hand still outstretched toward the handle that's growing further and further away as he pulls me back. Tears prick at the back of my eyes, both from fright and from not being able to draw enough oxygen in through my nose.

My thoughts scramble together and bounce off the inside of my skull as my pulse spikes, and I grow dizzier and dizzier.

"Scream, and you'll die," he warns, his deep voice digging its way into my bones. "Make any noise at all, and you'll die. Cross me, and you'll fucking die."

Something hard pokes me in my lower back. It only takes one glance at the reflection in the framed United States flag above Principal Gregory's desk to see that the hard something he's pressing into my spine is a gun.

This can't be happening. Not now. Not yet. I made promises. I have things to finish.

I struggle against him, but he only pulls me tighter against his hard, massive chest. He pulls on my arm and cuffs my wrist behind my back with one hand while the other stays firmly over my mouth. I pull my wrist away but am only rewarded with a yanking of my other hand and a tightening off the cuffs as the other is wrenched behind my back.

His lips are next to my ear. Never have whispered words carried such warning.

"You can either walk out of here with me SILENTLY and without incident or you can scream and call for help. Either way, you'll still be leaving this school with me. One way is neat and clean. Nobody gets hurt. The other will have me shooting our way out. Everyone gets hurt. Your choice, hellion. You understand?" he asks.

When I don't answer, he yanks on my cuffs, pulling me away from the wall. "You understand?"

I nod because I'm too afraid to speak. This man's threat is as real as the sky is fucking blue.

"Let's go," he barks, tugging me toward the door.

My knees give out, and I feel myself sagging. The man isn't having it. He roughly hauls me to my feet before I hit the floor.

"Walk," he demands, shoving me forward.

He has me. He has me, and I have no choice but to comply. There's no way I will allow innocent people to be hurt when this man is obviously only here for me. The door opens, and the hand over my mouth disappears. I swallow a huge gulp of air, forcing much needed oxygen back into my lungs.

Principal Gregory's standing outside the door. Her eyes go to my tear-stained cheeks first and then the handcuffs now binding my wrists together behind my back. "Is there anyone you'd like me to call for you, Miss Jackson?" she asks. "Your father, perhaps?"

The man tightens his grip around my bicep in warning.

"That won't be necessary," he answers for me. "Her father is already waiting for us at the station."

Principal Gregory nods her understanding, easily believing the lie. She shoots me a sympathetic look as she leads us through the hallway. Students part like the Red Sea to give us room to pass. I don't know what she thinks I've done to deserve being arrested, but it's the least of my worries.

I keep my eyes on the floor. Whispers and quiet laughter follow closely behind. We exit through the glass front doors, and Principal Gregory follows us to the police cruiser waiting at the curb.

"Have your father call me," Principal Gregory says with so much sadness in her voice I feel like I should be the one comforting her.

The fake police officer shoves me into the backseat of the police cruiser and slams the door. Again, I remain silent.

"Hey! Where are you taking her? What happened? What the fuck's going on?" someone calls out.

I freeze as I recognize Duke's voice.

No. No. No. I chant in my head.

I glance out the corner of my eye through a part in my hair. Principal Gregory has her hand flat on Duke's chest, preventing him from coming any closer. She shakes her head and guides him back up the stairs into the school.

"Sarah!" he calls over his shoulder. "Sarah!"

I say nothing as the car pulls away from the school. Away from my life.

It isn't a real life, but it's all I have.

HAD.

It's not just my life that's over.

I may have spared the lives of the people in that school with my silence, but if I can't complete my work, others will die.

The only question now is, *how many?*

CHAPTER SEVEN

FRANKIE

I pretend to be crying, bawling loudly complete with sniffles and moans so that the brute in the front seat can't hear what I'm really doing, which is picking the lock on the handcuffs with the small nail file I keep taped to the inside cuff of my sweater.

I knew my end was near, but that didn't mean I hadn't been preparing for it.

My kidnapper doesn't seem annoyed by my tears. He doesn't react at all. After sending a text message, his eyes are on the road without sparing so much as a glance at me in the rearview mirror.

When I've got the lock picked, I let out an exceptionally loud wail to disguise the click of the cuffs as they open, and my wrists are finally free, but I keep them behind my back.

The cop car I'm riding in has the cage thing that separates the backseat from the front. There is no handle because like most cop cars, the doors only open from the outside. Fortunately, it's a newer model cruiser, and I spot the red emergency release lever by my foot poking out from under the floor mat. I slip off my shoe, maneuver my foot, and lift the edge of the mat. It takes some work, especially because I can't move any other part of my body while doing it, but I finally manage to slip my big toe through the fabric of the handle.

Most logical people would choose to make a run for it while the car is stopped at a stop sign or a light. But this man is massive. His legs are long and strong, and I have no doubt that if I escape while we are stopped that he'll catch me before I have a chance to get further than a few feet.

On the other hand, while the car is in motion, is a whole other ballgame. I can push open the door and leap. If I don't crack my skull on the pavement or break a limb in the process, I can make a run for it while he's still slowing to a stop.

It's the best chance I've got.

It's the *only* chance I've got.

We enter the highway on-ramp. I sit up and watch the needle on the speedometer rise. Forty miles per hour. Fifty. Sixty.

It's now or never.

I take a deep breath and pull the release lever up with my foot. The door lock clicks its release, and I push on it with all my might.

"Fuck!" the man curses as I dive out of the vehicle. The painted yellow lines blur together beneath me as I aim for the patch grass lining the highway.

It's the last thing I remember.

CHAPTER EIGHT

SMOKE

Any and all thoughts I had about Frankie Helburn being smart leap with her from the fucking car.

Stupid bitch.

I yank the wheel and cross the grassy median, the tires vibrating beneath me as I speed through the unpaved terrain. I skid back onto the asphalt in a plume of smoke from the burning rubber. The door she somehow managed to open slams shut with the force of the turn. I slam my foot on the gas pedal and cross the median yet again, circling back around to where she ate pavement at over sixty miles per house. Seconds later I slam on the brakes and screech to a stop on the side of the road.

I spot her before I get out of the car—trying to hide in the tall grass in the center of the ditch with her face down. Her glossy main of black hair is what gives her away, doing nothing to conceal her in the green and brown weeds, hiding as well as an ostrich with its head in the sand.

I stomp over with a curse on my lips and a scowl on my

face. That is, until I realize why her attempt to hide is so fucking bad.

It's because she isn't hiding.

Shit.

I don't even know if the bitch is breathing.

CHAPTER NINE

FRANKIE

The smell hits me first.

It reeks like laundry left in the washer too long. Stale. Moldy. And something else. Something that stings my nostrils. Urine perhaps.

I struggle to open my eyes. After a few attempts they're open, but barely.

It's daylight. I know this much because dust is swirling around like a slow-moving cyclone within a beam of sunlight shining from under a torn window shade.

Where the hell am I?

But the answer doesn't come.

All I know is that I'm alone in what appears to be a run-down motel room. An old TV with a cracked screen sits on top of a wooden dresser missing two of its four drawers. The horrid floral wallpaper is more torn than not. Someone has even gone so far as to color in the gaps with pink marker as if no one will be able to tell wallpaper from the scribble of a highlighter.

A battering ram of pain crashes into my chest with a strength that causes my vision to blur as I try to roll over. I freeze and shut my eyes tightly as if that can squelch the burning of my ribs. My every muscle joins in, protesting my consciousness. My right arm aches and throbs. My thoughts are jumbled together, and my heartbeat is drumming against my skull as if I'd spent last night chugging tequila.

The pain eases slightly. When I can take a deep breath again, I attempt to rub my temples to soothe the throb in my head, but I'm stopped by the bite of metal into my skin. The tear-inducing pain vibrates up to my elbow. I glance up. My sweater is torn into ribbons, showcasing large angry purple and yellow bruises that take up more space on my arms than skin. My wrists are bound to the headboard by handcuffs.

I freeze as the sharp fangs of fear pierce the skin of my throat. I close my eyes tightly and attempt to see through the fog and panic.

Think, Frankie. Think. What's the last thing you remember?

The memory is right there within reach but it stays at the edge without so much as dipping a toe in the waters of remembrance. I growl in frustration but the movement causes me to hiss in more pain when the springs of the worn mattress beneath me stab into my back like I'm lying on a bed of knives.

The clanking and scraping of metal against metal echoes in my ears as I try to pull my hands free from the cuffs, to no avail. I try to swallow but my mouth is dry. I roll my tongue around in my mouth and taste the copper of dried blood on my teeth.

I hear a deep familiar voice just outside the closed door. It's angry and deep. "I'm not bringing her to you. Not fucking yet. Not until I'm through with her." Another pause. "Give me time and when I'm ready I'll either bring you the girl or her body."

"Shit." I curse when I try to sit up, forgetting for a moment that I'm bound to the bed. Sizzling pain drags along my muscles like a serrated knife. When it finally subsides enough for me to concentrate, I take a deep breath. A memory begins to wiggle free of the fog. A flash of red and blue. A man with dark hair and eyes. The principal's office at school.

Was it a dream? No. A nightmare.

Only, I'm not even sleeping. The pain is real. The restraints are real.

Everything is real.

It all comes back to me the second I see the blue policeman's uniform draped over a chair in the corner. School. The walk to the principal's office. The policeman. The man from the service station. Duke screaming my name.

Jumping from the car on the highway.

"Business is business, asshole," I hear the man say.

I can make out his large shadow pacing back and forth in front of the window.

"Save that shit for your own people." he grinds out. "I work alone. If you send someone out to check up on me, I'll make it so he won't be coming back."

He ends the call, and his heavy footsteps stop right in front of the door.

I pull on my cuffs again, ignoring the pain it brings. I glance around the small room for another exit, another means of escape, but even if I could free myself there isn't anywhere to go. I look again as if I can will another way to appear, but there's nothing but a small windowless bathroom and the ugly wallpapered walls.

The door creaks open, and heavy footsteps approach the bed. I close my eyes and pretend to be asleep although my heart is hammering in my chest like I'm darting for the finish line in a race I'm not winning. I try not to react as his large hand wraps around my forearm, but I'm panicking inside. He releases my wrists from the cuffs and lets them drop to the bed. I hear him walking about the room. I steal a glance through a slit in my eye. He's crouched over a black tote bag on the floor to my right.

The door is to my left.

There's no time to think.

I sit up slowly but the mattress creaks with my movement. The man's head swings in my direction, and I close my eyes again, hoping he'll think I'm just moving in my sleep. After a few moments, I dare another glance. His back is to me again. Slow isn't going to work this time.

I don't give the thought time to process because time is a luxury I don't have.

I spring from the bed and bolt across the room. My legs are screaming because something is clawing at them from the inside, raking down my every muscle like jagged knives being dragged across my skin. I run as fast as I can, but I know it's not fast enough because I'm limping like my feet are anchors I'm struggling to drag behind me.

I'm lifted off my feet and tossed through the air with ease, like a newspaper flippantly tossed onto a porch on Sunday morning. I hit the mattress with such force I bounce off, landing on my stomach onto the dirty carpet on the other side of the bed. The wind is sucked from my lungs on impact. My cheek stings as if I hit concrete instead of wiry shag carpeting.

My captor thuds over to where I'm gasping for breath. He growls, and it's like I can feel his anger sailing toward me with the dust in the air. I hear it in the way he cracks his knuckles. I see it in the way he cocks his head from one side to the other and his nostrils flare. I can smell it permeating off him like a new Calvin Klein fragrance. *Hatred, for men.*

He's dressed like he was when I first saw him at the service station. Tight black t-shirt revealing the vast number of interconnecting colorful tattoos running the length of his muscular arms. Plain black leather vest. Dark low-slung jeans. Black scuffed boots. He's got two thick silver bracelets adorning both wrists, a chain connecting each pair.

He moves closer. They aren't bracelets.

They're handcuffs.

A pair for each wrist.

Revulsion and loathing cross over his tanned face, twisting his thick lips.

How did I ever think this man was beautiful?

"Please. Don't hurt me. I'll give you whatever you want." I beg, hating the way I don't recognize my own voice.

"Yes, you *will*," he says, crouching closer, his breath on my cheek. He isn't touching me, but I can feel him everywhere. Around me. Against my skin, in the pit growing in the bottom of my stomach. In the spike of adrenaline surging through my heart. "Where the fuck is your old man?"

My old man. My *father*.

My lungs inflate, drawing in a much needed gulp of breath, bringing new life to my thoughts.

He wants my father, not me. He doesn't know the truth.

I'd feel slightly relieved because it means my work is safe, even if I'm not. At least for now.

"Answer me!"

"I...I don't know," I lie on a strangled exhale. I turn my head back to the floor, the curtain of my hair I'm used to hiding behind falls between us. But he isn't a high school kid. My hair isn't going to do much to protect me now.

"Bullshit," he growls, taking a handful of my hair and

twisting it in his hands so I have no choice but to face him. My scalp burns.

"Let's try this again," he seethes. He flips me over onto my back and cages my torso in with his big thighs on each side of my hips. He lifts my wrists above my head and holds them there. "Where's your old…" his words suddenly trail off. He leans closer. His brows lift then furrow again, lining his forehead in confusion. He's unmoving. Unbreathing.

I do the same, remaining as still as I've ever been in fear that even the smallest blink will trigger his rage and set him off down a path there won't be an escape from.

Eons pass before he blinks back through wherever it is he'd gone. He flips me over onto my back, keeping my hair firmly between his fingers. He twists it until I can hear hairs ripping free from my heated scalp. "The truth. Now," he demands.

I can barely think with the pressure mounting inside my skull. I'm at this man's mercy, and that's only if he has any.

"I haven't spoken to my father in years," I tell him. My eyes water.

He yanks my hair back so hard I have no choice but to look up at him. Tears leak from my eyes and spill down my cheeks into my ears and hair.

He scans my face again, this time not in confusion but like a human lie detector conducting a scan. He reaches up with his free hand. I try to pull away but only manage to inflict more pain on my own scalp. He surprises me by running his fingertips over my lips, slowly tracing both the top and then bottom. My stomach turns as fear stabs its way through my body.

"It's a fucking shame I can't keep you. You'd make a pretty little pet." His dark words are laced with even darker meaning. "Tell me, *hellion*." He says. "Why didn't you ask me why I was taking you? Or why you're here?"

"I...I..." I stutter.

Shit.

"I think it's because you already know."

He releases my hair and I fall forward onto the floor at his feet. Relief and pain crash into the top of my head.

"I don't know what you're..."

"Don't play dumb. That shit won't work. Not with me. Your old man stole from the wrong people," he grinds out. On the side of his neck is an elaborate tattoo of a pocket watch where a thick vein throbs directly under the second hand. "People who aren't as patient as *I* am."

"I'm telling you the truth. I haven't spoken to him in years," I tell him.

"The question is where he is, not if you've fucking chatted lately!" He leans down so close his nose is almost touching mine. His nostrils flare. He's losing his patience, and I'm losing my shit.

"I don't have any money," I tell him. "But I-I can get it. I just need a laptop, and I can—"

"Even if I believed you, that's not gonna fucking happen. Money isn't all your old man stole." He stands, towering high above me like a god looking down from heaven, peeking into Hell.

He's living proof that as humans our outsides don't always match our insides. His good looks are wasted. A travesty. A distraction. No more effective than marker filling in for wallpaper.

"If you won't tell me where he is, then we'll have to make him come to us. You know how we'll do that?"

"It doesn't matter. He won't come for me." It's the truth. I feel a little stronger for being the one holding the cards even if those cards are face cards, and that face is the grim reaper. I take a deep breath. One and then another. Each painful inhale gives me more strength. More determination. More will to fight.

"You're awfully smart for a girl who's so fucking dumb," he says with a shake of his head.

"I'm not dumb," I say through my teeth. "My father used to tell me I was dumb. He was wrong, too."

"Oh yeah? You jumped from a moving car," he points out, his voice so deep it rumbles like the engine of his motorcycle and I can feel his words as well as hear them.

"That was brave," I argue.

He's looking at me with interest but doesn't say anything.

"If you're going to kill me, then just do it," I challenge.

His chuckle is low and menacing. "You're not doing much to prove your point about not being dumb, hellion."

I meet his gaze. "Death on my terms? Seems pretty smart to me." I shrug. "I can't give you what you're looking for so I'm dead either way, right?"

"That's where you're wrong."

He crouches down again. He lifts his hand to grab my face, and when I turn away, he forcefully turns me back by grabbing my chin, his fingers digging painfully into my skin. His breath on my lips.

"Nothing about this will be on your terms. NOTHING."

What he doesn't know is that nothing about my life has ever been on my terms. This might be the first time I've ever been kidnapped.

But I've been a prisoner for years.

CHAPTER TEN

FRANKIE

"Do you want to know what's going to happen to you if you don't tell me where your father is?" The man asks, staring at me with cold, hard eyes.

I shake my head. What does it matter?

He tells me anyway. "I'm going to do more than just kill you." He lifts my hand in his and pulls on my index finger until the knuckle cracks. "I'll start by removing your fingernails."

I try to yank my hand away but he holds tighter and presses down on my thumbnail until I'm breathing through the searing pain. He releases me, and I wrap my hand around my finger like a brace.

"Then, I'll remove your fingers, one at a time." He grabs my wrist. "Then your hands."

He slides his hand up to my forearm right below my elbow squeezing painfully at the joint. My mouth opens in a silent cry.

"It's amazing how you can remain conscious and alert

while getting your arms and legs hacked off. I've seen men watch their limbs be removed one by one until more parts of them are hanging around the room than are left attached to their bodies. The human body can take a lot before it gives up. But I won't bore you with all the details. You'll find out for yourself soon enough."

He digs his fingers into the most menacing looking purple bruise on my bicep. I hiss and glare hatred into his eyes.

"You'll feel every fucking thing. Every snap of bone. Every severed muscle. Every pop of a vein." He pushes into the bruise once more before releasing me.

I rub my aching arm while he stays close, looking at me. Watching my every reaction like he's studying me. His gaze darts from where I'm rubbing the bruise to my face then back again. He looks like he's thinking about something and whatever it is, I don't want to know.

For a long while we just breath the same air, staring hatred into each other. He's waiting for me to crack and tell him where my father is, but I can't crack even if I wanted to.

I curse my father in my head. "Listen. Please. Frank wasn't a very good father, and later, I found out he wasn't a good person either. Honestly, I would hand him over to you if I could. He deserves whatever he has coming to him, but I can't do that. It's not possible."

The man says nothing but continues to stare at me for a long time.

"Get the fuck up," he finally orders.

Dread courses through me. I can hear it too. It's louder than my own heartbeat which is thudding in my ears like the heel of a hand beating out an unsteady rhythm on a drum.

I freeze.

"Get up, and take off your fucking clothes."

My stomach rolls. My eyes widen. My pulse quickens and

my fingers begin to twitch. "Please," I beg. "No. No. Please no. Don't. I'm sorry."

"Get. Up." This time, he repeats it through tightly clenched teeth.

He lifts me off the floor. His hands are large and rough as they wrap around my shoulders. I kick against him, but he subdues me easily, turning me around so my back is pressed tightly to his chest.

I'm trembling as he shoves his hand into a hole in my sweater and yanks. "No!" I yell as he tears what's left of my school uniform from my body, the sound of ripping fabric slicing through my last shred of hope. I'd rather have him take my limbs then take my body by force. I'm weeping for the first time in my entire life.

The man moves to my skirt next, and it only takes a few tugs at the seam before it, too, is in shreds, and I'm standing before him in only my panties and sports bra.

I'm terrified, but I resist the urge to cover myself with my arms. I tell myself that when it comes to it, I'll fight him off with all I've got, but if that doesn't work, which given our size and strength difference seems likely, then I'll try and think of a happier place and happier times. It doesn't take me long to realize that won't work either. I haven't had a real happy time since…well, ever.

His fingers trace the thick strap of my sports bra. I suck in a strangled breath. The hair on the backs of my arms stands on end. He chuckles as he circles me.

"As I said," he whispers, "so smart, yet so fucking stupid."

"What…what are you going to do to me?" I manage to squeak out. The heat from his chest warms my back as he comes to stand behind me once more. "I'll fight back. I won't let you. Please. Please don't…"

"Please don't *what*?" he asks, coming to stand in front of

me, crossing his big muscular arms over his chest. He's looking down at me at me as if my very presence offends him.

"Please. Just... *don't*." I can't find the right words, but I hope it's enough. I close my eyes and drop my chin to my chest. I'm pushed backward. I land harshly onto a rickety wooden chair with legs almost as wobbly as mine. My tailbone screams out in pain but it's nothing compared to the pain of not being able to do a damn thing to save myself. "Cut me or even kill me if you have to, just don't do...*that*. Please."

He looks me over like a spider assessing the fly caught in his web. Panic rises in my chest and gets stuck in my throat. I try, but I can't swallow it down. I'm prepared for most things, but I'm not prepared for *that*. No one could be.

He comes closer. His knees bump against mine. I open my mouth to scream, but he covers it with his hand. "Have it your way, hellion."

Suddenly, there's a gun pressed to my forehead.

I GO BLANK. I REGISTER NOTHING BUT WHITE, THEN THE man standing above me holding a gun to my head. The image is shifting in and out of focus.

"I'm not going to suddenly be able to deliver my father to you just because you have a gun to my head," a much stronger version of myself says.

My heart is trembling in fear, but my soul wants to fight like a suicidal gladiator and I want to live because I *have* to live. I've spent several years fighting for the lives of others and if I die, they die.

I shut my eyes tightly, preparing for the end. I make silent apologies to all the people I've never met who don't even know they're counting on me.

I'm so sorry I failed you.

I'm wondering what it's going to feel like, if anything at all, when the bullet sends bits of my brain splattering onto the wall behind me.

"I hope I make a big fucking mess, and you have to clean it up yourself." I say, coming back into my body, and staring up into his dark evil pools. The corner of his eyes wrinkle like a smile that doesn't reach his lips.

My heart is hammering in my chest when his phone buzzes, and he answers it on speaker without saying a word.

"Smoke," the man on the other end greets.

"Griff," Smoke replies, gruffly.

Smoke. My kidnapper's name is Smoke. And Griff? Where have I heard that name before?

"The bitch talking, yet?"

"Not yet," Smoke says, cocking the gun. He pushes the barrel harder into my skin until I'm pressing my head against the back of the chair as far as it will go. "I'm working on it."

It's not far enough.

"Send the pictures," Griff demands, sounding as if he's talking through a stuffy nose.

Smoke holds up the phone and snaps a few pictures of me with the gun to my head. He taps out a few keys then returns the phone to speaker. "Sent."

"I'll make sure they get sent to anyone who's ever had contact with Frank Helburn. One way or another he'll get them and more importantly he'll get the message. Show your face or the bitch dies." Griff says, sounding pleased with himself.

He can be pleased with himself all he wants. It's not going to work.

"You've got your picture. Flush the fucker out," Smoke says.

"We'll wait a week. If it doesn't work we'll throw her off the Skyway Bridge and come up with another plan," Griff says. "Better yet. Hang onto her for a week. Take out your pound of flesh as you see fit then bring the girl to me."

"I can end things just fine on my own."

"You owe me, Smoke. If he shows his face he's yours. If he doesn't, you have one week. Then the girl is mine."

Smoke grunts in agreement then hangs up. The gun leaves my head. He throws the phone into the drywall where it makes a pizza-sized hole.

I exhale the longest held breath in history and drop my chin to my chest. I'm shivering from both fear and adrenaline.

I'm still trying to catch my breath when something soft connects with my head. Another something falls on top of my bare feet. I'm surprised to find it's a black t-shirt and a pair of jeans.

"Put those on," Smoke orders, shoving things into his duffle bag.

When I don't move right away, he gives my body a slow once-over. For a second, I think I see heat in his eyes, and my entire body tenses, remembering my earlier fear.

"You have two fucking seconds to put those on before I take them away and you spend the next week naked."

I scramble as fast as I can to pull the jeans over my legs and the shirt over my head. The fabric of both is soft and stretchy, but still feels like sandpaper against my bruises and scabs. Regardless, I'm grateful to be covered again.

One week.

Just like that, my death sentence has been temporarily extended. I have seven days to figure out a plan. To escape. Whether I do it through bribery or by figuring out which god is the right one to pray to. Lucky for me, I still have a few tricks up my sleeve, and I'll use every single one of them if I have to.

I'm fully dressed, but I'm unsure of what to do next. Smoke comes over and pushes me back down into the chair and pulls my arm down, cuffing my wrist to one of the legs.

"I see that look in your eyes," he says. "It's best you put an end to that shit right now."

"What look is that?" I ask.

"Hope. It ain't gonna do you no fucking good. Not with me. It's best you stick to fear. Hope may feel like the beginning, but it will gut you in the end." His lips brush my ear. "Trust me on that one."

CHAPTER ELEVEN

FRANKIE

The strong stench of motor oil and gas clings to the inside of my nostrils, rousing me back to consciousness.

I'm groggy. The inside of my mouth feels as if I've been chewing on cotton balls and tastes sour. I'm sure he's drugged me, but I'm not sure with what. The sick part is that half of me, the half still reeling in pain, is grateful, while the other half, the half he kidnapped and threatened, is still both furious and terrified.

I'm laid out across the back seat. This time there will be no escape. No jumping out on the highway. He's made sure of it. I'm blindfolded. Bound at both my wrists and ankles. Thick tape covers my mouth. I'm strapped down with both sets of seatbelts.

I don't know what day it is or how long it's been since I was taken from school. It doesn't matter. The only thing that matters is escaping.

It takes a while for my brain to become fully awake.

I will not panic. That's the first rule.

I take a deep breath and try to recall the rest of the rules. They're from a book I read by Dr. Ida Kurshner. It's half autobiography and half 'how-to'. The book detailed the kidnapping and subsequent escape she'd experienced as a young woman at the hands of a plumber who came to her home to do work one day and decided to take her with him when he left. At the end of the book, she listed her TO DO's in case anyone reading ever found themselves held captive.

I recall Dr. Ida's list.

#1) Avoid being captured all together by screaming and fighting back.

That ship has sailed, lady.

#2) Retain your composure and dignity. Do not beg or become hysterical. Do not cry, if at all possible. Smile and offer compliments without appearing manipulative.

I think the good doctor was also the same one who wrote all those housewife manuals from the 50's. Curl your hair and put on lipstick before your husband comes home. Do not concern him with how bad the children might have been during the day. Smile often and make sure his dinner is hot and ready. You could end up with that new vacuum you've had your eye on if he thinks you're doing a swell job.

No.

#3) Do not challenge your captor.. Show them respect.

Over my dead fucking body, Dr. Ida.

#4) Do not engage them in any conversation that could be upsetting for them.

Hey, Mr. Captor Man! How's the family? See the game Sunday? Can you believe this weather we're having? How about you letting me go and we meet up for a game of one-on-one at the rec center next week? Sound good? Okay, see you there!

#5) Connect with your captor on a personal level. Share personal

stories. Make them feel like you have things in common. Better yet, make them care about you by relating to them.

Hey, you like killing and kidnapping? O.M.G. Me too!

#6) Seduction.

Number six is how Dr. Ida finally escaped. She convinced her captor she wanted him as much as he wanted her. She seduced him and they engaged in what she called a 'consensual non-consensual sexual relationship.' Over the course of a few months she gained his trust enough for him to let her go outside in the backyard on occasion where she eventually scaled a fence and ran to a neighboring house for help.

The problem is that Dr. Ida was dealing with a man having a psychotic breakdown. I'm dealing with a man who's straight up psychotic.

I'm going to have to improvise on the list, but I'm going to try. I must try. I'll do anything to make up for the sins of my father. I'll pray to every god. I'll sink to the lowest of the lows, because I *will* finish my work, even if it's with a gun to my head during and a bullet in my brain after.

One way or another, I *will* be free.

CHAPTER TWELVE

FRANKIE

Thinking you're going to die one minute and live the next is downright exhausting. I'm emotionally and mentally drained when I hear doors open, and I'm pulled from the vehicle. The blindfold is ripped away. The bright light that's creating a halo in my vision. Once my eyes focus, I can see the vehicle I was traveling in is an unmarked black van. Not the soccer-mom kind, but the industrial kind plumbers or electricians use. I'm set on my feet, but my legs are wobbly and my feet are still tethered at the ankles. I stumble but don't fall, held up by the large warm palm of my captor.

Smoke braces my bicep with one hand and bends to cut away my restraints with the other.

"Are you this rough with everyone you kidnap?" I bite out. I realize it's not smart to insult him. The Dr. Ida of my imagination is slapping a ruler against my palms.

"Sorry, I'm out of touch dealing with the living. Most people I encounter stop breathing after a few seconds. I'll try to be more fucking gentle next time," he says.

He's being sarcastic, but it's the truth in his words that hit me in the gut. He doesn't usually kidnap people. He kills them.

There's no aftercare involved in killing.

We're in the middle of a field in front of a large U-shaped building with broken windows that looks as if it's an abandoned school of some sort. Weeds, vines, and graffiti take up most of the chipped brick exterior. A dilapidated metal fence around the perimeter is missing entire sections I assume are somewhere under the thick brush growing between the chain links. The parts that are still standing have a metal slinky looking wire sitting at the top. Barbed wire. It's not a school at all.

It's a prison.

Or at least, it was.

There's no sign of life. No sounds except the crunching of the brush under our feet as Smoke leads me over thick woven brush at least a foot high. I get caught up in it several times. My foot sinking to the bottom of the tangled vines and holding me there until Smoke cuts them away with a long, serrated knife from his belt, urging me forward into the building.

We enter through a car-sized hole in the side of the building. We climb over a steep pile of crumbled brick in order to get inside.

I stumble, my foot slipping on the brick several times until Smoke picks me up with ease, setting me back on my feet on the other side of the pile.

He nudges my shoulders, and I slowly move forward into the prison, his heavy footsteps follow closely behind, echoing off the walls as if there is more than one of him behind me.

We move deeper into the cellblock down a wide hall. The building is two stories. One row of cells on top of the other. A corroded staircase stands in the very middle of the large room. Furry brown dust and mold clings to the air ducts running the length of the ceiling. Rust peeks out through the dozens of layers of prison green paint peeling from the walls. Graffiti is everywhere, even high above the cells where I'm left wondering how on earth the artist got all the way up there.

Broken windows let in an occasional breeze that can't be felt in the stagnant heat outside. A torn piece of paper floats across the floor in front of us like a prison tumbleweed. Warm air hits my sweaty skin. I shiver, the warmth doing nothing to stop the chill from stabbing its way through my skin down into my bones like an ice pick. My lower jaw vibrates. My teeth chatter so loudly the sound echoes around in my brain. To make it stop I clamp my jaw so tight I'm sure my teeth are about to crack.

It smells like death.

My stomach rolls.

Decay thickens the air and makes it hard to breathe. It's more than just a smell. It's a feeling. A feeling I fear I'll never be able to rid from my nostrils or my thoughts. It sticks with me, covers me, cages me in as if I need a reminder that, like the many who've been here before, I am a prisoner.

Bits of paper and clothing are strewn about the cracked concrete floor. Thin dirty mattresses are everywhere except on the iron bed frames, the welds thick at the joints from multiple repairs. Some of the mattresses are leaning against the bottom of the stairs. Some are stacked in the middle of the hallway. Some just lay about at various angles with tears exposing their springs like corpses left in the very spot they died in.

There's more graffiti here than on the outside of the building. Painted on the floor is a large red satanic star. I shut my eyes tightly as I cross over it. When I'm sure I'm clear I open my eyes again and look up to where an entire doorway of a cell appears to be stained in blood. A large splatter covers the right side, turning into thinner and thinner drip marks the further down the wall I look before turning into a black pool stain on the concrete.

Bile rises in my throat.

I can see the violence of the past all around me. It flutters in the air like ghosts surrounding me, making their presence known. They whisper in my ear, sliding across my prickly skin.

The breeze turns from warm to cold as the sun sets and the prison glows with a deep blue as the moon lights our way. I can hear the screams of the past. Banging against the bars. A last cry of whoever met their unfortunate end in that blood-stained cell.

"I'm not afraid," I say out loud. I'm not sure if I'm talking to Smoke or myself. But even I don't believe my own words.

Smoke chuckles, guiding me into a cell and slides the metal bars shut with a bang, creating a never-ending echo. He produces an ancient-looking key and locks the cell with a click that makes my heart jump in my chest.

The sun's almost completely set now and the light through the windows is dim at best.

"No lights?" I ask.

The second the words leave my lips I know it's a stupid question. The place barely has standing walls. Of course, it doesn't have electricity.

"Don't tell me you're afraid of the dark," Smoke says, tucking the key into his back pocket.

"No," I lie. "I'm not afraid of anything. Not even the likes of you."

The corner of his lip curls up into an evil, half-smile. He leans forward with his hands on the bars right above his head.

He looks me up and down. His eyes widen. He looks hungry. Angry. Feral.

"Oh, hellion. I very much doubt that."

I take a step back to gain more distance even though there are bars separating us.

"I've seen fear a million times in a thousand different ways," Smoke says.

He pulls out the key once more and turns it in the lock. He's inside the cell now.

I'm backing up and backing up until I'm trapped against the far wall.

Smoke approaches and leans down. He's so close his nose is almost touching the place between my neck and ear.

"You can't tell me you're not afraid. I know fear when I see it."

I'm trembling as he closes his eyes and inhales deeply running the tip of his nose runs across my skin.

"Fuck, I can smell it on you, kid."

"Don't call me a kid," I seethe through my teeth.

His eyes darken with fury. "I'll call you whatever the fuck I want to call you."

"My name is *Frankie*." I say with a sudden boost of confidence.

He's so close now, his chest is pressed against mine. "I know your name. I just don't *fucking* care."

We're still, locked in position, neither one of us wanting to make the first move. Smoke breaks first.

"Your eyes really are that color," he whispers. I'm taken aback.

"What's going to happen to me?" I ask, on a shaky whisper.

Smoke places his hands on the wall beside my head,

caging me in. I'm eye to emotionless eye with the ghost of Christmas kidnapping.

"Whatever the fuck I want," he growls.

"Fuck you," I spit.

He chuckles, and I can feel it in my chest. His lips brush against my jaw.

"Only if you *beg.*"

CHAPTER THIRTEEN

FRANKIE

I'm alone.

Smoke's gone. He left me a mattress and a few bottles of water. The cell has no toilet but a small metal sink with no running water. Since it has the only drain in the place, I use it to relieve my full bladder and lay down just as darkness blankets everything.

It's freezing. I'm awake, but I'm not sure if I've slept yet or not. I don't remember dreaming, but I also don't remember falling asleep. How long have I been in here? Minutes? Hours? Days? Long enough to make me understand how inmates in solitary go crazy.

Sitting alone in this cell is a lot like walking on train tracks in the dark when you know a train is coming along at any second. My skin pricks with anxiety. With the unknown.

When? When? When?

My stomach rumbles with hunger, but it's the least of my worries.

Every few seconds a whistling noise starts like wind

blowing through a pipe. It begins low and grows louder and louder until it sounds as if the ceiling above me might burst. It stops completely for a few moments before starting all over again.

I count the sequence of these whistles to keep my brain occupied. One. Two. Three. It's when I'm on four that the whistling stops and another kind can be heard.

One that's not coming from any pipe; it's coming from down below.

I pretend it's nothing until I hear footsteps on the metal stairs. The hair on the back of my neck stands on end. My palms begin to sweat.

He's back.

I sit up and pull my knees up to my chest. A barrier that can easily be breached.

The clouds shift through the large window on the far wall revealing a half moon which gives off just enough light to remind me I can see.

A shaky yellow stream from a flashlight bounces off the walls of my cell and hits me in the eye, momentarily blinding me.

A key turns in the lock and I hear the squeal of the door sliding open.

Holding in a cry I grip the mattress tightly.

My eyes strain as I peer into the blackness. The shadow standing above me is big but not nearly as large as Smoke. When the clouds clear and allow the rest of the moonlight to flood the cell and reveal more of the stranger in front of me.

This man is much shorter, skinnier, and dirtier than Smoke. He takes out the toothpick he's chewing on and smiles, revealing a missing front tooth. "Hello there, darlin'. I'm Wes," he says with a crooked smile.

"Did Smoke send you?" I ask, hesitantly.

The man shakes his head slowly from side to side, and for a split-second, I think I'm saved.

Saved is the last thing I am right now.

His eyes rake across my body like I'm wearing nothing at all. The hair on the back of my neck stands up.

He sits down on the bed next to me. I immediately jump up and run for the now open cell door. He reaches out and grabs my arm, pulling me back down on the mattress.

"Oh, no you don't. We just met. Let's get to know each other for a while." The man grins, and I shake my head.

"No, let me go."

"Why do you gotta be so rude? I just want us to be friends."

Wes reminds me of a snake slithering his way around a rodent playfully before squeezing the life from its body. He looks like a snake, too. Flat-headed. Beady, little, wide-set eyes, and a sharp tongue that might as well be forked.

This man is not here to rescue me.

A surprising thought crosses my mind. It sounds idiotic, even to me.

I hope Smoke comes back soon.

"Smoke treating you alright?" the man asks, sucking on his bottom lip and shuffling closer to me on the mattress. He's got my wrist in his grip and as much as I try, I'm too battered and bruised to fight him off. "I've been sent to check up on things and from the looks of it, things look *real* good."

Everything in me is screaming to fight, but I don't have anything to fight him off with. I'm weak. So weak. He palms himself through his jeans and my stomach rolls. If it wasn't already empty it would be now.

"Think of me like your secondary babysitter," he hisses, placing his thin cold hands on my ankles. He pries my legs apart, and I flip over, trying to crawl off the end. "Fiesty. I like 'em feisty."

I scream as loud as I can until my own ears hurt from the sound.

"Smoke's not here, darling. It's just you and me." I feel his knee on the mattress. "There, there now. It looks like you've had a rough day, let me make it better."

His grip around my ankle tightens. He uses his knees to keep my legs spread painfully apart. My sobs are silent because my voice is gone.

"Let me see that pretty, pink pussy," he moans, tugging at the waistband of my jeans. "My cock wants a taste."

He flips me over, and regardless of my empty stomach, I know I'm going to be sick. There's no stopping it. I try and swallow it down, but as he reaches for his belt and unbuckles his pants, I know it's only a matter of seconds before it erupts from my throat.

He manages to get my jeans down to my knees then reaches for his buckle. He frees his tiny ant-eater looking cock and tugs at it a few times. Groaning while keeping his eyes fixated on the space between my legs.

Slowly, I raise my knee and wait a few agonizing seconds for the perfect moment. When he licks his lips and reaches for my panties, I straighten my leg, kicking my heel into his crotch.

He howls in pain and I make a run for it, but I'm weak and slow. Within seconds, he's on me, pinning me to the ground.

"I was gonna make this good for you," he spits, his eyes bulging from his tiny head. "You stupid cunt!"

He punches me across my already injured jaw, and I see stars.

Wes covers my mouth with his hand, and I can't hold it

down any longer. I throw up against his palm but he keeps his hand pressed firmly over my mouth. My stomach keeps pushing everything upwards. I'm choking on my own bile; my eyes water. Everything's blurry. I can't breathe. I can't see.

"Now." He leans down, his putrid breath on my face. He holds a gun to my temple. He talks through his teeth, spraying his spit on my face. "I'm going to make you feel all the pain."

I'm so dizzy. The room is spinning. The bloodied and rusted concrete finds its way in and out of my vision over and over again. Wes is tearing at my clothes. My shirt is open. Even with the gun to my head, I'm fighting and fighting him, but I don't feel myself moving.

This is what it means to be all out of fight.

I thought I had seven more days.

I was wrong.

An explosion booms through the cell. It's so loud it temporarily replaces all other sound. All I hear is a high-pitched ringing in my ears. Wes's weight leaves my body, his gun drops from my head. He disappears into a mist of red and pink, falling lifeless against the iron bed frame. His mouth is open, and so are his eyes but he sees nothing.

Wes is dead.

I try to catch my breath but can't get off the floor. I watch motionless as Wes's blood seeps into the dingy yellowed mattress, staining it a deep red.

Smoke walks over to him, gun in hand. He crouches down and smirks.

"How'd that feel, motherfucker?"

CHAPTER FOURTEEN

FRANKIE

Smoke's shadow in the moonlight covers every inch of my body and blocking every bit of the light from the window. I heave again, but there's nothing left in my stomach.

And nothing left of my hope.

There's only so much one person can take, and I fear I'm nearing the point of no return.

I wipe my mouth with the back of my hand. "You…You killed him," I whisper.

"He interfered," Smoke answered. "No one interferes." He lights a cigar and takes a puff, blowing smoke rings into the cell.

I spot Wes's fallen gun. It's within reach.

I have an idea. It's a stupid and reckless one, but it's all I've got.

Dr Ida Tip: If you see an opportunity to escape, take it.

I pretend to heave again and stretch my fingers, connecting with the gun. My mouth is inches away from bits of Wes's skull. My fingers brush over soft chunks of his brain, and if my stomach wasn't already empty, I really would be heaving again. I can smell the copper in his blood and feel the heat escaping his freshly opened skull as it rises from his corpse.

My fingertips contact the gun. I wrap my hand around it and place my finger on the trigger. Smoke's standing behind me, I can feel his eyes on my back. I sit up slowly onto my knees only to be met with the barrel of his gun on the back of my head.

"You going to kill me, *hellion*?" Smoke asks, sounding amused.

I'm glad my torment and agony is so entertaining for him. I don't see how I can save anyone right now. Let alone myself. I feel all hope draining from my body, from my soul, like someone has pulled the bath plug.

I make a decision.

A vengeful spiteful stupid decision.

One I won't be around to regret.

"No, I'm not going to kill you." I say, shifting the gun into position. I turn around slowly so he can be rest assured it's not pointed at him.

It's in my mouth.

CHAPTER FIFTEEN

SMOKE

Impatient bitch.

This girl would rather kill herself then wait for someone else to do it.

I'm pretty sure the asshole with his brains scattered all around the cell is one of Griff's men. He's checking up on me and I won't fucking tolerate that kind of bullshit. I told Griff I'd bring him Frankie in a week's time I'll make good on my word.

I'll also bring him this motherfuckers head in a box.

But first I've got to deal with the issue at hand.

I think it's safe to say that boredom isn't a problem of mine. Not anymore.

Not where Frankie Helburn is concerned and not since I've seen her body back in the motel room.

And what a fucking body it is. Even scraped and cut up, maybe even because of it, I was rethinking my plans for her.

A week isn't nearly long enough when I think of how much pleasure I could get from taking my revenge out on the body of Frank Helburn's only daughter. I could hurt her. Her body. Her mind. I could destroy her and hand him back an empty fucking shell only capable of retelling the stories of what I've done to her over and over again. I could ruin that beautiful body of hers in every single way possible. Frank Helburn would get the message loud and motherfucking clear.

Fuck with me and suffer the consequences.

But my revenge plans are ruined and so is my deal with Griff if the bitch is dead.

I lean against the wall with one leg raised, my boot flat against it as if she's about to sing me a song instead of threatening to blow her fucking brains out. No matter what I can't let her pull the trigger. It will destroy all my plans and I won't fail. Not at this. As much as it pains me to rely on something or someone else, I need this crazy bitch.

I try to appear as calm as I can, but my blood is boiling. I'm angry, and I'm irritated. She could ruin everything on one pull of the trigger. "You're gonna let this shit-bag be the reason for the end?"

She closes her eyes, and I can see by the way the hand holding the gun is shaking that she's trying to grow the balls to pull the trigger.

"I'll give it to you. You're creative, but in this situation, suicide is the coward's way out. I didn't take you for a coward," I tell her.

That part's true. She's not the shy meek girl I thought she was while watching her. She's stronger than I thought. Defiant.

Wild.

Not to mention, out of her god damned mind.

Frankie's breathing heavy. Her t-shirt is ripped down the middle exposing her taut stomach.

Her waist is small and trim and the way she's breathing so

erratically I can make out the shadows of her abs beneath her bruised skin. Her thighs and calves are shapely. I've never seen her workout in all the time I've watched her, but there's no doubt the girl does more physical work than just walking to and from school every day.

Her banging body isn't the only thing that throws me. Well, besides her complete lack of self-preservation. It's her eyes. Originally, I thought her eye color was just another distortion in that grainy picture on my phone, but it turns out it was the only accurate thing about that picture. Bright yellow-gold with spots of orange. I've never seen anything like it. She's got fucking *flames* in her eyes.

Fitting.

"If you wanna take the coward's way out, go right on ahead. Pull the fucking trigger. I'm not gonna fucking stop ya," I make a large sweeping motion with my arm.

She opens her eyes and slowly removes the gun from her mouth only to place it against her temple. My gun is still in my hand, but only in case she decides to swing hers my way.

"How is this the coward's way out?" she asks. Her pupils dilate. Her bottom lip is bruised and swollen, a dried patch of blood in the corner.

I want to bite off the scab and catch the fresh blood on my tongue before it spills down her chin.

"I might as well die when and how I say so. There's no other way out as I see it. If there was I'd take it. But at least this will be *my* choice. Not yours! Not my father's. Not *his*!" Her eyes dart to the corpse on the floor. She lowers her voice and straightens her shoulders. There's a determination in her words that makes me think I'm losing this battle.

And I don't lose.

"That's where you're mistaken. Is this how you want to go? Is this WHEN you want to go? Pulling that trigger is going to make you meet the dirt, that's for sure, but you're lying to yourself if you think doing it this way is dying on your own terms. It's a coward's way out," I remind her.

"Then I'm a coward," she says, closing her eyes again and taking a deep breath.

Shit.

Something inside me clicks. I don't want to see this girl blow her fucking head off. I don't want to see the fire in her eyes die.

What a fucking waste. I think to myself.

I can't take any joy in getting my revenge on Frank if his daughter is the one who pulls the trigger.

Frankie's lips are moving silently. She's counting to herself.

Fuck.

One.

Two.

I'm on her just as she squeezes the trigger. The gun goes off, the bullet missing her and grazing my shoulder. I've got the gun, and I've got her back to the floor, her wrists pinned above her head.

Her gaze is its own kind of bullet, shooting hatred straight through me.

"Face your fucking end like a man," I say, tearing the gun from her hands and tucking it in the waistband of my jeans. I'm fucking fuming because some chick I don't know and should want dead wanted to kill herself. My confusion is just as fucking infuriating as the girl fighting against me.

"I should have just killed you!" she grinds out, trying to free her hands from my grip.

In a really fucked up way I'm beginning to admire this girl. She's got balls bigger than a lot of men I've dealt with in this business. Her unwavering rebellion stirs something deep inside of me. Something unfamiliar. I write it off as irritation because god-fucking-damn-it does she irritate me.

She's kicking and punching.

I hold her still. I lean down close. "Yeah you should have killed me, hellion. It would have been the smart thing to do. But I'll admit, it's kind of fucking cute how you think you can take me out that easily. Try something like this again, and I'll make you wish that bullet would've hit the fucking mark." I produce my blade and run the sharp tip across her collarbone, slicing into the first few layers of skin to show her how serious I am.

She winces but then corrects herself and stares up at me unflinchingly as if she can't feel the pinch of pain or the scratching of the blade followed by the droplets of blood running down her chest, staining her bra.

"There she is," I say.

My cock twitches.

I lift the blade and hold it down between her legs, pressing the flat side up against her pussy through her panties. "I'll cut you up from the inside out. Your death won't be a pretty one. I hold the control here. Not you. You'd be wise not to fucking test me."

Her eyes widen, her breaths are short, quick.

"Why?" she asks, her eyes wide and determined. "Why are you doing this? Any of this?"

I chuckle because I can't help myself. She's trying my patience and testing my restraint. "Because I took you, hellion. You're all mine. Only *I* get to say whether you live or die."

"You're a monster." she whispers on a shaky exhale.

You have no fucking idea.

I withdraw the blade and tuck it away. I brush a lock of dark hair from her eyes, tucking it behind her ear, my fingers lingering on the delicate curve of her bruised and sliced neck.

"You're right," I whisper. "I *am* a monster." Roughly, I grab her chin, forcing her to look me in the eye.

"I'm *your* monster."

CHAPTER SIXTEEN

FRANKIE

I wake up from a dreamless sleep and even though I hurt all over I'm grateful to be alive.

I don't know what I was thinking by trying to kill myself. Actually, I do know. I felt scared and desperate and backed into a corner. That's not who I am. I won't make the mistake again. I'm going to write it off as a moment of weakness and concentrate on escaping.

I look around and realize I'm no longer in the cell. I'm in a bed. A big one. It's soft and the sheets and blankets are simple but smell clean.

I'm also completely naked.

Fuck.

I sit up slowly, pulling the blankets with me to cover myself. The pain doesn't hit me like a hammer although I'm still very sore.

Smoke appears in the doorway, naked from the waist up. His chest is broad and so are his shoulders. His abs flex from underneath the colorful tattoos that cover almost every inch of his skin. He walks past me, crossing the room, He opens a door in the far corner. He disappears inside, and I hear water running. He comes back out and rips the sheets from my body.

I'm naked, and his gaze is trailing over my body. I can feel his stare on me. His eyes grow darker.

"No!" I shout, pushing him away as he grabs me by the waist. I turn over on my knees and try to scramble from his grasp.

"You want a bath or not?" he asks.

I still and turn toward him, covering my chest. I search his face for any trace that this might be a joke, but I don't find one.

I nod because there's nothing in the world that sounds better to my aching muscles than a bath. He lifts me again into his strong arms as if I weigh nothing, and I breathe through my nose deeply and try to calm the urge to push off his chest and run.

Smoke is much larger than me, but I don't realize how much until I'm cradled in his arms. He's massive. Taller than me by a foot and outweighing me by at least a hundred pounds.

He carries me over to the bathroom while I try and keep myself covered the best I can with my hands over my chest and my legs crossed at my thighs. He sets me on my feet beside the tub but I'm weaker than I thought. My legs shakier. I stumble.

Smoke catches me. His arm around my waist. He dips his hand into the water to check the temperature.

"I'm surprised you even check. Imagine what joy you could get out of tossing me into scalding hot water."

"Don't fucking tempt me, hellion."

I look around at the white tile and high window. "Where are we?" I ask. The last thing I remember is the prison cell.

"We're still at the same place," he says. "This is the warden's house. Or at least, it used to be. I figure I can keep a better eye on you here."

The small bathroom doesn't look anything like the abandoned prison. There's no graffiti or peeling paint. Everything in it is at least twenty years old, but it doesn't appear to be abandoned at all. The white tile lining the bottom half of the walls and covering the floor is clean and the claw foot tub, although rusted at the drain, is otherwise intact.

Smoke, seemingly satisfied with the temperature of the water, lifts me again.

I brace myself to cringe from the contact against my bruised skin but he's surprisingly gentle as he sets me down in the tub.

Why the hell is he bothering?

He's been a brute. Rough. Now he's suddenly Florence fucking Nightingale? I think I liked the aggression better. At least, it wasn't confusing.

I hiss through my teeth as I sink down in the warm water as it makes contact with my wounds. It's only a temporary sting. After a few minutes, my muscles begin to relax. I moan out loud. I'm so far gone, lost in the wonderful sensation I drop my hands from my chest and almost forget that I'm not alone until Smoke speaks.

He's looking down into the water. "That guy in the cell, did he…was I too—"

"No!" I cut him off, repeating my answer. "No."

"Good," he says with a curt nod. His lips turn up in a snarl like he's remembering what had happened.

"Why do you care?" I ask.

Smoke crouches down next to the tub. "Because you

belong to me. Your fear, your anger, your fury, your fucking defiance. It all belongs to me. And nobody fucks with what's mine but ME."

I gasp, his words twisting my insides into a mess that can rival the tangled vines of the prison yard.

ME, not Griff, the man he's supposedly working for, the man my father stole from. His one eyebrow, the one with a scar through it, twitches. He looks down into the water. There's more to this situation than he's letting on.

Much more.

I remember my nudity and cover my body to shield myself from his gaze.

He chuckles. "Who do you think is the one who undressed you? Hate to tell you, hellion, but I've already seen it all. Every inch of your bruised and cut flesh."

He might have a point, but I refuse to uncover my body. He may say he owns me, but it's a lie.

I own me.

No one else.

I close my eyes as if to block him out in every way I'm capable of, but they spring open again when I feel a sting at my lip. "Ouch!"

Smoke is holding a cotton ball to the corner of my mouth, a medical kit open on the side of the tub, a bottle of rubbing alcohol open on the floor. He's cleaning my cuts. I'm about to ask him why but choke down the words. I can't think of a single positive outcome that will come of that question so I ask him another one.

"Who was that guy? The one in the cell?" I ask.

"An asshole sent to check up on me by an even bigger asshole," he grates out.

"He doesn't work for you?" I ask.

Smoke shakes his head. "No. I work alone. At least, I do

now." I can see the regret on his face the second the words are spoken.

I remember Dr. Ida's rules. *Relate to your captor.* "I'm better by myself, too," I say.

Smoke raises an eyebrow and moves the cotton ball to a scrape on my shoulder. That's when I notice the gauze covering the top of his right shoulder and the bloodstain underneath from the bullet I meant to shoot into my own head.

Smoke stills and turns his head to the side. There's an unspoken question lingering on his lips.

"What?" I ask. "You think you're so different from everyone else in the world? You're not. There are a lot of people out there like you. Hell, I'm even more like you than you think."

"That's not fuckin' possible," Smoke mutters, closing the kit.

This is the first time I'm attempting to relate to him in a non-panicked state so I take a moment and choose my words wisely.

"Well, you're a lone wolf. Just like me. Governed by nothing and no one except his own fucked up set of rules and morals, and believe it or not, that's just like me." I meant to lie to him, but the words I've spoken are the truth. I am alone in this world and so is he.

"You think that matters?" Smoke asks.

"Yes. I think it does." I argue then decide to stretch the truth a bit. "We both use what we've got to make others do what we want. I use my looks to get the guy from the grocery store to make deliveries by promising him things I'm never planning to go through with. I get the neighbors to fix the door hinge or rewire the stove by offering hints of a friendship I'm not capable of giving them. You do the same except you use your intimidation to get what you want. It's your own brand of manipulation. So, you see? We may have our differences, but there's a lot between us that's the same too. And I have a feeling that you're just as lonely as I am."

"Maybe," he says calmly.

I'm taken aback by his agreement. Stunned.

This might actually work.

Smoke washes my body with a washcloth. He's gentle and careful. His face twists in concentration as he maneuvers around the worst of the road rash on my arm.

This man is a lot more complicated than I initially thought.

He washes between my legs, never taking his eyes from mine. He drags the washcloth up, dragging it lightly over my nipples then lingering over the cut below my collarbone where he stares down with an expression of awe.

A LOT more complicated.

Smoke blinks rapidly, dropping the cloth into the tub. With a small plastic cup, he rinses my hair, careful not to get any water in my eyes. "There is one major difference between us you're forgetting about. The most important one."

"And what might that be?" I ask, as Smoke helps me to stand and wraps a towel around my shoulders.

Something cold and hard juts into the base of my spine and trails up the bone until my entire body is taut.

Smoke's lips move against the tip of my ear, his voice rolling through me like thunder.

"I've got the balls to pull the trigger."

CHAPTER SEVENTEEN

SMOKE

Frankie is a shit actress. She's worse than Rage because even Rage was convincing, at least for the first twenty minutes before you realize there is something very off about the blonde with murder written in her blue eyes.

But Rage was Meryl Fucking Streep compared to Frankie's pitiful getting-to-know-you performance.

I toss her one of my large black t-shirts. It'll be enormous on her but I'm exhausted and don't feel like rummaging through the storage bins in the other room to see what other clothes might be there.

Frankie goes to put it on but winces when she raises her arms above her head. I walk over to her and steady the shirt helping her pull her arms through and then get back in bed. I go to remove a set of handcuffs off my wrist to tether her to the bed again.

"No! Please. No!" she begs, holding her already bruised and cut wrist.

It's the first time I've really heard her beg. It sparks something within me, making my cock jump to attention.

I'm too fucking tired to do anything about it and I'm too fucking tired to think things to death. There will be time for all that shit tomorrow.

I secure the cuff back around my wrists. I kick off my jeans and can practically feel her panic as I get in beside her. I pull her back against my chest, wrapping my arms around her tiny body, resting my hands on her flat stomach. She smells like the lavender shampoo I just used to wash her hair. I begin to relax with my chin on top of her head when I feel her tremble against me.

"What are you doing?" she asks with a shaky voice.

"It's this or the cuffs," I tell her. It's aggravating to even feel like I should explain why I don't want to fuck her right now.

No matter how beautiful her trembling is. No matter how hard my cock swells as she takes a deep breath to steady herself, but doesn't stop shaking.

Defiant little hellion.

"I fucking can't sleep with you trembling like a frightened Chihuahua," I scold.

"I just don't know what you...I don't want you to..." she says.

I sigh. "What you want doesn't matter. Your 'no's' don't fucking matter. YOU don't fucking matter. Now get some fucking sleep, before I cuff you, strip that shirt from your body, and show you first hand that you belong to me."

"No. Please. I'm in high school," she whimpers. "I'm seventeen. I'm too young—"

I roll my eyes. "I don't give a shit how old you are, even though I know you're twenty-two."

I don't know why I feel the need to defend myself.

Especially to *her*.

She stops trembling and eventually falls asleep, making a soft snoring sound through her dried blood clogged nose. She's small and warm and I find myself nuzzling my nose and lips into the crook of her neck inhaling the fresh scent of the bath soap.

"Tell me where your old man is and I'll make this all go away," I tell her even though she's sleeping. It's not true either. If her old man came to the fucking door right now and turned himself in it's not like I could just let Frankie go. She knows and has seen too much.

She's mine now.

I close my eyes, not expecting her to answer. I get one anyway. To my ears her words sound and feel like the beginning of the end.

"That's where you're wrong."

CHAPTER EIGHTEEN

FRANKIE

I'm lying on my side in a grassy field. Various rocks and pebbles stab into my back as I try to move. It smells like sour milk and rotten meat. I hear the crackling of fire along with echoes of screams in the distance.

Then nothing.

Slowly, I raise my head only to find that I'm surrounded by thousands of bloodied bodies. I sit up and realize I'm on the top of a pile directly in the center. Not just a mound of bodies. But parts. Men and women, all in various stages of death and decay. All bent in unnatural positions. Grayish skin sagging from broken bones. Thick red turns to black as the blood on their clothing dries before my eyes.

I scramble to my feet. My stomach rolls but there's no time to get sick, there's only time to run. I stumble between limbs and torsos as I try to climb down, lifting my knees high. I free my sunken foot by pressing my hand onto hard cold flesh that contains what feels like teeth, but I don't look to see what I've touched.

My feet finally hit the ground, and I'm free of the pile. I freeze. There are more bodies than grass on the field where I'm standing. As far as I can see. I can't process what's around me because the need to flee is stronger than the need to contemplate their mortality or even my own for that matter.

I navigate the field the best I can, jumping over human obstacles like they're land mines and not corpses. I try not to stare too long at the bulging eyes staring up at me, or the mouths frozen-open in deadly screams, but I can't help it. I look then quickly turn away, but it's too late. Now, I can hear them. Their screams. Their last pleas for their lives. Begging that went unanswered.

It's too much. It's all way too much. I move faster. Push harder. But I'm too fast. I trip over a leg, and when I brace myself, my hands land on a severed head. Not just any severed head.

My mother.

Now, it's me who's screaming.

I pick the head up in my hands, but when it hits me what exactly I'm holding, I drop it at my feet and it lands in a position that looks like she's buried up to her neck in the ground except I know there's no body beneath. I turn to the side, and the churning of my stomach finally emerges as I purge its contents until I'm sure there's nothing left. I bend over with my hands on my knees and try to catch my breath while trying to turn off my thoughts. I won't be able to get free of this field if I concentrate too hard on what's around me. I have to keep going, keep moving, but the screams of the dead around me grow louder, holding me in place. They're so loud now I cover my ears and shut my eyes tightly in an attempt to silence them. It doesn't work. I'm lost. I don't know what to do. I'm going to die by way of scream and soon I'll be just another body on the already bloodied field.

I'll take it. I'll die right now. Eternal silence has to be better than the shrill screams adding to my own.

"Be quiet, girl," I hear my father's voice echo from somewhere above me. I take my hands from my ears and look around, but he's not there. It's like he's speaking into a microphone from the clouds. His voice is

distant and echoing all around me. The screams become muted. "He'll hear you."

"Where are you?" I ask, spinning around in a circle. I can barely see through my unshed tears. But still, he's not there.

There's an explosion in the distance. It takes me by surprise, and I take cover, diving behind a tree stump. I can't tell if it's me shaking or the earth beneath me. However, it might be me because I can hear my teeth chattering. After a few minutes, I realize it's not my teeth, but my mother's as her head vibrates from the aftershock of the explosion.

There's another explosion. A flash of yellow then red appears from over a small hill in the distance followed by a huge plume of grey.

I don't know where I'm going I just know that I need to leave. "Run, Frankie. Run," My father orders angrily, his voice surrounding me on all sides. I'm drowning in his voice, but he's still nowhere to be seen. "Run," he commands again. "Be smart. Stay safe and RUN. He's coming for you, Frankie. RUN RUN RUN!"

"Where?" I cry, looking to the cloud covered sky above me. "Where do you want me to run? And if you want me to be safe then why won't you rescue me yourself! Where are you? Why aren't you here?" I shout at the sky, growing angrier at the man who won't show himself. I ball up my fists and dig my fingernails into my palms.

Only the sky answers with a rumbling roll of deep thunder that rattles my bones. From over the small hill, a shadow of a man appears from the smoke. Not just any man. He's as massive as a bear. My spine straightens with awareness, fear, and familiarity. His strides are sure and wide, and I realize it's because he knows where he's going.

Or WHO he's going to.

Me.

He pays the bodies around him no mind. As he walks, the ground shakes again like the thunder has crashed to the ground, causing an earthquake. His dark gaze is solely focused on me. My blood turns to ice. Fear strangles me. My throat grows dry and thick. I can't swallow. Finally snapping out of my haze, I heed my father's advice and turn to run, but my feet have sunken into the soft ground. I'm held in place. Stuck.

Panic constricts my breathing.

He's so close now that I can see his face. His tanned skin. His dark, emotionless eyes that convey nothing but his determination to get to me.

The sun emerges from behind the clouds, and I immediately notice the man has no shadow. He's got to be some demon. He smirks. No, a devil. There is no doubt in my mind that the carnage surrounding us is his doing. He's a one-man army walking across the bloodied field of his sin, and I'm next to face his wrath, but there's nothing I can do but stare as my end nears.

Before he reaches me, he kicks over my mother's head like it's a beach ball in his way, and I again feel sick. I close my eyes tightly and wish away the feeling while waiting my turn to become just another corpse in the field. I just hope it's over fast.

I flinch when I feel his rough hand against my cheek. "Open your eyes, hellion," he says. I refuse and shake my head. He grips my face with his hand, holding it still. I can feel his breath against my skin. "Look at me, my love."

My love?

Confused by his words, I finally obey and come face to face with evil. He's hatred personified. There's something terrifyingly beautiful about the purity of his evil. There's something else there too. Deep in his eyes. Lust. Admiration. Awe.

He strokes my face in a way that's almost loving. This time I don't flinch. In fact, I find myself leaning into his warm touch.

The man looks all around us with a proud smile on his upturned lips. "This is better than I expected," he says, pressing his lips to mine in a brief soft kiss that makes me feel like I'm floating.

"Better?" I ask, my head spinning. "What's better?"

He lifts me from the mud into his strong tattooed arms with ease and cradles me against his hard chest. "Rest now, my love," he whis-

pers, carrying me back across the field, gliding over the bodies with ease without ever looking down at the ground.

I find surprising comfort in his arms. I sigh and settle myself against his body, nuzzling against his warmth. The fear that had me frozen just moments before has vanished. I feel safe now.

Whole.

"I'm so tired." I hear myself say. I yawn and close my eyes. The weariness begins to take me under.

"Look," he whispers, spinning me around in his arms slowly.

I open my eyes and lift my head. I take one last look at the aftermath. The chaos. The gore. The blood. The death.

He chuckles and kisses the top of my head. "Of course, you're tired. Look at all you've done."

I WAKE UP FROM ONE NIGHTMARE ONLY TO BE THRUST BACK into another.

Smoke is standing in the doorway. His hair is wet from a recent shower and combed back. He's not wearing a shirt just his leather biker cut and jeans. His feet are bare.

"Get dressed. Something in there should fit you," Smoke says, pointing to the large black storage container at the foot of the bed. "There's food in the kitchen. Come out when you're done. The windows are all bolted shut and the back door is bolted and only I have the key so don't waste your fucking time. If you aren't out in five minutes, I'm gonna come back and dress you myself."

All the gentleness from the night before is gone.

My stomach growls with emptiness and twists with disappointment.

Smoke disappears from the doorway. There's an open first aid kit on the side table. I raise my arm which is less sore than it was the day before. Band-Aids and butterfly stitches over my various cuts. Orange circular stains peek out from underneath the dressings and I spot an open bottle of iodine in the kit.

I slide to the edge of the bed and wince from the pain and soreness although today it's bearable.

I dig through the large plastic container which is filled with women's clothes and shoes of various sizes. Some items still have the sales tags attached. I find a simple and soft pair of light colored jeans and a white fitted tank top. For shoes, I find a pair of Converse that's a half size too big but will work. At the bottom is a zip lock bag with various combs and brushes. I brush out my hair and dig through for a hair tie, pulling my hair on the top of my head in a messy bun. I also find something else that interests me in another small bag tucked into the side of the bin. Not knowing if I'll need it, I tuck it away under the mattress in case I don't have access to the bin again.

I go into the bathroom, and what I see reflected in the mirror doesn't surprise me. My bruises and scrapes still ache but the swelling has gone down and they aren't so purple or angry anymore. I find a new toothbrush in a small travel kit in the bathroom and help myself to it. I savor the feeling of brushing my teeth until my gums bleed.

Remembering that I'm on a time crunch I make my way through a small hallway where there's one other door partially open. I peek in hoping to find a computer but I'm not that lucky and Smoke's not that dumb. It's another small bedroom, or at least I think it is, it's so filled with black storage containers with yellow lids from top to bottom it's hard to tell.

What the hell is in them? More clothes? For who? Why?

The main living area is almost as small as the bedroom. The entire house can't be more than six hundred square feet total. A single loveseat sits against the wall with a brick fireplace lining the wall. It doesn't look like it's ever been used but then again, it's a fireplace in South Florida, why would it ever be used? A little square two-person table is tucked into the corner of the open galley style kitchen. Everything out here is just like it is in the bathroom. Clean, but old. The sofa is a faded brown color and has a tear on the top of one of the cushions, exposing the stuffing. The dining room table has duct tape around one of the legs. The chairs are mismatched as well as the cushions tied to the seats.

On the table, there's a glass casserole dish steaming with something that looks like biscuits floating on the top. It smells like salt and gravy. My eyes roll back in my head.

My mouth waters, and my stomach growls.

"Eat," Smoke says, pointing to one of the chairs.

I don't like taking orders, especially from him, but this is one order I can't turn down. I don't care if it's fucking poison. I'll go out with a full stomach, and right now a full stomach is all I can think about.

How long has it been since I've eaten?

I try to remember, but as Smoke ladles out a heaping scoop of biscuits with sausage and white gravy onto a plate in front of me I realize it's been at least a day. Maybe two. Smoke drops a spoon next to my plate. "You're not getting a fucking fork."

I inwardly smirk. Oddly enough his comment makes me proud. I straighten a little more.

Smoke isn't underestimating me or what I'm capable of. He knows I'll use anything to my advantage, and he's right. Him knowing this will make escaping harder, but I'll cross that bridge when I get there.

After breakfast.

Smoke nods to me, and I waste no more time shoveling the

food into my mouth. The biscuits are hot and fluffy and the sausage gravy is salty and savory. My tongue rejoices, and when I discover the bottom of the pan is coated in sliced potatoes I practically jump out of my chair with joy.

Smoke's standing in the kitchen watching me with those dark dangerous eyes.

The hair on my arms stand on end. Dr. Ida's rules run through my head.

Escape. Befriend. Seduce.

"Did you make this?" I ask, with my mouth ful.

"No," Smoke answers gruffly.

"Then, who made it?" I'm chewing and swallowing at record speed. "It's really good."

"Someone."

How articulate. I'm reaching for more food from the dish when I feel his eyes on me. I look up.

"Listen, when you…" he starts, but he quickly shuts his mouth and pulls out his phone, tapping something out.

"What?" I ask, curiously.

"Never mind," he mutters, shutting me down.

Friendship, even a fake one meant to secure survival, is going to be impossible with someone who won't talk to me, but I'll keep trying. Stopping means I've given up and I've learned my lesson. I'm not going to give up. I have more than myself to think about, and I'll use the thought of them to keep me going.

I down the entire glass of water sitting next to my plate and put down my spoon when my stomach feels like it's about to burst.

"Thank you for this," I say, raising my bandaged arm and giving him a small, fake smile. It's all I can muster. Thanking the man who kidnapped me doesn't exactly come easy or naturally.

Smoke nods but doesn't speak.

"Can I ask you why?"

"Why what?" he crosses the kitchen to stand over me at the table.

From this position, his size is even more intimidating. I almost lose my nerve, but swallow hard and find the courage to continue from deep within.

I crane my neck to meet his eyes. "Why did you take care of my cuts and bruises? Why are you feeding me or bothering if I'm to be tortured and killed in seven days anyway?"

"Six," Smoke corrects.

My stomach sinks. My eyes fall to my empty plate. My chin to my chest. "Six," I whisper to myself.

"Tell me where your old man is, and it won't come to that."

"I can't do that," I say.

"Can't or won't?"

"Both."

Smoke lifts me by the elbow and takes me back into the room where he cuffs me to the bed again. I don't think he's going to answer my question of why he's doing all this when he turns to leave, but as he disappears down the hallway I swear I hear him say just loud enough for me to hear, "Because, you'll need your strength, *hellion*."

CHAPTER NINETEEN

SMOKE

Crickets chirp. Frogs croak. A wolf howls in the distance. The old warden's house creaks and groans with every shift of the breeze like a crotchety old man complaining about the weather.

I could torture her for the information about the whereabouts of her old man like I promised, but I'm good at reading people. She's telling the truth. Not the entire truth, but at least about the part where she hasn't spoken to him in years. Torture is fucking pointless unless there's something to be revealed and torture on an innocent isn't nearly as fun as it sounds.

And not as fucking fun as spilling the blood of her old man will be.

I press play on the boom box on the floor and sink down onto the couch. Creed's "Arms Wide Open" fills the empty space in the room, but not in my cold black heart.

That one can't ever be filled.

It's officially been one year since that night, and I feel like drowning my fucking sorrows. Funny, until that night, I didn't think I was capable of sorrow.

I sit silently in the dark only able to see slightly past the cherry end of my cigarette. I'm alone except for a half-empty bottle of Jack and my own fucking thoughts.

This morning, I almost told Frankie the real reason I need to get to her father.

Instead, I bit my tongue and locked her in the room for the rest of the day to avoid talking to her for fear of letting it slip again. She don't need to know all the reasons why. She's bait. Bait don't need to know shit.

I set down the bottle and pull out the picture I keep tucked into the inner pocket of my cut. It's dark, but I don't need to see the picture. I know what's on it. I just want to feel it between my fingers. I've memorized every curve and line and detail of the ultrasound. Some people claim they're hard to make out, but not this one. Not for me. I see every curve of skull, the outline of a little heart in the center. Tiny lips sucking an even tinier thumb. At least, that's what Morgan told me the baby was doing, although to me it looks as if it's giving the finger. I chuckle, but it's short-lived. I reach for the bottle, tilting it high and downing several swallows before setting it back down.

It's said that you don't know who you really are or what you're capable until you're connected to another human being. This baby, who never had the chance to be born, is that connection for me.

I know who I really am now. What I'm really capable of.

And what I'm capable of is the stuff of nightmares.

I'll do those things, and I'll do them gladly because I'm close. So fucking close to setting things right. Or, as right as I can set them if Griff gets a hit from Frank on the picture of his daughter we've sent out into the world.

I pull out a new burner phone and dial Rage's number. It's a knee-jerk reaction. A habit I thought I'd broken myself of that whiskey has apparently made me forget.

I tuck the phone back into my pocket before I can press send. It's too late. Too fucking late to rebuild a bridge that's better off burned. I'd broken my own number one rule. No loyalties. And look where it's gotten me.

Making that call would be like trying to revive a chicken after its head's been chopped off and all its feathers plucked.

I was Rage's mentor. She was sixteen years old when I first saw her kill a man. The emptiness in her eyes changed to sheer fucking pleasure in that moment. I wanted to help her harness her skills and reign in the shit that would've resulted in her either in the ground or on death fucking row. I wanted to teach her because there was no one there to teach me and figuring that shit out on your own is like climbing uphill while the fucking hill is turning into a mountain.

Rage proved she had feelings, even though they aren't like the rest of society's, when she fell in love with a biker named Nolan. Good kid. The problem is I helped her rescue him from some shit one night and that shit went to complete shit. Nolan was saved.

Can't say the same thing about my relationship with Rage.

I look to the closed door of the back bedroom where Frankie is asleep and cuffed to the bed.

I sigh and clutch the ultrasound to my bare chest. I drain the bottle of whiskey. I comfort myself with thoughts of revenge. Of bloodshed.

That's why I'm here.

That's what this is all about.

It's why Frankie Helburn will die.

CHAPTER TWENTY

FRANKIE

It's well after midnight when the door squeaks open and Smoke comes in. The smell of whiskey and cigar smoke reach me well before he does, bumping his shin into the bed.

"Fucking bed," he whispers.

Shit. Shit. Shit.

I hate to see what he's capable of in this state, but I know I don't want to find out, so I pretend to be asleep.

Smoke sits down on the end of the mattress and wrestles with his boots, dropping them to the ground one after the other.

I don't hear him move again, so I wait, counting silently to twenty in my head. Still nothing.

I risk opening my eyes, and when I do, I blink through the darkness until my eyes adjust. He's still there, sitting at the edge of the bed. He's hunched forward, his wide back bathed in moon light. His elbows are propped up on his knees, face in his hands, fingers tangled in, and pulling at his hair.

For the first time since I've been held against my will, the monster looks a lot less…like a monster. Gone is the cocky smirk and even cockier words. He looks like a man right now, a very troubled one.

Smoke sighs, then rounds the bed, pulling off his shirt. I close my eyes as he slides under the blanket.

He leans over me, and I freeze in fear. I feel his breath on my cheek. He unlocks the cuff tethering me to the bed. I exhale without making it noticeable which is a feat. He doesn't take the cuff off completely though, this time he wraps his arms around my waist and attaches the side he's removed from the bed to his own wrist, adding to the handcuffs already adorning his wrists that I've yet to see him without.

He pulls me against his chest the same way he did the night before, and within moments, he's asleep, lightly snoring in my ear, his warm chest rising and falling evenly against my back.

"Are you awake?" I ask into the dark.

Smoke doesn't so much as stir.

I pretend to be trying to roll over and elbow him in the ribs.

Nothing.

I exhale.

"I need to talk to someone and since you're the only person around, I figure it might as well be you, and since you're passed out and probably drunk, I don't think you'll mind too much."

I sigh, then laugh to myself. This is all so ridiculous. Talking to the man who kidnapped me because I feel like a chat.

"I remember seeing you, before you came to the school," I say. "You were across the street at the gas station. I felt you before I saw you. I was aware of your existence before I even knew you existed. I know that sounds stupid, but it's true. I felt you there, and when I saw you, I thought…this sounds even more stupid, especially considering all that's happened, but I thought you were the most beautiful man I'd ever seen. I've never thought that of anyone else before. One face blends into another for me, one no prettier or more handsome than the next for the most part, but you. You stood out."

I look over my shoulder to make sure he's still asleep. His long lashes lay against his tanned cheeks. His brows are furrowed, even in sleep.

"I guess that shows what a great judge of character I am. Someone so beautiful can do such ugly things. Write that down. You can use it as the title of your autobiography one day."

My eyelids grow heavy. I close them and adjust my head on the pillow. Smoke's warm breath floats across the back of my head.

"Now you're going to either kill me, or turn me over to someone else who's going to kill me," I say, followed by a yawn.

Smoke suddenly shifts, his arms tighten around me like I'm about to escape. I jump in his grasp and turn my head only to find him still sound asleep.

I rest my head back on the pillow. I lower my voice to a whisper as sleep takes me under.

"You wanna know what the really fucked-up part is?" I sigh. "You're still the most beautiful man I've ever seen."

CHAPTER TWENTY-ONE

SMOKE

You're still the most beautiful man I've ever seen.

I'll give it to her. Frankie's not as much of a shit actress as I may have thought. She's good enough to have me believing for half a second that she might even mean it. But it's a trick. I know it is. I ain't falling for it. I will not be manipulated.

Not by her. Not by anyone.

Fucking, *hellion.*

Fucking sweet tits, fat lips, curvy hips, high-rounded ass, and fakest fucking smile I've ever seen.

I've got to make a run into town for supplies, and I have to run an errand and check up on something too important to risk using the phone.

I sure as shit am not taking Frankie with me, but I also don't trust that she won't gnaw her hand off to free herself from the cuffs while I'm gone.

I go as far as to reach for my phone. This time it's Morgan's number I begin to dial.

Shit.

Without a shit-ton of other options, and not being too far from Logan's Beach, I clear the screen and dial a different number.

The greeting is exactly what I expect considering who it is I'm calling.

"Yo yo yo! County morgue. You grill 'em, we chill 'em. You've reached Preppy. How may I service you today?"

Even though I roll my eyes it's good to hear a familiar voice. "Prep, it's Smoke."

"Smokey! What the fuck, dude? I've been searching for you ever since you saved my ass in that hospital. Where the fuck you been? I thought you mighta got sucked into that mega sinkhole that swallowed up half of Highway 28."

"Still above ground. For now, anyways."

"You know, I've missed these really detailed conversations of ours," Preppy says with an exaggerated sigh.

"We can sing by the campfire and braid each other's hair another time. Right now, I need a favor. I'm in the middle of a job. Need a babysitter for some cargo I'm toting."

"How big is this cargo?" he asks, jumping into business mode.

I look back to the house. "In weight or attitude?"

"Ah, it's like that."

"Weight wise she can't be more than a buck twenty, tops. And let's just say she wouldn't make it through a truck stop weigh in with the size of her fucking attitude."

"Noted. When do you need someone?"

"ASAP, brother."

"Alright man. You got it. I'd come out myself except Taylor and Miley have been up nights and I'm on duty so Dre can get some sleep." I hear a baby cooing in the background followed by another baby crying. There's a crash. "Bo, what did I tell you about the kitchen knives!" Preppy shouts away from the phone.

"Who can you spare?" I ask. There's a shuffling on the phone. Another crash in the background. "Bo, if you're making another fucking pipe bomb your mom is going to be really, really fucking mad. Like no TV for a week mad."

"Sowwy," I hear a little sad voice sing.

"It's okay. Go play in the backyard, and I'll bring your sisters out in a minute." Preppy comes back to the phone. "Kids, you can't live without them and you can't leave them alone with household items they can create explosives from."

"Is that what the saying is?"

"How the shit would I know," Preppy says. "Text me the location, Smoke, and I'll have someone out there tomorrow. I might have to dip into Bear's bitches, but someone will be there for you, bro. It'll be someone you can trust. I swear to that on a stack of motherfucking pancakes."

"Appreciate it, Prep."

"You know, I owe you more than sending someone out to help babysit even if you may or may not have allegedly abducted this someone. I owe you everything, man. You saved my goddamned life."

I shake my head. "I was just in the right place at the right time," I say.

"Yeah, whatever lets you sleep at night," Preppy says, "Shit, I gotta go." The phone sounds like it's tossed down, but the line doesn't go dead. "Bo, do not run that lawn mower over your…" his voice trails off.

I hang up, tap out the location of the prison and send it over to Preppy. I dig into my pocket and pull out my smokes. I light one and take a long slow drag.

I may not get close to people, not anymore and never

fucking again, but you can't make it in this world of ours, this life we chose, if you don't trust someone every now and again.

And just now, I've chosen to trust someone who named his daughters after fucking pop stars and whose son is the youngest on record to be on the FBI watch list.

There ain't many people out there who have my respect. Respect needs to be earned. Preppy's got mine. The man might have a case of verbal diarrhea there ain't no cure for, but he's been through hell and back. He's been tortured and brutalized the likes of which most folks can't begin to imagine. Most men, the strongest of men, in both body and spirit, would've caved after that.

Not Preppy.

Not Samuel Motherfucking Clearwater.

I take another drag of my smoke.

Anytime I've ever worked with Preppy, he could get me to laugh about the stupidest shit, but right now, I feel like I haven't really laughed in fucking years.

I'm tired. Worn the fuck out. Revenge is fucking exhausting.

I feel older than my thirty-five years.

I pause because something about that doesn't seem right. I double check the year on my phone and roll my eyes.

Probably because I'm thirty fucking six.

CHAPTER TWENTY-TWO

I've been going about this all wrong. Escape isn't a long-term solution. Not for me anyway. It's impossible. I'm trapped inside a prison, after all. Human workers are long gone, but overgrown brush and mangled fences now stand guard watching over a single prisoner.

Me.

All I need is time. A few hours. Just long enough to get to a computer before I'm found out.

Consequences be damned.

Smoke's on the phone on the front porch. He's left me uncuffed so I can shower and change. I've only got a few minutes. I'm dressed in a pair of short black athletic shorts and a fitted, white, Beatles t-shirt from the storage container. I take an extra thirty seconds to rip the collar off the shirt so it hangs off my one shoulder just like my favorite Veruca Salt shirt.

A shirt I'll probably never see again.

I look out the bedroom window. All I see are weeds. I

climb up on the dresser and stand, craning my neck to see what might lie beyond the tangled green and brown mess. I see something off in the distance just beyond the prison fence, and unless I'm seeing things, I'm pretty sure it's a roof top.

Now, if I can just find a way out of this damn house.

I shove my feet into my chucks and peek my head out the door down the hallway. I spot Smoke through the open front door. He's still on the phone, puffing away on a cigarette.

I creep toward the back door. It's locked and, just as Smoke had warned, it's also bolted shut.

There's got to be some other way out.

There's a potted plant in the corner. A plastic twin palm in a gigantic clay bowl. It's not the tree that interests me so much, but what I see that's hiding behind it.

A plastic doggy door.

No bolts.

I use all the power in my legs and ignore the pain shooting down my spine as I dig my toes into the carpet and push the plant from the wall until there's just enough room for me to shimmy behind it and crawl through.

I have no time to celebrate my short-lived freedom because there's an entire field of brush and debris to navigate.

I make a run for it.

SMOKE

The house is quiet. Too fucking quiet.

I run to the bedroom, but I already know it's empty. I dart back out and spot the plant and the doggy door, the plastic panel in the center flopping in the breeze.

I'm calm as I grab my gun and walk out the front door. I'm whistling as I round the house and spot her stumbling across the prison yard.

Game on, Hellion.

I'm a product of sin and violence. I was born with rage sizzling through my heated blood. With every crack of my knuckles, it consumes me until it is me.

I can't be the good guy, and I don't wanna be. Frankie Helburn is the only thing standing between me and Frank Helburn and I won't let it all go because of pussy.

I'm the arrow. Frankie's my target.

I never fucking miss.

CHAPTER TWENTY-THREE

FRANKIE

Beads of sweat fall into my eyes. I wipe them away with an even sweatier palm. My limbs shake as I lift my knees as high as I can, navigating my way over the tangled vines. I stumble a few times, scraping my hands on short spikey thorns.

I cannot fail.

I *will not* fail.

I step over the downed sign for Broward County Correctional Facility where the ground is smooth. My breaths are labored. My chest burns.

I make a beeline for the house, running and tripping over a hose. I growl at my own clumsiness and leap up the rickety porch steps.

I hear something inside and I hold in a scream of relief.

Foototopol

I bang on the door loudly and wildly, checking over my shoulder every few seconds. "Come on. Come on. Open the door," I chant to myself, shaking out my hands and jumping from foot to foot.

"What's the trouble, my dear?" A woman comes to the door, wiping her hands on her apron. She's older, maybe in her late seventies or early eighties. I'm just about to tell her everything when I stop.

If I tell her too much or the wrong thing, I could be putting her life in danger too.

Shit.

"Uhhh…no troubles exactly. I'm just lost and a little winded from walking over all the twisted weeds," I tell her. "I'm staying with my…boyfriend in a cottage around here, but I went for a walk, and now I can't find my way back."

"Oh my. Well, come on in, dear. I'm Zelda, it's very nice to meet you." She stands aside to usher me in.

"Thank you," I say, entering the house. It's just as small as the warden's house, but it's much cozier. Everything is yellow. Curtains, wallpaper, placemats on the table. Every wall has a high plant shelf running across the length of that wall and connecting to the next. Except there aren't plants on the shelves, instead they're lined with wooden statues. Mostly of animals, and most of those animals are some variation of dog. Some are crude little things that look as if a child made them with a dull knife and some are so smooth it's obvious they were sculpted by the hand of a skilled artist.

"Lovely, aren't they?" Zelda asks pointing up to the wooden statues on the shelves.

"Yes, very," I respond.

"Are you staying at the warden's cottage?" she asks, taking me off guard.

I don't want to lie and the truth might get her in trouble so I do what I think is the next best thing. "Is that what it's called?"

"It's the only house around here besides this one. No one's been there in quite a bit." Zelda says, shuffling her feet into the kitchen.

"We're just visiting. We won't be staying long," I explain. I'm trying not to jump to my point and worry her. It takes every ounce of restraint I have not to ransack the house in search of a computer.

"Have a seat, my dear." Zelda points to a yellow chair at an equally yellow kitchen. "Do you need to use the phone?" she asks.

"I'd actually like to use your computer if you have one. I dropped my phone and don't have my boyfriend's number memorized so I'd like to send him a message online that I'm alright before I try and head back." I glance out the corner of my eye toward the window. A chill runs up my spine, and it's as if I can feel his anger from across the field.

I don't have much time.

Zelda nods. "Would you like some tea?"

"Sure, I'd love some." I twiddle my thumbs on my lap and tap the toe of my shoe against the table leg.

Zelda puts an old yellow kettle on the burner. "I got one of them fancy lap-stops," she says, speaking slower and slower as the moments pass. "Friend of mine gave it to me for Christmas. He set up the internets and all, but I have no idea how to use it. Grandkids use the WeeFee when they visit, but they bring their own lap-stops. Let me just go fetch it for you."

Zelda pushes her glasses up the bridge of her nose and slowly shuffles from the kitchen. When she comes back, she's holding a laptop, but it's at least four inches thick and dark blue in color.

It wasn't *a* laptop, it was the *first* laptop.

"You got this for Christmas, you said?" I open the ancient computer praying to every god I can think of that the internet connections works. My fingers fly over the keyboard. I ask Zelda for a password, but only to be polite. I've already hacked the connection.

I'm on.

"Password is Christmas1993." Zelda says proudly, setting a cup of tea next to me.

"Is that the year you got the computer?" I ask.

"Yup! That's the one!" she holds up her own teacup and takes a sip.

"Thank you so much," I say, taking a quick sip. I set the teacup down and go back to the computer.

"You're awfully banged up. You get in a fight with some livestock and lose?"

"Oh, this," I say, touching my fingers to the corner of my lip. I forgot about my bruises and scabs. "Car accident."

Zelda twists her lips. She's not buying it.

"With a truck," I add. "I uh. I mean, a truck hit my car." *Shit.*

Zelda nods, but I can tell she's not sold on the story, and I don't blame her.

I wouldn't believe me either.

I'm in the deep web. Here, I'm not a clumsy young woman who's never experienced even a fraction of what life has to offer. No, here I'm at home. I'm comfortable navigating barriers and obstacles put in place to keep people like me out with practiced ease.

I could use my time to put out an SOS call instead of locating the file that needs to be transferred, but I decide not to. Not just because I can't spare the time, but because I can't put Zelda at risk. Lord knows what he'd do to her if he thought she aided my escape in some way.

After a long series of replacing bank code with my own, the money is there and the transfer is finally happening.

It's sloppy and not my best work, there are some other channels I would've liked to delete along the way, some ends I would've liked to tie up to cover my tracks, but there's no time for painting scenery today. This is abstract art. A few splashes on paint on the canvas, and I'm done. I'm so tempted to send an SOS message. It would only take a few minutes more. I look to Zelda.

There just isn't enough time, and it's too much of a risk.

I sigh in both relief and disappointment, then wipe Zelda's computer, making sure any trace I was ever here is erased from the memory before shutting it down and sliding it across the table.

"Thank you," I tell her, picking up my cup and taking another sip of tea.

Zelda stands and moves into the kitchen. She opens the fridge and takes out a large block of cheese. She opens a drawer and pulls out a huge kitchen knife. She flashes me a slow grin, the sun catches on the blade. My heart skips a beat, and slowly, I put down my teacup, realizing that this woman might not be the friendly home-making granny she first appeared to be.

I swallow hard.

Zelda brings the knife down hard into the block of cheese. She whistles as she cuts it into cubes.

She's just an old lady trying to be hospitable, Frankie.

I inwardly laugh at myself. My paranoia is still around. The thought is weirdly comforting. Paranoia is normal for me, and right now I'll take any taste of normal I can get.

I slide out my chair. "Thank you again, but I really can't stay—"

"Frankie," a familiar and very angry voice grumbles from behind. The barrel of his gun jabs at the base of my neck.

I freeze. The nerves in my spine jump. My chest tightens.

He might as well be strangling me because I can't catch my breath, but even with a gun to my back I can't help but feel relieved and even…a bit smug.

"What did you DO?" he asks through clenched teeth.

Zelda turns around with the plate. She sees Smoke standing behind me, and much to my surprise, she isn't startled.

"I didn't hear you come in," she says to him. She turns to me. "This the truck?"

"Zelda this is…" I go to make the introduction, to show Smoke I haven't told this nice woman anything that would warrant any harm coming to her, but Zelda laughs, cutting me off.

"I know who he is, dear." Zelda rounds the table and Smoke bends down so she can plant a kiss on his cheek. "I wasn't expecting you, or I'd have set out the good china," she says with a roll of her eyes.

"You of all people know I'm a paper plate kind of guy." He's cocky with her. Calm.

Who the hell was this man, and what did he do with the guy who threatened to cut off all my limbs while I watched?

Zelda's gaze drops to the gun. She holds out her hand. "You know the rules," she says sternly, and for the first time, I hear the slight trace of a Scottish accent in her voice.

Smoke leaves her hand empty but tucks the gun in his waistband. "Gotta break house rules this one time." He glares down at me. "Can't exactly trust this one."

"She don't seem so bad to me. We were just having some tea. She giving you trouble?"

"Something like that," Smoke replies.

Zelda leans on the table and winks at me. "Give him hell, lass." She pinches my cheek and smiles then turns back to

Smoke, pointing at his gun. "A Glock17, Smoke? Thought you were a Beretta man?"

"People change," he answers, still looking at me.

"You don't change," she laughs, swatting at him with a dishtowel.

"What alternate universe did I just fall into?" I ask, looking from Smoke to Zelda in a daze.

They both ignore me.

"Let me get another cup for tea out of the china cabinet in the den. I'll just be a minute," Zelda says.

"Make my tea a whiskey," Smoke says, taking a seat beside me. He lights a cigarette and turns to face me, his long legs spread, his knee knocking into my thigh.

"Did I say china cabinet? I meant liquor cabinet." Zelda shuffles from the kitchen.

We're alone. Suddenly, I'm not feeling so brave about my big, albeit temporary, escape.

Plus, Smoke's…calm.

Too calm.

"What did you DO, hellion?" Smoke taps the closed laptop with his index finger.

I shake my head. "Nothing. I really didn't do anything. Didn't get a chance to. Open it. Check for yourself."

He's not buying it. He opens the laptop and types in Zelda's password. Christmas 1993.

"How do you know her password?" I ask.

"Who do you think bought me the computer?" Zelda sings, coming back into the room with a bottle of Jack Daniels on a silver tray with a doily underneath.

She sets in on the table and opens the bottle. "I'd get you a glass, but I know how you are," she says.

Smoke grabs the bottle by the neck and tilts it to his lips, looking at me as his Adam's apple bobs up and down with each swallow.

He somehow manages to make drinking whiskey straight from the bottle look graceful. Grace and violence. What an oddly beautiful yet horrendous combination.

Smoke sets the whiskey on the tray and turns his attentions back to the computer.

Something about the way his nostrils flare, how he gets so heated at the littlest thing, makes my blood boil while simultaneously making me afraid. There's more to this man than kidnapper/killer extraordinaire. If I didn't hate him so much, I might be curious to find out more about him.

"This is bullshit," Smoke mutters, slamming the laptop shut. "You're lying."

"Language," Zelda corrects, setting the cheese plate on the table along with a box of cookies. The fancy ones with cupcake papers delicately cradling each different kind.

"What did she do?" Smoke asks Zelda.

Zelda shrugs and pops a cheese cube in her mouth, talking around it. "Nothing much. She told me she was lost and staying with her boyfriend. She needed to use the computer. She didn't do nothing. I was watching the entire time. She looked at the screen, then told me she changed her mind and shut the thing down. We're just having ourselves a little visit," Zelda says. "But if you want me to check the back way I can. Just to make sure she didn't bypass...standard methods." She looks to me and smiles, showing off the many fine lines around her mouth.

I was right. Zelda isn't some old woman who doesn't know shit about shit.

This is a woman who knows *everything*.

She knows what I did, and she just lied to Smoke for me.

But why?

"Why didn't you ask to use the phone?" he asks skeptically.

"Stop houndin' her, you brute. She didn't want to get who she saw as an innocent mixed up in your affairs. She's a smart one. A kind one to boot. A good combination, if you ask me."

Zelda pushes a lock of curly red hair back up into the handkerchief tied around her head and takes the bottle of whiskey off the table. She chugs down twice as much as Smoke did before setting it back down on the table and wiping her mouth with the back of her hand.

I smile at her because I can't help it.

She's fucking glorious.

Smoke lifts me out of the chair by my arm and tugs me toward the door. "Unfortunately, we can't stay," he grates.

"Understood," Zelda says, without breaking her big smile. She stands and follows us out.

"Just remember, boy," she wraps her wrinkled hand around Smoke's bicep. "The best jobs are the ones you don't ask for. The ones you don't get paid for. The ones you *learn* something from."

Zelda leans in and whispers in my ear. "Stay strong, lass. When he gives you hell, show 'em your horns."

"Thank you," I say to her, returning her smile and putting on my bravest face. I just met her but I don't want her to worry about me, and something in her eyes tells me she would do just that.

Zelda speaks in riddles. She also likes to feed people. She knows her guns. She lied for me. She's a friend of Smoke's.

Despite the last item, I decide I like Zelda.

I like her VERY much.

Smoke drags me over the weeds and brush by my arm. I feel the anger wafting off him. Despite this, I wave and call back to Zelda, "Thank you for the tea!"

When Zelda is back inside the house and out of earshot, Smoke grunts, "That was a stupid fucking move."

"I know." This time, I agree with him. It WAS stupid. But I don't regret it. Not for a second.

"I don't know what you're fucking playing at, but you need to stop before you get yourself or someone else killed," he growls.

"Before I get myself killed?" I raise my voice. "I'm dead in less than a week. You know it. I know it. My father isn't coming for me. Don't you get it? It doesn't matter what I do. I'm dead anyway!"

I turn and run through the field back toward the warden's house, but I'm no match for Smoke's long legs.

He connects with my back, tackling me. The air goes whooshing out from my lungs as I fall face first into a mud puddle. Mud fills my nose. My mouth. My eyes. My throat.

I'm pulled up by my hair. I spit and cough brown sludge until it's no longer standing in the way of breathing. I wipe my eyes with my forearm since my hands are covered in mud.

Smoke stands and yanks me up with him. He bends at the waist, his arm at the back of my knees like he's going to lift me into his arms.

I punch at his chest. "Don't fucking touch me!" Desperation and terror along with frustration fill my raspy scream.

"What did I tell you?" Smoke digs his fingers into my skin. "You're mine to do with as I please. If I want to touch you I'll god damned touch you."

He grunts, picks me up, and carries me into the house, not stopping until we're through the bedroom and in the bathroom. He sets me on my feet and holds me with one arm while he turns on the shower. He doesn't wait for the water to run warm, tugging me under the cold spray while still fully clothed.

I shriek. My teeth chatter.

"Take off your clothes," he demands.

Freezing under the spray, it takes a few beats for me to gather my nerve again, but when I do, I look up at him with all the contempt I can muster.

"No," I say, shivering under the cold water. It eventually turns warm, but my shivering doesn't stop. Just because I'm oppositional doesn't mean I'm not fearful, and there's nothing about Smoke's hard glare telling me otherwise.

"Why don't you just fucking listen?" Smoke seethes.

I roll my eyes. "Haven't you figured that out by now? That's not who I am. Not now. Not. EVER." I stare straight into his dark villainous eyes.

He growls and lunges for me. I leap back, but there's nowhere to go. I'm trapped between him and the shower wall. He steps behind me, tearing my clothes from my body until I'm completely naked, wearing nothing but mud and my insolence.

"Stop! No! Don't!" I scream.

The water's now steaming hot. He holds my naked body against him. I struggle and flail until the stinging heat of the water is all I feel. Against my will my aching bones and muscles sag in relief. I moan without thinking.

I let my forehead fall to the tile on the wall in front of me, the steaming water washing away the mud and grime, soaking into my sore muscles and warming my bones. I dig my nails into the grout and wish I could claw my way through this shower and out of this hole I've dug myself into.

I'm naked in front of this strange man for the second time, but I see it as more than just exposed skin. I feel vulnerable. Shaken.

Exposed inside and out.

"These few days? The rest of this week?" I start, without

looking over my shoulder. "According to you and this Griff person it's all the time I have left on this earth. I won't run away again. Just…just don't keep me cuffed to the bed or locked in a room." It was an honesty he didn't deserve, but with few options left, I have no other choice. "I could have called for help today, but I didn't. I wouldn't."

Smoke releases me and I hear the slap of his wet clothes against the tile as he undresses. "I don't think you'll do this because you know her, but I have to say it. Just in case. Please don't hurt Zelda. I swear she doesn't know anything. I didn't tell her anything. She doesn't deserve to get hurt or die because of me."

I wait for Smoke to answer. When he doesn't and I no longer hear him rustling around, I assume he's left until I feel him. His skin against mine.

His *naked* skin.

"You are concerned that I'll hurt Zelda? A complete stranger to you?" Smoke asks, sounding perplexed. He reaches over my head and I flinch, relaxing again slightly when I realize he's only reaching for the soap. "Why would you care?"

I tell him the truth. "Because, I can't NOT care."

Smoke pulls the soap out of the dish slowly then rubs the bar down my back and thighs. I push my body against the tile to put as much distance between us as possible, but he grunts and pulls me off the wall. He drags the bar of soap back up, sliding it across my wet ass cheek. The shower begins to smell like him. Like Irish soap. Clean and fresh.

The opposite of how I feel.

Dirty. Used. Trapped.

I'm still shivering, even under the scorching heat of the water.

"I'm not going to hurt Zelda," Smoke says, taking me by surprise. "I wouldn't."

"But you'd hurt me?" I ask.

"That's different," he argues.

"How—"

"Enough!" he barks.

Smoke leans forward again to place the soap back on the dish mounted to the wall. His nose at my neck, his chest against my back. His entire body pressed against mine. He's hard.

Everywhere.

I gasp and shut my eyes like I can make this all go away if I concentrate hard enough.

"You WILL be punished for that shit you just pulled, hellion." Smoke says, rocking his hips so that his erection slides against my soapy ass. He feels warm. Like soft silk wrapped around hard steel as he drags his erection over my skin again and again.

I can barely hold myself up.

"Fuck you," I seethe. I'm talking half to Smoke and half to my body who's betraying me. My nipples are hard pebbles. I'm achingly wet between my thighs. It only infuriates me more.

"Is that what you want for your punishment, hellion? For me to *fuck* you?"

"No…no," I stutter, but his words send a new kind of chill sputtering through me.

My clit throbs. I can't think straight while he's so close.

I don't want this. I don't want him.

"Liar," Smoke accuses, brushing my long hair off my back and pressing his lips to the back of my neck. "I can smell how turned on you are." His hand snakes around my waist, trailing down my flat stomach until they're splayed across the crest of my thighs. "Almost as well as I can smell your fear." He squeezes my flesh between his fingers. *Hard.* "I can't decide which turns me on more."

I freeze, my blood turns to ice.

"I...I..." I stutter. "You said you didn't want me," I say, recalling his words from the first night we slept in the same bed.

"I said no fucking thing. But even if I did. Don't you know by now?" He breathes. "I'm a liar. Just. Like. *You.*" He licks the skin at the back of my neck, traveling up to my ear.

Desire pools low in my stomach. Fighting the feeling is as impossible as fighting off Smoke and winning.

I open my mouth and close my eyes in a silent moan, suppressing the need to rock back into him with all that I have.

"Are you trying to scare me?" I grate.

"Why?" he asks, nipping at my earlobe, dragging his teeth along the edge. "Are you afraid, hellion? Afraid of what I might do to you? Or afraid you might love it? Scream my name? Beg me for more?"

Yes.

"No," I lie, staring at the tile in front of me. "You're just toying with me. Trying to scare me. You just said that you're a liar. This is a lie. A trick to screw with my head."

"Does *this* feel like a lie to you?" He presses against me again, letting me feel every inch of his thick rigidness as it slides against my ass crack. The tip of his erection grazes my bare pussy, and the sensation that follows is nothing like I've ever felt before. A type of warm electric current.

My lower stomach contracts. My inner walls squeeze onto something that isn't there.

No, no it does not feel like a lie. It feels like desire and confusion and lust. It feels like being out of control and adventure and possibilities, and I want it. I want *him.*

And I hate myself for it.

"All these bruises and marks," he muses. "And none of them caused by me." He trails a hand up my arms and down my flat stomach. "Pity, but I still have time to leave my mark on you yet."

My entire body stiffens. I'm as rigid as a corpse.

Smoke chuckles against me, and I'm glad I'm facing away because his laugh is pure torture, causing his erection to vibrate against my folds which are aching for more contact.

"You will be punished, hellion. You can be sure of that."

I look over my shoulder and meet his dark eyes which darken even further as his pupils dilate. His lingering gaze rakes me over from my feet to my breasts and back down to the space between my thighs. He licks his full bottom lip.

My stomach flips. My will to fight him off doesn't waiver, but my body isn't getting the message. My core clenches again. I turn back around to face the tile, digging my teeth into my lower lip until I taste my own blood.

His chest presses against my back, and his hardness pulses between my legs, rubbing against my inner thighs. He squirts some shampoo in his hand, working it into my hair. He tilts my head back and rinses my hair, then slides his slick and soapy hand down my body.

I'm breathing rapidly now. Short, quick breaths I can't control. There's a deep rumble in his throat. His hand travels lower and lower on my stomach until it's between my legs, and he's working his thumb over my swollen nub, sending sparks of need, pangs of pleasure, and a wave of self-hatred, surging within my battered body and bruised soul.

"What...what are you doing?" I ask, seeing flashes of white hot lust behind my closed eyes.

"More questions..." his voice a hearty amused rasp. His fingers circle my clit while he continues to rock his hard cock between my legs. The pressure building is so strong it borders on painful.

Tears leak from my eyes. I'm so fucking mad at myself for being turned on. For Smoke being right. I'm so wet. He feels it. There's no way he *can't* feel it.

He leans in close. I'm stone still except for the tremors gripping my body. He licks the tear off my cheek and groans. He dips the tip of his finger inside of me, and I tighten around the intrusion. It's a foreign sensation. Strange. It feels both wrong and right. Pleasurable and painful. "Your tight little pussy is weeping too. I wonder if its tears taste the same."

I look over my shoulder as he withdraws his finger and sucks it into his mouth. He groans. "Fear or desire. They both taste real fuckin' good to me."

He places his hand back between my legs. When I try to squeeze my thighs together to keep him out, he parts them with his knee on a grunt and begins circling my clit again. This time harder. Faster.

I'm staying as still as I can, but when I feel something begin to happen inside my body. The sparks he ignited within me all crashing together. I can't hold back. My face scrunches as I try to fight the orgasm fighting its way out, but it's no use. I can't fight it. It's too fucking strong. I'm so fucking close.

I arch my back without thinking, pressing my ass against him, begging for more. For what I need to push me over the edge.

Smoke hisses. "Oh, what I could do to this beautiful little pussy."

The pleasure builds and builds as he strokes me harder. Faster. I'm about to come all over his fingers when the feeling is lost.

I spin around.

Smoke is gone.

I can't see through the steam so I shut off the spray and wipe the water from my eyes only to see Smoke toweling off in front of the sink on the other side of the bathroom.

The only proof I have of what just happened between us was real is his cock. Erect. Thick. Huge. The purplish swollen head bobs against his abs, jutting out over the top of the towel he wraps around his waist.

"What...what just happened?" I stammer, leaning back against the wall for support.

Smoke steps forward, and when I go to jerk back, he reaches out and pinches my nipple painfully hard. I yelp and leap back, slipping on the tile, falling on my ass, taking the shower curtain down with me.

Smoke rips the curtain off my head and glares down at me with a triumphant grin on his evil beautiful face. "What just happened was called punishment and you got off easy. Next time, I'll split that tight pussy in two with my fucking cock."

He goes to leave but stops. "You want pain?" he asks. "I'll give it to you. You want pleasure? Now, that's something you're gonna have to earn."

He leaves, slamming the door behind him.

I release a shaky exhale.

I'd hoped the rest of my time with Smoke would be tolerable, but there's no fucking way that's going to happen. Not now. Not with my skin crawling with need. I'm losing my mind. About where I am. About what this is all about. About this beautiful horrible evil man.

I feel like I've already been split in two.

What Smoke did to me was far more than a punishment.

It was pure fucking torture.

CHAPTER TWENTY-FOUR

SMOKE

Trouble ain't nothing new for me. I've been in trouble before. With the law. With women. With the men I've done jobs for. Name the trouble, and I guaran-fuckin'-tee I've been mixed up in it a time or twenty.

Frankie Helburn is a whole new level of trouble.

One my gut, my brain, and my cock can't quite fuckin' agree on.

Her fucking brazenness. Her audacity. The way she challenges me. Stands up to me like I couldn't crush her with a single blow.

Then, there's the way she looks at me like she wants to claw my fucking eyes out.

God fucking damn it.

I'm hard just thinking about it.

She was so wet I could feel it leaking from her even though we were in the shower. How fucking sweet she tasted.

How she was hiding that tiny waist, full tits, and epic ass underneath that baggy school girl uniform is a mystery. Now that I've seen her curves in all their glory, I can't ever unsee them.

Even battered and bruised the bitch was beautiful and I don't think I've ever thought about a bitch as being beautiful before. Hot? Sure. Sexy? Sure. Stacked? Sure. Down to fuck? Sure.

Beautiful?

Just Frankie.

I left Frankie alone in the bedroom un-cuffed so she can get dressed. Ain't no way she's escaping again. I've taken care of that pet door and bolted it shut.

I'm on the porch waiting for the babysitter Preppy texted and told me would be here shortly. I expect he sent his kid brother who's been working with him for a while now, or one of Bear's prospects from the Lawless MC.

That's not who shows up.

A familiar high-pitched sound starts in the distance, and my swollen cock and Frankie are temporarily forgotten. The sound is coming from a small motor. One I've worked on before. A wheeze more than a roar. It grows louder and louder, and I know who's coming long before the baby blue Vespa pulls up the dirt path and parks with a dramatic skid in the middle of the grass.

"Fuck," I swear, shrugging on my cut.

I light a smoke and walk out to greet someone I never thought I'd see again. Someone I've made a mission out of avoiding. My one-time partner and friend.

Rage.

Rage sets down her kick stand and removes her pink helmet revealing her trademark long blond hair pulled into a tight ponytail. She smooths it down with the palm of her hands.

Rage looks like a typical teenage girl. That's how she gets

away with being a stone-cold killer for hire. Most men can't see past her tight body and pretty face.

Until it's too fucking late.

Rage spots me and doesn't smile, doesn't react. She grabs her duffle bag from the storage compartment below the seat and drapes it over her shoulders. She walks up to me with her hands on the strap. Her shirt is tight and pink and says BITCH PLEASE across her tits.

"Nice shirt, princess," I say.

She shrugs. "Well, they didn't have one that said STEP BACK OR DIE so I went with this one."

"Good call." I stub out my cigarette.

"Surprised to see me?" Rage asks.

"Understatement," I reply. "Why you here?"

"Where's my ward?" Rage asks, peeking around my shoulder and ignoring my question.

"Changing," I say. "I didn't expect to see you."

"Now or NEVER?" she asks with a smile I know to be fake because I've seen her practice it in the mirror a million times.

I shrug. "Can't say."

The guilt I've felt since the night we parted ways has never left and standing in front of her now the whole shit-show of that night hits me in the fucking gut, and I want to puke and shoot someone all at the same time. "Didn't think Preppy would send you of all people. Thought I'd get a Lawless prospect."

Rage narrows her eyes at me. "First off, you of all people know that no one SENDS me anywhere. Second, he didn't send me. He was sending his brother, but I volunteered instead. And third..." she reaches into her duffle bag and pulls out what appears to be a small version of a biker's cut and shrugs it on. "I am one of the Lawless."

Rage spins around to show off the cut and sure enough, the back has the Lawless MC logo. The front has a patch that would normally hold a title like Sergeant at Arms but hers reads *Don't Label Me.*

"Cute," I say, amused as all hell. "Can't say I'm surprised though. Only you can get a fucking MC to make you a member. What brought this on? Thought you didn't like tying yourself to any one group."

Rage follows me up to the house. "You mean besides the threats of violence against them if they didn't let me in?"

"Yeah, besides that."

She stops on the porch and circles around to face me. "You."

"Me?" I take a drag of my smoke.

She exhales and shakes her head. "Smoke, you were my mentor. My dahli-fucking-lama. You were my only connection to humanity before you inserted Nolan into my life because you knew I needed him and others around me. I didn't understand it until him." She lowers her voice. "You and I were a team, and then you left. I wanted another team. I needed to belong again."

"Thought you didn't have feelings," I say, the pain in my gut growing.

"You of all people know that's not true. It's me who didn't know it, but you showed me. And then you LEFT me."

She pokes her little index finger into my chest.

I look away and stub out my smoke on the railing, lighting another one. "We don't gotta do this right now."

"We do! You left me. I didn't realize it then, but I realize it now. You were like my brother. You were family. Then, you left."

"What a fucking brother I was. I left because..." I lower

my voice, unable to say the fucking words. "You *know* why I left."

"No, I don't," Rage says, shaking her head and setting her duffle bag down on the porch.

"I raped you, Rage," I say, my chest burning with anger toward myself. Bile rising in my throat. "While your man was forced to watch. You didn't deserve that. Nolan didn't deserve to watch that."

Rage's small hands grab hold of my cut. She's the only person in the world that can get away with this shit. Any other man would be missing that hand by now.

"Look at me!" She yells, yanking on my cut. I look down into her blue eyes. "Smoke! There was NO RAPE! That shit-bag forced us to have sex at gunpoint. That's not rape, and if it is, then, I raped you, too. 'Cause this isn't all on you. You can't take all the blame."

"It's different for you!" I shout, raising my voice above hers.

"Why? Why is it different for me?" she challenges, releasing my cut and jutting out a hip. Her head cocked to the side.

"Because you zoned out. I saw that look in your eyes you used to get when you would wash the world around you away and crawled inside your own head. You weren't there. I...I got hard. I fucking came for Christ's sake!"

Rage rolls her eyes and shrugs. "Eh, different strokes for different folks. I once read about a guy who can only come with a gun to his head. Nobody's screaming rape at the lady holding it. That's biology, asshole. What else you got? 'Cause that excuse is as weak as nonalcoholic beer. I AIN'T BUYING IT."

Rage smiles and this time it's genuine.

"What the fuck do you know about biology?" I ask, feeling

the mood lighten around us. She doesn't blame me. Don't mean I can't blame myself, but maybe I don't have to fucking hate myself so much.

Not about this anyway.

"Besides being a germ expert, as you know, I am also a college graduate now."

"You went to college?" I look at her with disbelief. "In a year and a half?"

She wrinkles her nose. "More like a half an hour. Just for enough time to threaten the dean into giving me a degree. It's real pretty, too. I framed it. It's hanging in my room at the MC. Come by. I'll show it to you sometime."

I chuckle. "Same old Rage," I say, then reconsider my words. "Yet not the same ole Rage."

Rage stills. "Don't move, okay? I'm gonna try something," she whispers, taking a step toward me.

I shift my feet. Rage is unpredictable, but she's still Rage, and I trust her even though I know I shouldn't. "Okay, but what are…"

"I said don't move!"

I'm stone still as her tiny arms wrap around my waist, and she leans her head against me. I'm so much bigger that her head only comes to the bottom of my ribs.

"Thank you for helping me all those years ago," she says. "Thank you for being my friend when I didn't know what a friend was supposed to be. Thank you for setting me up with Nolan although you did it in the weirdest way possible. Thank you for knowing I needed him before I knew I needed him. Just, thank you, Smoke."

"I…" I sputter, not knowing what to say. I feel myself soften, and before I know it, I'm placing one of my hands over her tiny head. I kiss the top of her hair.

"It's all done. It's over!" Rage announces, pulling away

and clapping her hands together. "Now, let's kill something and string its intestines up like Christmas lights." The crazed look in her eyes returns, the one I've known and loved since the first time I saw her when she was sixteen years old.

"Yep, same ole, Rage." I chuckle. "You got all this feelings shit down pat, don't ya?"

Her shoulders drop. "Yeah, but it's *exhausting*. There are so many layers of feelings, and sometimes, I just want to blow shit up and forget about it all, but…it's worth it. *Nolan's* worth it." Rage points at me. "You're worth it."

"Thanks for coming, princess," I tell her. I mean it.

"You're very fucking welcome. This place isn't nearly as gross as I thought it would be, so that's a plus. Now, what the fuck do you have going on here, and please, please, *please*, can I do something involving knife play to whoever you have tied up back there?"

I think about how much to tell Rage.

"All of it. Tell me all of it," she says knowingly. She skips into the house and props herself up on the kitchen counter. I shake my head and follow her inside.

I grab a bottle of whiskey from the table and take a long pull. "You remember Morgan?"

Rage nods. "Yeah, the brunette. Walked in on you banging her one day. I liked her. Great tits. No over the top moaning. Seemed clean."

Clean to Rage means a lot since she's a germaphobe and OCD and a lot of other things I don't know the specific terms for.

"She's dead," I tell her, looking down at the bottle in my hand.

Rage doesn't react because Rage *doesn't* react. She lifts her chin and waits for me to continue.

I sigh. "Short version is that I found her in a pool of her

own fucking blood. Hacked to bits. Couldn't for the life of me figure out who did it until I got a lead from Griff. Frank Helburn, a hacker scumbag, is the one who did it although I have no clue why. The girl in the back room? She's his kid. Using her to flush her old man out."

"That all?" She asks, knowing me better than I know my fucking self.

I shake my head and light yet another smoke and take an even bigger swig of whiskey. "Nope. That's not all. Morgan… she was carrying my kid."

"So, this is a revenge mission," Rage states, swinging her legs. There is no apology from her lips because Rage isn't sorry. She didn't know Morgan and she isn't built that way.

It's comforting in a way. It's familiar. And shit if I need her pity or anyone else's.

I nod.

Rage is processing, looking to the ceiling, deep in thought. This isn't the time to try and shake her out of it unless you want to be on the bloody end of her crystal studded blade.

I take another swig of whiskey and decide I'm glad Rage came today.

Frankie enters the room and pauses when she sees Rage sitting on the counter. Frankie's eyes widen in surprise, and she looks to me. "Who's that girl?"

"That ain't no girl," I say setting down the whiskey. "That's Rage."

CHAPTER TWENTY-FIVE

FRANKIE

"Sit," Smoke says, sliding out one of the chairs from the dining room table.

"Is she okay?" I ask, not taking my eyes off the blonde with the white shorts and matching flip flops. She's gorgeous. Weird with that unblinking robotic look in her bright blue eyes, but gorgeous none the less.

"Depends on what your definition of okay is," Smoke answers.

"Why is she here?" I ask, wary of this new person in the room.

"To watch you. I've got some shit to do in town."

"*She's* going to watch me?" I ask.

A knife, no, a dagger, spirals through the kitchen and lands with the blade in the table less than an inch from my arm, its white, crystal handle sparkling in the sunlight.

I look up.

"Yeah, I'm gonna watch you," Rage says, her eyes now focused. "We're gonna be BFF's, I'm sure."

There's no emotion in her voice and something off about her words. About *her*.

About the way she just threw a fucking knife at me.

"Is she your..." I start to ask.

Rage laughs, her head thrown back. "Negative, crime fighter."

"Can't I come with you?" I ask Smoke, not taking my eyes from Rage who's now staring at me again.

She's not blinking.

"No," they both answer in unison.

"She's pretty, Smoke. Even all banged up. I like her hair. And she's got cat-colored eyes," Rage says, as if I'm on display at the zoo and not in the same room.

"More like fire," Smoke says, staring at me for a few seconds before looking away.

Rage tosses him something that isn't a knife.

Smoke drops to his knees on the floor and tugs my leg so my calf is lying against his thigh.

"What are you doing?" I ask.

"Do you always have to question everything?" he groans, adjusting a thick black bracelet around my ankle.

"What's this?" I ask.

"I'll take that as a yes." Smoke says.

The bracelet has a black square attached to it slightly smaller than a pack of cards.

"This, is insurance," he explains. "An ankle monitor," he checks to make sure it's secure.

"Like for someone on house arrest?" I ask, remembering seeing it in movies when the convict gets sentenced to time at home instead of jail. They're monitored by the police and used to make sure the criminal remains at home for the duration of their sentences.

"Yes, the same concept."

"Except," Rage sings, pressing her lips together and swinging her legs off the counter. "This one's waaaayyyyy more fun."

"How is it more *fun*?" I ask, dread pooling in my stomach.

Rage's eyes go wide. She smiles maniacally.

Smoke locks the device in place and tucks the little key into his pocket. He stands.

"Mostly, because it'll explode," Rage squeals with joy, staring with an uncomfortable amount of interest at the little box now tethered to my leg.

"It's a bomb?" I exclaim, jumping up like I can somehow distance myself from the thing, but it's too late.

Smoke continues, "I've set the perimeter guidelines to the fence which goes around the prison. Zelda's house is included. If you go outside the perimeter, it'll give you a warning beep then you've got yourself ten seconds to get back inside before it goes off. Same goes if you try and fuck or tamper with it in any way."

"Boom," Rage whispers, making an exploding motion with her hands.

Terror dances up my spine.

"You put a bomb…on my leg," I whisper. I sit and look down at my new explosive ankle jewelry.

Smoke smirks. "You can look at it that way." His eyes meet mine. "Or, you look at it like I'm giving you some freedom."

"Freedom…with a *bomb* on my *leg*."

Smoke nods.

Rage whistles.

"But I thought she was here to watch me," I say.

"As I said. Insurance," Smoke answers.

He was giving me what I asked for. Some freedom during my last few days.

Never in my life did I ever think I could be grateful for a bomb strapped to my leg, but I am.

Smoke holds up something that looks like a controller for a DVD player. "I can also set it off remotely," he says, tucking it into his back pocket.

"Oh, can I have it?" Rage asks, making grabby hands in the air.

"No," Smoke and I both answer.

I close off the part of my brain freaking out over the explosive factor of my situation and instead focus on the tiny bit of freedom aspect. I begin to dance around the kitchen, the weight of the ankle monitor making me feel freer than I have in days. Smoke watches me expressionlessly until I dance myself right into a cabinet. The monitor vibrates on impact, and I freeze, looking up to meet Smoke's eyes.

Smoke covers his mouth, and I realize it's to hide a smile. I'm disappointed because I would like to have seen it.

Rage leaps off the counter.

"It's sturdy," Smoke crosses his arms over his chest. "It won't go off if you kick it around or knock it into things. It doesn't work like that."

I exhale. "Thank God."

"No. Thank *Smoke,*" Rage corrects.

"Thank you, Smoke." I say, and I mean it.

For a few moments, we just stand there, staring at one another silently until Rage clears her throat.

"I gotta go," Smoke says. "I'll be back in the morning."

Smoke leaves the kitchen and heads into the back bedroom where I hear him rifling through the storage containers.

"So," I say. "Your name is Rage."

"Yep. It's short for Ragina."

"No, it's not," Smoke says, crossing back through the

kitchen with a bag in his hand. He pauses at the door and looks at me, then Rage.

"Go," she says to him. "No boys. No parties. No booze and no rated R movies. We got it, Pops. Now, go!"

Smoke pushes out the door, shaking his head as he leaves.

I follow Rage onto the porch where we watch Smoke fire up his bike and roll out down the path past a blue scooter parked in the yard.

Smoke could have left me cuffed. In a cage tied to a bed. Starved me. Tortured me. But for some reason, he's given me room to run. A babysitter. An ankle monitor.

"I know what you're thinking," Rage says.

"No, you don't," I argue.

"I do. You're thinking that maybe Smoke isn't so much of a monster after all."

Shit.

"You're wrong you know," she sings.

"How so?"

Rage brushes past me back into the house. "The man did strap a bomb to your leg."

I look down to the black box around my ankle.

Shit.

CHAPTER TWENTY-SIX

FRANKIE

"Do you mind if I ask you a question?" I'm sitting on the front porch in one of the tattered rocking chairs looking over the landscape of the prison.

My curiosity has gotten the best of me, and I've been wondering something ever since Smoke left.

"That was a question," Rage says. She turns the page of the bridal magazine she's reading and makes a face of disgust. She rolls her eyes and closes the magazine, tossing it on top of a tall pile stacked next to her. She reaches in her bag and pulls out another, opening it and making the same face at the very first page.

"You're very literal," I observe.

"And Smoke was right. You're very *question-ey*," Rage gives up on the magazine, shoving it aside. She sits up in her chair and folds her feet underneath her body. "So what's this mystical question you've got for me? Spoiler alert, I don't do horoscopes."

"How do you know Smoke?"

"It's a tale as old as time," she says with a sigh. "You might even say a song as old as rhyme."

"Are you trying to tell me you're Beauty and the Beast?" I ask with a laugh.

Rage wrinkles her nose. "No, why?"

"Uh, no reason."

Rage pauses to think. "I guess you can say that Smoke is the Mr. Miyagi to my Karate Kid, but I haven't seen him in a long while."

"What happened?" I ask.

Rage lifts her hand, examining her nails. "All was not well in the dojo."

"So you guys have never..." I don't know why I'm asking, but even I realize the question comes off as jealous when there's no way that's possible. Curious. That's all I am. It's human nature to be curious of those around you and right now those around me are Rage and Smoke.

It's as simple as that.

"THAT is a lot more complicated. We've never felt that way about each other, but some shit went down where we were forced to..." she makes a finger in the hole gesture with her hands. "At gunpoint," she adds.

I don't know what I was expecting but THAT certainly wasn't it.

"He felt guilty and took off. Today is the first time I've seen him in years."

"Smoke felt *guilty*?" I ask, taken aback. I didn't think he was capable of guilt."

"Don't get it twisted. That man is capable of much more than you or he even knows," Rage answers cryptically.

She reaches behind her back, pulling out the dagger she'd thrown at me earlier. The one with the shiny crystal handle. She fiddles with it, rotating it in her hand, pressing the pad of her index finger against the tip, testing its sharpness.

"You know," she starts. "I see the way he looks at you. A couple of years back, shit, even a year back I would never have seen it or recognized what it was. Even if I did it would only be an observation, something to mimic while I'm on a job and have to pretend to feel the same way everyone else does." Rage spins the handle of the blade on the table between us. "But I saw it today. He looks at you like he wants to..."

"I don't know what you think you saw—"

Rage cuts me off. "You're a smart girl, Frankie. I can tell. But you might be more clueless to what people are feeling than I ever was because Smoke looks at you like he wants to stick a flag in you and claim you for the homeland."

I raise my eyebrows in question.

Rage rolls hers. "I've been watching these emotional movies lately. It's this therapy thing my parents want me to try. The stake a claim thing is from *Far and Away* with Tom Cruise. He goes out West and..." She stops. "Never mind. I've probably got it all wrong anyway."

Rage looks down to the blade in her hands.

Feeling the need to lift whatever burden is sitting on her shoulders I tell her. "I like that movie."

After a few moments of silence Rage turns to me. "Be honest. What's your story? How did you end up Smoke's captive?"

"He didn't tell you?"

"He told me his side. I want to hear your side."

"Why?" I ask.

"Because I care about Smoke, and I need to know if I should bury you in the prison yard before he gets back," she says.

My eyes widen.

She rolls hers. "Don't worry, I'd totally tell him you offed yourself so he wouldn't blame me. We'd still be buds."

"Good to know?" I say. It comes out like a question.

There's no doubt in my mind it's the truth but she says it so casually, like she's planning what to eat for dinner or talking about the weather.

I know Rage's loyalty lies with Smoke, I don't know if I can trust her. Actually, I know I can't trust her.

I tell her everything anyway.

Well, ALMOST everything.

I tell her about my father and how he was negligent toward me after my mother died. About taking a false name and re-enrolling in high school to avoid the fallout from my father's bullshit. The abduction. Smoke. Smoke. SMOKE.

I toss one truth after another at her like clothes on a laundry heap until there's a huge pile between us to be sorted.

"Well, that was…educational," Rage says, twisting the end of her ponytail in her hand. She pulls up her legs and sits cross-legged on the rocking chair. "But I guessed it."

"Guessed what?" I ask.

"He named the bacon," she whispers.

I'm not sure if she's talking to herself or to me.

"Huh?"

"Think of Smoke like a pig farmer," Rage starts to explain. I have no idea where she's going with this.

"Let me guess. Am I the pig in this scenario?" I ask, pointing at my chest.

She nods. "Yes, for this metaphor anyway. Smoke, or anyone who does what we do, are pig farmers and pig farmers don't name their pigs, they don't treat them like pets because they're not. They might be walking around breathing, but they're food. You don't cuddle and play with food. You don't tie pretty bows around your food's neck." She holds out her hands, palms up, and shrugs. "You don't name the bacon."

"And you think Smoke did?"

Rage nods. "Oh, Smoke's a pig namer alright. Never thought I would say that about him. But if he isn't careful, then soon he'll be a pig..." Rage pauses and presses her lips together. A burst of laughter escapes, and she covers her mouth with her hands.

"A pig *fucker*?" I barely get the word out.

Rage and I look at each other, and we're lost to laughter until our stomachs ache and our eyes tear. It feels so good to laugh that once I start I can't seem to stop.

I've got a death sentence looming over my head. I've been abducted by a killer, and I'm sitting across from another who just compared me to a pig being lead to slaughter.

And I'm *laughing*.

"I will say this though," Rage says, wiping the tears from her cheeks. Her back straightens as she looks me in the eye. Her expression grows serious. Her smile falls. "There's a lot more to us monsters than we let on."

I look out over the prison. "I think I'm beginning to understand that."

"So, what's your next plan of action?" She asks, clapping her hands together.

"What makes you think I have one?" I pull my knees up to my chest.

Rage stares at me for a long moment, then flashes me a knowing smile. "Nothing makes me think you don't. But, whatever it is, you better get moving on it. And soon."

"Why is that?" I ask, curiously.

Rage sighs. "Because, if I know Smoke, you have a lot less time than you think."

CHAPTER TWENTY-SEVEN

FRANKIE

You have a lot less time than you think.

I'm on my knees, fishing under the mattress for the garments I've hidden while Rage's words play over and over again in my mind. She wouldn't tell me why she thought I had less time, but whatever the reason, it's time to try out Dr. Ida's last tip for surviving captivity.

Seduction.

Smoke wants me. I saw it in his eyes. I *felt* it against my back.

It's all I have to work with. A hope. A feeling.

Smoke was only gone for a few hours. Rage left shortly after Smoke came back. He hasn't spoken a word to me since. He's colder than before. If Rage was right and Smoke *named the bacon,* then maybe, he's trying to place distance between us. Or maybe, it's simpler than that and he doesn't want to be around me.

I'm nervous, shaking all over as I take a shower and scrub

my skin with a washcloth until it's smooth. I towel dry and brush my hair, then shave and groom using the electric razor I find under the sink. I dress quickly and look in the mirror, adjusting where necessary.

My pulse is pounding in my ears as I give myself a once over. It's only been three days since I jumped from the car, but I've always been a fast healer. My bruises have mostly faded except for the scrapes on my right arm, which are scabbed over.

It's the best I can do with what I've got.

But will it be enough?

I take a deep breath and push open the bedroom door. I find Smoke sitting on the couch with his arms stretched over the top, a cigar in his mouth. A bottle of whiskey at his feet. He looks deep in thought. His legs spread. His arms resting across the back of the couch.

There's a radio in the corner playing "Take it Out on Me" by Florida Georgia Line.

"I like this song," I say to get Smoke's attention.

Smoke turns his head toward me and freezes, cigar halfway to his full lips. His eyes widen as he takes me in, looking me up and down.

"What the fuck are you doing?" He asks between gritted teeth. He's angry. His vein pulses under his neck tattoo. His nostrils flare.

I let his anger fuel my determination, and I walk with as much confidence as I can muster into the center of the room wearing only a sheer black bra that pushes my breasts up and amplifies my cleavage, along with a matching pair of sheer panties, leaving nothing to the imagination.

"What?" I ask, feigning innocence. I look down at my body. "You don't like the way I look?" I'm teasing him, or at least I'm trying to. The fire blazing in his eyes tells me that I'm either doing it very right or very wrong. It doesn't matter. I can't give up now.

I sway my hips from side to side, hooking my thumbs in the sides of my panties.

"What are you trying to prove, hellion?" Smoke rasps. His pupils dilate.

"I'm not trying to prove anything," I say, leaning over I pluck the cigar from his hand and take a puff before placing it in the ashtray on the end table.

Smoke clears his throat and shakes his head. "You don't know what the fuck you're doing," he grates. His eyes linger on the scrap of fabric between my legs then travel up to my breasts where my nipples pebble under his gaze.

"I think I do," I say in the seductive tone I'd practiced in the bathroom earlier.

"Such big words for such a little girl," Smoke drawls.

"I'm not a little girl!" I shout, taking a step forward, before reminding myself of what I was trying to do and freezing.

Smoke smiles, knowing he's gotten to me. "What exactly are you playing at here, *little girl*? 'Cause no matter what happens," he grabs the whiskey off the floor and tips it to his mouth. He swallows and sets it back down, licking his lips. "You're gonna lose."

That's what you think.

I don't answer. Because I'm focused on his full lips. The way his tongue darts out to catch a falling drop of whiskey.

Shit, get it together, Frankie.

"You might be twenty-two, but all I see is innocence. You ever been *fucked* before, hellion? 'Cause, I'm betting on no."

"Does it matter?" I ask, running my fingers across my breasts.

My heart is pounding so hard it shakes me the way hard-hitting bass rattles a trunk. I never pictured my first time. There were never enough minutes in the day for myself, never mind for fantasies or daydreams. Even if I had pictured it, attempting to seduce my kidnapper while quaking like the floor beneath me is shifting would probably not have come to mind.

I put on my best smile and unhook my bra with shaking fingers. Slowly, I drop it. He's watching my every move. When my bra hits the floor, his mouth gapes open, but he quickly corrects himself as if he's given too much away.

"I've seen plenty of naked women before. I've seen YOU naked before. You ain't gonna shock me, hellion."

"I'm not trying to shock you, *Smoke,"* I say, dragging out his name on my lips as if I'm enjoying the way it sounds rolling off my tongue.

"You're playing a very dangerous game, *little girl,"* Smoke warns. "Stop before you lose."

"So, play it with me," I say, rubbing circles around my taut nipples with my fingers. The way he watches me makes me want to grab his head and thrust his lips against my breasts. "And we'll both win."

"I'm not fucking around. This is your last warning to cut this shit out before you end up in a position you're going to regret…" His eyelids are heavy. Hooded. "And I'm going to enjoy."

"I just want to feel good. Don't you want to feel good?" I snake my hand down into my panties and rub my clit painstakingly slow. I'm supposed to be putting on a show for him, making him want me. It's supposed to be fake.

Then why am I soaking wet?

"Alright, Hellion," Smoke smirks wickedly. "You think you can handle it? Then, come the fuck on."

He unzips his pants and pushes them down far enough to reveal the V underneath. It leads down his trail of abs to a very large bulge straining beneath the fabric of his boxer briefs.

Doubt. Panic. Worry. Unease. Terror. Horror.

They all crash into me at once along with a surge of arousal so strong and so unexpected I stagger on my feet, drunk with it, with lust.

"A fuck is a fuck. It won't buy your freedom. It ain't that easy."

I kneel on the floor and spread my fingers on his hard thighs, hoping he can't feel me shaking. I smile up at him through my lashes and lick my lips.

He grabs my wrist roughly. "It's not a fucking joke, little girl. You think you're smart, and I know there are a lot of motherfuckers out there that will fall for this bullshit, but in case you haven't noticed, I ain't like other guys. I can see right through this act of yours. I ain't buying it. So, I'll warn you one last time before shit gets real and your pussy is too full of cock and your head too full of regret. You can't buy your freedom with pussy because your freedom ain't. For. Sale."

"It's not an act," I lie, defensively. I try to yank my wrist from his grip, but he holds me tighter, his fingernails biting into my flesh.

I gasp.

A current passes between us and I know he feels it, too, because our eyes both drop to where he's holding me. It runs through my skin then back to his.

Smoke releases me so suddenly I fall back onto the carpet.

"Fine, have it your way. I'm calling your bluff."

He reaches down and grabs me again, forcing me to stand. He rips my panties down my legs and groans when he sees the wetness on my thighs. He leans back on the couch, arms spread across the cushions. His deep voice lowers to a rumble.

"Take my cock out and ride me," he orders, his voice low. Rough. Demanding.

Chills dance down my spine. I glance down at the large bulge between his legs and swallow hard.

"I-I..." I stutter. I'd hoped to turn him on, but I never expected to be turned on myself. Plus, I kinda forgot the part where, when it comes down to it, I don't know what the hell I'm actually doing.

Shit.

"What's wrong?" Smoke asks, grinning. "Change your mind?"

No, I just don't know what to do.

I shake my head and try like hell to get a grip on my breathing.

Smoke crooks his finger at me. "Now," he orders.

I come closer, standing in front of him with my knees against the cushions. He reaches out, grabs me by the waist and sets me on top of him so I'm straddling his large body, my legs spread impossibly wide while his hard bulge nudges my naked entrance from within his boxers.

The current between us sparks again, except this time, it courses straight through to my center. I close my eyes and groan at the sensation. I blink them back open and find Smoke staring at me with both confusion and wonderment.

There's a shift in the air all around us and right now I imagine that in this moment he's not my captor and I'm not his captive. He's just a beautiful hard man and I'm just a lonely girl starving for human contact.

"What...what was that?" I ask. My voice is shaky. My breaths are short. Real true fear and lust break through the mask I've been wearing, and I squeeze my thighs around him because I HAVE TO.

Smoke's mouth falls open. His fingers dig into my hips. He can see it now. He can see me. The real me. I'm both terrified and excited. My skin is flushed. My wetness is soaking through his boxers. He takes my wrists and binds them with his hands behind my back, keeping me in place. He gazes deeply into my eyes like he can see my every thought, my every dream, my every nightmare.

My every *lie*.

My nipples are impossibly hard. Painfully hard. He blows a breath across them, and I drop my head back at the sensation. He pulls me against him, and when my nipples meet the warm soft skin of his muscular chest, I groan.

"Fuck," he swears, releasing my hands. I place them on his shoulders. His hands go to my hips again. He moves me. Rocking me against him. His hard cock rubs mercilessly against my clit sending that same electric current zapping over and over again with each glide. My lower stomach tightens.

My thighs flex involuntarily around his muscular thighs, and the groan that leaves his lips vibrates to my very core.

Fuck games, even if I'm the one who started it. Now, I only want more.

So much more.

I want *him*.

My body can't lie. My reactions to him are real. Primal. My need is real. The pressure building in my lower stomach threatening to explode is very, very real.

"This is so fucked up," I whisper.

"Makes it even better," Smoke says, his lips on my collarbone, his hands on my ass.

I know it's fucked up. I know it's wrong. And he's right. The wrongness of it is only making me want him more. If I'm going to die, I don't want to do it without ever knowing what it feels like to have a man inside my body.

This man.

This monster.

I'm your monster.

His words echo in my brain.

The pressure is building. Smoke's muscles flex underneath me, my nipples rub against his chest. My clit is aching. "What...what's happening?" I ask although I don't know what it is I'm actually asking.

Smoke's eyes grow impossibly dark. He drags the pad of his thumb across my lips. "I have no fucking idea," he says, pushing his other hand into my hair. He tugs on the back of my head, pauses for a moment, then presses my lips to his.

A kiss.

Smoke is kissing me. His lips are hard, yet soft. His facial hair tickles my cheeks. His tongue seeks entrance, and when I give it to him, we moan into one another's mouths while our tongues dance an unfamiliar dance where they already know all the moves. It's rough and hard and tender and needy. He pulls my hair harder, and the searing pain gives way to even greater pleasure.

I grind myself shamelessly against his lap.

Our connection is like TV static. Loud and confusing. A million buzzing black and white dots flying into each other all at once. It doesn't make sense, but it doesn't have to. I'm not in control.

And for the first time in my life.

I don't want to be.

I've never felt anything like this.

It feels too good to stop.

Too good to be real.

I'm sure now that I'm not kissing the man who kidnapped

me. I don't have to pretend anymore. Because I really am kissing the man I saw across the street. The one who captured my attention without saying a word.

The most beautiful man I've ever seen.

I'm desperate to give my body to the man who may very well be the one who takes my life.

And right now, I don't fucking care.

Because in Smoke's arms, I've come alive.

Smoke

I know there's no limit to what Frankie will do to gain her freedom. As much as I tell her otherwise, I know she's smart, capable, and I just learned what else she is when she came out into the living room wearing next to nothing.

The girl is cunning as fuck.

She wasn't waiting for me to toy with her. To mind fuck her past the point of no return. Not when she has a mind-fuck of her own planned.

It's a show. A scam. I should toss her off me and give her what she doesn't realize she's asking for. I should fuck her up her perky little ass without preparing her first and show her that tricks aren't going to get her anywhere or anything, but truly *fucked*.

But I don't. At least not yet. Not when the smell of her fucking wet pussy hits my nostrils and renders me stupid. It's a mistake to go along with her, but god fucking dammit, mistakes shouldn't feel this good. I want inside Frankie's sweet innocent pussy. I want to pound into her with every bit of hatred and desire in my veins.

She's playing you, and you're letting her.

Fuck my inner voice. Fuck everything except the here and now. Because in the now, I've got a hand threaded through

Frankie's thick, silky mane. I tug on it, and she gasps into my mouth, making my cock jump in response. I deepen the kiss, plunging my tongue into her mouth because I want more of her lush lips and soft tongue.

I'm harder than I've ever been. I want her more than I've ever wanted a piece of ass. I lie to myself. I say that I'm going along with her seduction to teach her a lesson not to toy with me. To show her that I won't be manipulated, but those thoughts fade as she grinds against my cock with her hot, soaking, wet pussy.

She's fucking dripping for me.

There's no doubt in my mind that Frankie hates me. As she should. But trick or not, she wants me. She wants this. Maybe, she didn't mean to want it, but there's no mistaking the lust in her eyes. Her gasps of pleasure. The parting of her thick lips I imagine wrapped around my cock, taking me deep into the back of her throat.

My balls tighten. My spine tingles.

I'm downright ravenous for her. Her smell, her taste. Her fucking insubordination.

Her *fear*.

I want all of her and I want all of me inside of her. I'm going to explore every inch of her perfect body with my mouth, fingers and aching cock. Her nipples are hard and in my face, creating an urgency to dominate her body, her mind, her fucking soul, that's about to detonate.

I've jerked off three times since the shower incident, picturing her ass in the air, her back arched as she leaned against the shower wall.

"I need more," I groan.

"More?" she asks breathlessly.

I grab her by the waist and dig my fingers into the curve

of her hips. I guide her to grind her hot pussy against me harder.

"I need it all," I rasp.

We're breathing in each other's exhales. Devouring each other's mouths. If the world burned down around us, I wouldn't notice.

I wouldn't stop.

I'm hanging on by a fucking thread. Frankie's mouth tastes sweet, and I wonder how her pussy tastes in comparison. The taste of her I got in the shower has lingered. No matter how much time has passed or how many times I've brushed or chugged whiskey, nothing has been able to rid it from my tongue.

The thought causes me to groan into her mouth, and I rock her harder against me. The warmth of her pussy on my lap is like a fucking drug. Stronger and more addictive than blow.

She's cocaine with legs, and I'm a fucking addict before I've even had a taste.

The phone buzzes on the side table. I reach over blindly to shut it off, but I can't reach it. I lean over to hit the ignore button when I read the words that slam the brakes on this train before it barrels off the tracks and crashes into the motherfucking station.

GOT A HIT ON FRANK HELBURN YESTERDAY. REMOTE LOG-IN THROUGH DARK WEB. WORKING ON HIS LOCATION NOW. NOT LONG BEFORE THE FUCKER IS OURS. I'LL BE IN TOUCH.

My brain is still processing the text when another bucket

of water is doused over our heads as Zelda enters through the front door carrying a steaming casserole dish.

"Fuck," Frankie curses, pressing herself up tighter against my body to hide her nakedness.

Zelda doesn't look the least bit shocked. She places the dish on the counter and looks over at us with an eyebrow raised and a fist on her hip.

"Shit, Rage was right. You really did name the bacon."

CHAPTER TWENTY-EIGHT

FRANKIE

Smoke took off. Cold hard eyes in place of the ones filled with lust just seconds before. He tossed me off his lap and threw my clothes at me like *nothing* changed between us when EVERYTHING has changed. He made some excuse about a phone call and having shit to do, leaving me alone with Zelda at her place.

I set out to seduce him, but in the process, I'd managed to seduce myself right into his arms.

Idiot.

I look out over the prison yard and contemplate making a run for it since now I know Zelda wouldn't be held accountable for my actions, but I remember the ankle monitor strapped to my leg.

Blowing myself up seems a bit counterproductive.

We're sitting on the back deck in silence, teacups in hand. Zelda's lips are pressed together like she's trying not to smile.

"Are we going to talk about what you saw or are you just

going to sit there and try not to laugh?" I ask, now fully-clothed. I pull my knees up and sigh.

"Oh, Frankie," she says with a chuckle. "I'm gonna do what all good Scottish mamas do and weave this situation into a life lesson you won't understand." She nods. "Just as soon as I figure out how."

"I'll be waiting," I say.

"While you're waiting, maybe, you should do something to occupy your time," Zelda suggests. "Do you have any hobbies?"

"No," I say. "I don't know a lot about my mother. She died when I was young but I found a bunch of paintings in the attic once with her name on them. I'm okay at drawing but I've always wanted to try my hand at painting."

"Why haven't you?" Zelda asks.

"I've been...preoccupied."

A big yellow lab comes bounding out from the weeds with a snake in his mouth, tail swinging proudly from side to side. He's only got one eye.

"Have you met The Warden?" Zelda asks, leaning down to scratch behind the lab's ears. She takes the black snake from his mouth. It's still alive, hissing and showing its fangs. "Oh hush," she says, plucking the snake from his mouth and tossing it over the railing. "He lost his eye fighting a snake. Looks like he still hasn't learned his lesson."

The dog comes over to me next, resting his head on my lap. He closes his eyes and sighs as I scratch his neck. He's obviously not one of those dogs who needs time to get used to new people.

"The Warden?" I ask, patting his head in long slow strokes. The dog makes a noise that sounds curiously like purring, keeping his eyes closed. "That's his name?"

Zelda chuckles. "Every prison needs a warden. I named

him before I realized that he's about as stern and watchful as a baby bunny. Good at catching snakes though. Now, if he would just kill 'em instead of trying to be friends with them..."

My mind wanders back to Smoke.

The dog isn't the only one who needs to learn that lesson.

I shift in my chair. The Warden glares up at me with one eye open as if to say he doesn't appreciate being jostled around. I scratch between his ears some more, and his eye closes once again. His hind leg bounces off the floor in appreciation.

"He's downright menacing," I joke.

"Not all who appear menacing are what they seem," Zelda comments. I know instantly she's talking about Smoke. I stop petting the dog who only stays a second more before darting into the yard to lay belly up in the grass under the bright sun, long tongue hanging out of the side of his mouth.

"I'm not so sure about that," I say. I feel disappointed and stupid and rejected and then stupider still because the whole thing is ridiculous. I'm a captive who's about to be offered up for slaughter, not some girl whose been ditched before prom.

"Did Smoke tell you how we met?" Zelda asks, then, without waiting for me to answer, adds, "Of course, he hasn't."

She sets down her knitting and looks out to the yard where The Warden is now scratching his back against the grass in some sort of weird lying down dance, shifting his hips from one side to the other with his legs up in the air.

"Smoke was just a boy. About nine years old. Barney, my late husband, was a retired Navy man. He found Smoke covered in blood and dirt, wondering around the prison yard. He was half starved to death, and his eyes...his eyes were all wrong. Barney called me over, and I tried to coax the boy into the house, give him a bath and some food and shelter but he looked at us like he was a wild animal. He lunged at me with a knife. Thankfully my husband punched him before he could reach me. Knocked him out cold."

She laughs like it's a fond memory and not the opening scene of a horror movie where everyone dies in the end and the serial killer heads to another town to start his murdering spree all over again.

"What happened after that?"

"While Smoke was passed out, I bathed him and washed his clothes but they were so flimsy they fell apart in the wash, so I mended some of Barney's things, altering them on the fly so they'd fit him. I placed some food by the bedside. When he came to, he disappeared again. The food was gone off the nightstand, but the clothes were still on the foot of the bed.

"Where did you find him?" I ask. On some level, I'm beginning to identify with the kid she's describing, and it's sitting like a rock in my gut.

Zelda sighs, knitting her brows together, still disturbed with whatever it was she was recalling. "He was under the porch in the crawlspace. Naked. Eating the beef stew and biscuits with his hand like a wild animal. He was shoving it into his mouth so quickly he was choking."

"How did you get him to come out?" I ask, my heart squeezing for a young Smoke.

"He came out on his own, after a while. He let me dress him, but he didn't speak, just watched me like I was an alien. We tried to get him to tell us who his parents were. When we couldn't get it out of him, we decided to call the police, but he must have heard us talking about it because he was gone before they arrived."

The Warden leapt up when a bird landed in the yard. He barked and chased it back into the weeds.

"Over the next few years, he'd come around time and

again. Sometimes, he was crazed like we'd found him the first time. Sometimes, he'd just leave wild flowers on the front porch for me. He never stayed the night no matter how many times we'd ask. He never took anything from us more than a meal. I started putting clothes and food in the porch box so he could come and take them whenever he wanted. After a while, I left other things in there. Sometimes he took them. Sometimes he didn't. Years passed this way until my Barney died. Smoke was a teenager by then. Then, it was Smoke who started leaving stuff for me. Flowers. Cash. Gifts." Zelda takes a sip of tea. "It's because of him I was able to keep this house after my Barney passed."

I know how it feels to grow up neglected. Not on that kind of scale but on some level. My heart breaks for the kid version of Smoke. Out there alone in the world. Having to find his own way. I realize the pain in my chest isn't just for him.

It's for me, too.

I reach over and grab Zelda's hand in mine which she covers with her own. She closes her eyes, and when she opens them, a single tear drips down her cheek, getting trapped in the many lines of her face.

"He still takes care of me, sometimes from afar," Zelda says looking at the screen door falling from the hinge and to the porch railing which was rotting and crumbling before our very eyes. "Which is why I take care of the main house for him so when he's around, he has a place to stay."

"And you still make him food," I say, remembering the biscuits and gravy from my first morning at the prison.

"That I do," she smiles.

"Wait, the main house? You mean The Warden's cottage?"

Zelda nods. "Yes. This house, the warden's cottage, and the prison have all been combined onto one parcel of land."

"Who owns it?" I ask, already knowing the answer.

"Smoke, dear. Smoke owns it all."

"Why?" I look around from the weeds to the main prison building, crumbling and littered with graffiti. "I mean, if he could afford all this surely he could afford to buy a house somewhere that isn't so...prisoney?"

"Sometimes you don't get to choose where home is. Sometimes home chooses you," Zelda says, wiping her hand on her apron.

"Zelda, why do you think he tried to push you away all those years ago? What happened to him?"

"He wasn't pushing us away," Zelda argues. "Quite the opposite. He was staying away because he didn't want to bring his troubles into our lives. Don't you see? He was loving us, the only way he knew how."

"By staying away from you," I say with some semblance of understanding beginning to sink in.

"Yes, and I'm afraid he still thinks that way no matter how many times I try to tell him otherwise." Zelda smiles and shakes her head. "I wish things were simple, but Smoke...he's not a simple man."

"But you two are close now? I mean, you seem close," I say.

"In some ways, yes. In others...well, some things never change." Zelda stands up. "I'm going to go freshen my tea."

She leaves me alone on the porch. I hear barking in the distance and look up to see The Warden with another snake in his mouth. He's tossing it around in the air like it's a Frisbee. My eyes fall on the porch box in the corner, and I can't help my curiosity.

I kneel and lift the rusted metal lid. It's empty...except for a bouquet of fresh wildflowers.

Zelda comes back out to the deck just as Smoke comes into view carrying a huge bundle of wood over his shoulder.

He's shirtless, wearing only his jeans, boots, and a pair of work gloves. His tattooed body is glistening with sweat. His long dark hair is tied into a knot on the top of his head. He sets the wood down with ease in front of the dilapidated fence and using his hands, he grips an old crumbling post and lifts it from the ground, tossing it to the side with ease before replacing it with a new one.

Zelda sees me watching him.

"You know, just because a relationship doesn't conform to the standard shapes you were taught in preschool doesn't mean they don't fit together. We may not all be triangles or squares, but we're still shapes. That boy over there," she says, pointing her teacup at Smoke.

It sounds odd her calling him a boy especially when he yanks another post from the ground with one hand.

"He's my child in every way. Not every child requires three squares a day and a story at bed time. Some just need a box on the porch and the freedom to run free."

She gives my shoulder a squeeze. "Just give him time."

Time for what?

"Time isn't something I have much of," I say, looking down to my hands.

Zelda doesn't ask why, and I suspect she knows a lot of what I'm not telling her already. She squeezes my shoulder again and sighs. "Time isn't something any of us really have."

It isn't. I look down at my lap.

"Rage was right, you do feel something for him." Zelda says, watching my expression. "I can't blame you. I was always attracted to the complicated ones myself. My Barney being the most complicated of them all."

My eyes snap to hers.

"I know everything, dear," she says with a sweet smile. "Let me tell you this one thing." She leans in close and gently tucks a lock of my hair behind my ear, cupping my cheek. "Never ever underestimate a woman, especially yourself. We are in charge despite what anyone might say or think. You have more control over your life than you give yourself credit or blame for. Also, Smoke seems to think he don't feel things like a normal person. That he was born without a conscience or a heart but he's wrong."

"He is?"

She nods. "He is. It's not that he doesn't feel anything, it's that he feels *everything*. And for a man capable of such atrocities it's hard for him to justify it any other way."

It hits me. I've been blaming Smoke for ripping me away and holding me hostage, but really, none of this is his fault. It's *mine*. I'm the one who stole the money from Griff and set the wheels in motion. I'm the one who embarked on some sort of deep web crusade to save the world without fully appreciating the consequences of my actions.

Zelda and The Warden make me think of all I had in the world before I was brought here, and it wasn't much. A sort-of friendship with Duke. A one-sided love-hate thing with neighbor's meddling cat.

Smoke isn't the problem at all, I realize.

He's the consequence.

CHAPTER TWENTY-NINE

SMOKE

Griff is close to finding Frank. Soon, revenge will be mine. I'm in shock that Griff got a hit on Frank. I was beginning to believe Frankie when she said her old man wouldn't materialize no matter what we threatened him with.

But it was hard to focus on revenge after that shit-storm on the couch and the text from Griff. I find myself needing a release like a snake bite victim needs anti-venom. I'm dying, or I'm already dead, because visions of Frankie gyrating her hot pussy up and down my lap are all I can see. Even hard physical labor of replacing Zelda's fence posts didn't tire me out enough to stop my imagination from running wild with what could've happened. What I'd wanted to happen.

What Frankie wanted to happen.

After taking Frankie back from Zelda's, I spend half of the night in the same bed with her trying to pretend this thing between us isn't a thing. It's better that way. I promised I'd deliver her to Griff. That was the deal. I can't go back on my word when Griff was the one who gave me the Frank Helburn lead to begin with.

Frankie's asleep. Her warm body just inches from mine. The covers slip, and I'm staring at a perfect pink nipple on a made-for-my-mouth pale creamy tit.

I'm rock fucking hard. I salivate, imagining my tongue lapping against her nipple. Sucking it. Making her moan as it peaks in my mouth. Imagining her wet and ready for me to take her any fucking way I goddamned please.

I wipe my mouth with the back of my hand. I'm a grown fucking man, and I'm drooling.

I have needs. I'm a man. That's all this shit is.

I slip out of bed and make sure the cuff tethering her to the bed is tight. I leave the house, get on my bike, and head over to a local dive bar. Within minutes, I find a busty and willing redhead who I take back to the house.

I bring the redhead into the living room, but I leave the door to the bedroom open. I tell myself it's because I want to make sure I can keep an eye on Frankie as she sleeps, but as the redhead unzips my fly, I realize it's because I want to keep my eyes on her. As my cock enters the stranger's mouth, it feels all wrong. I try to close my eyes, but all I see is Frankie.

I open them again, and all I see now is bright red lips and dark blue eyeshadow bobbing up and down on my dick. I feel myself softening. I look at the ceiling and thread my fingers through the redhead's hair, impaling her on my cock. She makes a choking sound followed by a moan, and I lift my hips to fuck her mouth, but I can't reach the release that's so close. I just need...

A clinking sound grabs my attention away from the ceiling. My eyes land on Frankie who's shifted on the bed. She's awake. The clinking was her cuff against the bedpost. Her eyes are open and staring straight at me. Wild and offended and something else. Jealous? Turned on?

The truth is I'm keeping my eyes locked on her because it's the only thing bringing me to the fucking edge. It's Frankie's mouth I'm imagining as I grow thicker. Harder. It's the taste of Frankie's pussy on my tongue that's driving me to fuck the back of her throat. I want it to be Frankie who swallows every drop of what I give her.

The redhead pops up and rolls a condom over my length. She raises up and takes a hold of me in her hand but before she has a chance to impale herself I spin her around by the hips so she's facing away from me.

I push on her shoulders so that she's slightly bent and not blocking my view of Frankie who's still watching, but the redhead doesn't notice her.

After a few exaggerated moans, she's either come or faked it, but I couldn't care less. I grab her hips and take control even though she's the one on top. I thrust up into her roughly as I lock eyes with Frankie with every intention of annoying her or smirking at her or pissing her off. Punishment for what she's already done to me, even if she knows it or not. But I can't bring myself to do it. I'm too lost in her eyes. When I come, I don't tear them from hers as I come harder than I ever have, so hard I'm seeing stars. I'm so lost that it's a while before I come to, but when I do, the redhead is gone, my pants remain open, and Frankie's eyes are closed once again.

I take a quick shower, feeling worse than I had before I went in search of relief that never came.

I should feel better. More powerful. I showed her who was in control, and in return, I've never felt so out of control. Because one inhale of her scent on the pillow, one little tease of her essence, and any satisfaction I might have felt is gone, and I am rock hard again.

My stomach a hollow pit. My soul a shade blacker than it was this morning.

I slide into bed and reach for her, pulling her against my chest. She tries to wiggle from my grasp, but I hold her steady until she stops resisting.

"Sssshhhh," I tell her. "Go back to sleep."

"I hate you," she says. I hear the tears in her words, and they fucking sting. For the first time in my life, I can feel the pain of words strike like a shiv to the ribs.

You and me both.

Despite the unwanted and unwelcome new pain, I feel something else. Something that feels a lot like pride. She's still defiant. She hasn't given up. I haven't broken her.

I kiss the top of her head and sigh into her hair.

"Good. You should."

CHAPTER THIRTY

FRANKIE

I mechanically throw the ball for the fifteenth time, and The Warden brings it back within seconds, sitting at my feet and waiting eagerly for yet another toss. It's all I can do to keep the anger from exploding inside of me, making me do something I know I'll regret.

Like tell Smoke the truth.

"Alright, boy. Time for a challenge." This time, I throw it as far as I can. I think it's going to stop at the fence, but the ball hits the ground and goes bouncing over it instead.

"Shit," I curse as The Warden leaps over the fence like a miniature horse jumping barrels. He lands with a yelp, and I leap to my feet and run toward him.

I'm not sure of where the property line is that will end in my demise if I cross over it, but Smoke assured me of a warning beep so I make my way slowly to the other side of the fence, careful not to make too much noise so I can hear the beep in case the warning isn't a loud one.

I jump down on the other side and look around. I don't see the ball or The Warden. "Where did you go, boy?" I call out.

The Warden whips past me, a big furry yellow blur, almost knocking me over. I watch him cross the field and dart into the open door of a small run down shed with rusted metal roof. I trudge through the long grass still listening for the beep when I hear a noise that sounds like a woodpecker hammering his beak into the trunk of a tree, but it can't be a woodpecker. It's much slower, and then it stops completely.

As I approach the shack the scent of pine hits me, reminding me of the tall trees covering the vacant lot around the townhouse. It's only been a few days since I've seen it but it feels like a lifetime ago.

"There better not be spiders in there," I grumble, carefully pushing open the door, peering into the darkness of the shack. The walls of the tiny room are covered with shelves and those shelves are full to the edges with wooden statues of all kinds and sizes, similar to the ones I saw in Zelda's home.

There are several dog statues that look like The Warden along with many torsos. Women's torsos. Some with large breasts, some with small. One with a large rounded pregnant belly on a center spot above the dirty window.

All are extremely beautiful. I stand there for a moment in awe with my mouth agape, taking it all in. The noise starts again, startling me. I look down from the shelves to the other side of the shack where I see movement in the shadows.

I approach slowly until I can make out the source of the noise which isn't a bird at all, it's the sound of a soft hammer banging against the end of a chisel, and that chisel is in the hands of none other than Smoke.

I'm surprised.

He's shirtless. His trap muscles flex, tightening and rotating as he rotates a block of wood upon a lazy-susan type of rotating wheel. One of his bare feet is propped up against the table leg, the other is flat on the floor.

Smoke created all this?

The Warden approaches me with the tennis ball in his mouth. He drops it at my feet, and that's when Smoke looks up. "What are you doing in here?" he asks.

"The Warden jumped the fence looking for his ball."

"Get out!" Smoke orders.

I barely register him speaking because my eyes are glued to the piece he's working on. The woman's figure isn't like the others. It's larger in scale, and it isn't smooth and perfect like the others. The wood is knotted and cracked as if representing bruises and scrapes. There's even a ding right below the left collarbone that looks just like…

"Get the fuck out," Smoke warns. His stool falls to the floor as he stands with his fists clenched at his sides.

I spin around and run back with The Warden hot on my heels, the ball still in his mouth, as if we're playing a game and he's chasing me.

I jump back over the fence and run to the porch. I don't stop until I'm inside the house with the door shut behind me. The Warden drops the ball at my feet, but I step over it on my way to the bathroom.

I rip off my shirt and look in the mirror at my now faded bruises and scrapes. I remember the piece Smoke was working on.

My eyes go wide as I trace my fingers over the small mole right below my left collarbone.

CHAPTER THIRTY-ONE

FRANKIE

I can't sleep.

It's late when Smoke climbs into bed. I smell the whiskey surrounding him along with cigar smoke. I pretend to be asleep while he takes off his clothes and gets into bed. He wraps his big arms around me as he usually does and pulls me against his hard chest.

I hate that I find myself relaxing into him instead of fighting him. I hate that I want his touch instead of being repulsed by it.

I hate that, despite everything, I *don't* hate him.

"I promise I'll try and find another way," Smoke whispers. I turn around to ask him what he meant by that, but he's already fast asleep.

His eyelashes are long and dark on his cheeks. His full lips are slightly parted. I don't know what comes over me, but I can't help myself. I crane my neck and lightly press my lips to his. I pull away only to find his eyes are now open, and he's looking at me with a mix of confusion and lust.

"I'm...I just..." I begin, but I don't get to finish because I'm rolled over on my back with Smoke on top of me and his lips on mine.

He rolls his hips against me, his long, hard erection pressing up against my sensitive nub igniting a carnal lust inside me like a flint to fire. His lips are against my neck, and I'm arching into him. His lips part and his tongue connects with my skin. I break out into delicious gooseflesh.

Then, he's gone.

The bathroom door slams, and the sound of water hitting the porcelain can be heard under the door as the shower turns on.

I creep out of the bed and watch him through a crack in the door. He's naked, leaning against his forearms on the wall of the shower. Water drips down his sculpted body as he lets his forehead rest on his arm. His other hand snakes down his chiseled abs where he grabs hold of his massive erection and begins to stroke himself.

I should look away. I should look anywhere but at him, but I can't help myself. I want to hate him for bringing that girl here. I want to not feel this pain and fear and anxiety every time I look at him. I want this desire for him to disappear as quickly as it came, but none of that happens. I can only stare at Smoke with wonderment and awe and fucking slicing pain.

I'm silently sobbing as his pace quickens, his breaths short. He shuts his eyes tightly. He's rough and almost violent with himself. His eyes open and find mine through the crack.

I stay still. Frozen in place. A tear rolls down my cheek.

He keeps his gaze fixed on mine as he strokes himself once more, coming with a deep groan on his lips; long streams of white coat the tile and his fist.

I'm panting along with him except now my sobs aren't so silent.

CHAPTER THIRTY-TWO

FRANKIE

In search of my sneakers, I move Smoke's cut off one of the chairs hoping to find them underneath. Nope. Not there. I place his cut back where I found it when something falls to the floor. I think it's a picture until I realize it's an ultrasound. Morgan Faith Clark is the name on the top left corner. The date is from last year.

"What the hell is this?" I ask myself out loud. And why does Smoke have it?

When I hear Smoke's heavy stomp, I tuck the photo back into his cut just as he opens the front door.

"Come out here," he says.

"I can't find my sneakers."

"You don't need them," he assures me.

The last thing I'm expecting is to be led out to the porch and presented with a large standing easel. But that's what's waiting for me on the far-left side. It has paint from past creations splattered on it all around the legs. It's secondhand, which to me, makes it even better, having already lived another life.

"What's that for?" I finally ask.

"It's for painting," Smoke says sarcastically, leaning against the door. "Thought you'd know that."

"I got that much, but why is it *here*?" My feet don't wait for his response. In fact, I'm already across the deck inspecting the materials by the time the question leaves my mouth.

Stretched canvas. Several bottles of Acrylic paint. Primary colors only with a larger bottle of white paint and wooden palate for mixing colors. There's also a water dish already filled to the top on the side table and several rags in the holder connecting the two front legs. A dozen or so paint brushes of various sizes sit in a cylinder attached to the side of the easel.

"Do you paint?" I ask because even after our conversation, I can't possibly believe this is all here for me.

"No," Smoke answers with a small laugh. "But, you're about as good at being bored as I am. Zelda told me you mentioned you've wanted to paint. Thought you might like to try."

I don't know what his endgame is here. All I know is that I want to be mad. I want to rage on him and tell him that trying to occupy my time until my death isn't going to work. I want to tell him to shove this entire easel up his murdering ass, but another part of me is itching to give it a shot. Tears prick at my eyes, but I keep my back to Smoke. I won't give him my fear, and I sure as hell won't give him my joy.

I wonder if Dr. Ida ever wanted to both thank someone and stab them at the same time. "So, this is a bribe, so I'll be less difficult? Because I don't know if a few paints are going to do the trick." When I'm sure the threat of tears is gone, I turn around and stop just in time to see the screen door flap shut.

Smoke's the one gone now.

I turn back to the easel and run my hand over the blank canvas. I look out over the porch and close my eyes. I breathe in the fresh air. I observe the way the sunlight feels on my face. I open them again and I'm already popping the tops off the paints and mixing the colors until I get the results I want. I choose a brush, dip it in the water, and shake off the excess.

Then, I'm gone. I'm in another world. One without fear. Or ankle bombs. Or fathers who abandon their children, or men who'd rather take lives than save them. In this world, only I and the canvas exist.

For a very short time, I am free.

Smoke

I've been trying to get a hold of Griff with no fucking luck. I know he said he'd reach out to me but I need to know how much closer his people are to finding Frank. I close the phone and sigh.

I need to know how much time is left.

I go outside for a smoke. Frankie's still at the easel, where she's been for the last several hours. Her foot's tapping to the beat of the song on the radio, and she's singing along. Her voice isn't that of an angel. It's pretty fucking horrific, actually, but I find myself watching her anyway as she sways from side to side while painting away.

I don't know what I expected her to paint or why. I didn't give it all that much thought when I bought the damn thing from the art store in town. I just wanted to keep her occupied so she'd stop asking questions, stop wanting to tell me stories. Stop making me like her. Want her.

The problem is that she's stopped making the effort, but I still find myself liking her.

Wanting her.

I light my smoke, and my foot brushes against a canvas drying in the sun on the top step. I crouch down and turn my head to get a better view of what it is. It's a very large and very realistic looking eye. A blueish circle lines the bottom giving it the appearance of being tired.

Damn. She's good. It isn't just an eye either. Inside the pupil is where the real art begins. It's a landscape of some sort. No, it's here. The prison yard. Only, it's different. The sky an apocalyptic-looking orange with brown clouds.

I stand up to take in the bigger picture. I take a drag of my cigarette and choke out a cough when I see the blood. The bodies strewn about what looks like a prison yard turned battlefield. In the very center is a man carrying a woman.

Holy shit. It's me. It's *us*.

More specifically, it's me... carrying Frankie into Hell.

CHAPTER THIRTY-THREE

FRANKIE

"Why do they call you Smoke?" I ask.

It's late afternoon, and we're sitting on the porch. We haven't spoken in a long while and despite my anger I'm tired of the silence.

Smoke's drinking whiskey straight from the bottle, and I'm reading a novel I found in a container in the guest bedroom. Or I should say I'm *trying* to read a novel. We've been out here for over an hour, and I've read the same paragraph a hundred times without yet understanding a single word. It's hard to focus when all I can think about is his lips on mine. The way he rocked me against him.

The redhead.

Smoke pulls the cigar from his lips and holds it up before my mind can wander further and before my blush has a chance to reach my cheeks. He raises his eyebrow like the answer to my question about his name is obvious, but I can sense there's more.

"No," I say. "That can't be it. If smoking cigars was the reason to call you Smoke then you would have already told me." I think for another minute and decide to change tactics to find out what I want to know. "What's your real name?"

"Smoke," he answers around the cigar now back between his lips.

"Will you tell me if I guess?" I ask, deciding to ignore the obvious lie about his real name being Smoke.

"Sure," he says. "I'll play along. What you got?"

"Max?" I ask.

He shakes his head.

"Jerry?"

He rolls his eyes and gives me a look that says *try harder.*

"Tim? Killer? Sven?"

He scrunches his nose. "Those all sound like dogs," Smoke scoffs, taking another puff of his cigar. He blows it out, clouding his features in puffs of white. "I'll save you some trouble. It's also not Fido, Spike, or Spot."

"Well, all the other names I can think of are so…regular. So…boring. They wouldn't suit you," I tell him, although I could be here all night, and I still think I'll never come up with something that does besides Smoke.

"I don't know my real name," he admits, flicking the ash at the end of his cigar into an empty beer bottle. "Some shit went down with my folks, and after that, I just couldn't remember it. Still can't."

I'm taken aback and don't know what to say to that. Thankfully, I don't have to come up with something because he continues after taking a long pull from the bottle of whiskey. He wipes his mouth with the back of his hand.

"The first time I went to a group home, they wanted to know what to call me, and since I didn't know my own name, they called me Johnny, for a while, anyway, but it didn't stick."

My heart stung for the child version of Smoke. Abandoned without so much as a name. And not JUST abandoned.

Thrown away.

Smoke clears his throat and looks out over the horizon. He seems almost peaceful here. Well, as peaceful as Smoke could be. His hard edges are still there but not so sharp I'd prick my finger on them if I stand too close.

"The kids there were cruel, especially the older ones. Those little shits thought they were better than me because they had it in their heads that their mom and pops were coming back for them someday."

"But not you."

Smoke put the cigar in his mouth. "No, not me. The running joke around the home was that my parents took one look at me after I was born then vanished into thin air. Gone. Poof." He met my eyes. "Up in smoke."

Smoke was right. Kids can be cruel. "So *that's* why they call you Smoke?"

He nods. "Yeah, I figured it's better than Johnny," he says, taking another long puff of the cigar.

"Wise call."

Smoke chuckles, and there wasn't a single bit of malicious intent in the laughter. No mocking. No eye roll. No threat of punishment or manipulation. This laugh is genuine. Like this one single sound is the gateway through which all sexual things began. My body needs to chill the fuck out. "I don't think anyone has ever called me wise before."

"I'm not going to make a habit of it," I say, and then the moment is lost, and we're both silent. Both thinking the same thing. There isn't time for a habit.

“I’m getting tired,” I lie. “I’m going to go inside.”

I stand up off the chair and head into the house. I pause at the doorway when he calls my name, and for a brief moment, my hopes rise, and I think he’s about to tell me that he’s changed his mind. That he’s found some way for us to both get out of this situation whole.

“What?” I ask my back still turned to him.

There’s another pause.

“Nothing, never mind,” he says, turning his head away.

My hopes fall along with my shoulders. I’m glad he can’t see the tears that instantly spring to my eyes. I keep my voice as steady as possible although I’m shaking inside.

“Nothing,” I repeat, pushing open the door. I shake my head. Now, I really am tired. Exhausted is more like it. “Funny, *nothing*, is exactly what I thought you’d say.”

I go back into the house, and the door slams behind me. I’m not surprised when I hear the door screech open and his heavy footsteps follow me into the bedroom where I’m already under the blankets with my back to him. He can’t even allow me to have one moment of peace to clear my head.

I hear his boots hit the floor, the jingle of his belt as he undresses and gets into bed beside me. It’s not even dark out yet.

He pushes the heat of his body against mine. He smells like cigars, whiskey, and soap, and it takes everything in me not to inhale deeply. Not like I have to. His scent is already imprinted into my brain, and I’ll remember it for the rest of my life.

However long that is.

Smoke wraps an arm around me, and I stiffen. His affection is just making it all worse.

“I wish I could hate you,” I whisper, feeling the world around me closing in more and more with each passing hour.

"Me, too," he responds, his lips kissing the back of my head. "What do you want from me, Frankie?"

I'm not sure what he wants me to say. It's not like it matters.

"Nothing," I whisper, closing my eyes. "I want absolutely nothing from you."

CHAPTER THIRTY-FOUR

"You remind me of someone," I say to the messy-haired man standing in the kitchen. Smoke had introduced him as Kevin before taking off to god only knows where. Maybe he's creating another wooden bust of me to throw off the roof when I'm long gone.

"Actually, they call me Nine now," he corrects after Smoke's long gone. He smiles proudly. "And let me guess, I remind you of someone…from your dreams?" He wags his eyebrows suggestively.

Nine opens then slams every cabinet and drawer in the small kitchen in search of whatever it is he's looking for to make his 'world famous pasta sauce'. His words, not mine.

"Not quite," I say.

Nine is big but not Smoke big. He's leaner than Smoke, and a few inches shorter. He's also about a decade or so younger from my guess, which makes him around my age.

There's a newer-looking tattoo on the side of his neck depicting a bleeding heart with a knife stabbed through it. It's gruesome but skillfully done, whoever created it is a true artist.

Nine's smile is lopsided. His eyes bright. His eyelids naturally hooded. He's chain-smoking cigarettes as he barrels his way through the kitchen as gracefully as one-footed duck.

It hits me who he reminds me of.

"I was thinking that you remind me of a friend of mine actually. His name was...*is*...Duke. His name is Duke."

Nine puts out his cigarette under the tap and plucks a joint from behind his ear. "Duke? Is there a duchess?"

I smile because I can't not smile at Nine. He's attractive and witty and, unlike some people, warm. "Why Nine?" I ask.

He thinks for a few beats. "Because I once took out an entire gang with only a nine millimeter?"

I give him the universal look for 'come on', cocking my head and crossing my arms.

"I'm like a cat, and I've got nine lives?" He tries again.

I shake my head. "You'll have to do better than that."

"The truth is..." he leans in and whispers. "I can't tell you the truth. If I tell ya, then I'll have to kill ya."

I wince.

"Fuck. Sorry about that. Wasn't thinking. I'm kinda new to all this," he apologizes. "I'm usually the tech guy, at least up until now, that is. I don't know the whole story here, but from the look on your face, I realize that a happy ending may not be in the future."

I'm normally the tech guy...

"No, but it's alright," I say. "In a way, it's no one's fault but my own." I pause, an idea forming. "I know how you can make it up to me, though."

"Do I want to know? Because I don't know if you've seen Smoke," Nine points a knife to the front door. "He might be a big scary as fuck dude, but what he'll do to me is probably nothing compared to what I'll have waiting for me back home if I let this all go to motherfucking shit. My brother and the guys he runs with would all take turns killing me. And then?" he shakes his head and shivers. He lowers his voice to a whisper. "And then they'd hand me over to the scariest one of them all…"

"Who?" I ask curiously,

"My sister in law," Nine says, taking a drag from the joint and handing it out to me. I shake my head, needing to stay sharp if I'm going to get my way.

"It's nothing big. Nothing that would bring down the wrath of those in charge. I just need a favor," I raise my shoulders to my neck and look up at Nine with an exaggerated tight smile. I have to go about this carefully, make him think the outcome is his idea.

Nine starts chopping onions. A ton of them. Most of them don't stay on the cutting board. Half of them fall to the floor and the other half fly from the knife as he chops with the joint dangling from his lips.

"I'm not taking the bomb off your leg," he says without looking up from his onions. "I feel like that would be the beginning of the end. For both of us."

"No, I mean, yeah, that would be swell, but that's not what I want."

He puts down the knife and leans forward. "Spill it."

"I want to use your laptop," I blurt, balling my fists and pressing them to my chin, looking up at him over my knuckles.

Nine rolls his eyes, continuing his chopping.

"Just for a few minutes!" I add.

"What makes you think I have a laptop with me? Or that I'd let you use it?" He swipes the chopped onions into the pan on the stove which sizzles. He brings the cutting board back to the island and begins on the mushrooms.

"Nine, you said you're a tech guy." I raise my hands to my chest. "Well, I'm a tech guy, too. And tech geeks like us don't go anywhere without their laptops. Not if they can help it."

Nine adds the mushrooms to the pan and gives them a stir. He grins and surrenders with a sigh, raising his hands in the air. "Okay, you got me. It's in the van, but I can't let you use it. Smoke would strangle me and that, my dear, is not my idea of a good time unless there's a hot chick connected to the hands wrapped around my neck."

"Can I ask you something?" I shove my laptop question to the side on a temporary hold.

"Shoot. But I don't guarantee I can answer it," Nine says.

"Why are you so loyal to him? To Smoke?"

"That's easy. He saved my brother's life," Nine sucks off the tomato juice dripping down his hand.

"He did?" I'm taken aback. Way back. It's the last thing I ever expected him to say.

"He sure as fuck did. He stopped some motherfucker from taking Preppy out in the hospital. I would never have met my brother if it weren't for Smoke. Didn't find him until recently. Wouldn't have my nieces now and would never have met my nephew or my sister-in-law, who I fucking love, despite my earlier comment. Although, she *can* be scary as shit when it comes to protecting my brother and those kids. Even me. So, you see, I owe Smoke a lot more than babysitting you. That's why as much as I'd like to help you, my hands are tied."

"He was *paid* to rescue your brother?"

Nine shakes his head. "Nope. He was there. Saw Preppy was in trouble. Put the breaks on the whole thing."

"Really," I say, drawing out the word. "Smoke has *friends*?

Well, I've met Rage and Zelda, but I kind of imagined them to be it."

"I probably shouldn't be answering that. Or anything."

"How does answering that affect me or you watching me in any way? How can I use that against Smoke or better yet how can I possibly use that information to escape?" I raise my leg and set my foot on the counter, pointing to my ankle. "I've got a bomb on my leg. Remember?"

Nine sighs. "Fine. Yes, Smoke has friends. Or at least, he has people in his corner. That's what I get when people talk about him anyway. He's a legend over in Logan's Beach. The people I know are loyal to him because over the years he's been loyal to them. But he's a loner. That's pretty much all I know."

I rest my chin on my fist. "Interesting. He makes it seem like he puts mountains between him and the rest of the world."

Nine laughs and leans forward with his elbows on the counter. "He does. The thing is, my people, our mutual friends? They're really fucking good climbers."

I laugh and taste the sauce on the spoon he's holding out to me. It's so spicy I cough and choke. "How much red pepper flake did you put in there?" I ask, my mouth hanging open.

Nine hands me a glass of water and I chug it so fast most of it spills down the corners of my mouth onto my shirt. When I'm done, I hand my glass out to Nine who refills it. My eyes are burning. My throat is seizing up. I chug the next one down just as fast.

"Uh, this much?" Nine holds up the now empty bottle of dried red pepper flake that was full only a few minutes before.

"That might be a tad too much," I rasp.

Nine takes a big mouthful of the sauce and swallows it

down. I wait for him to react, but he shrugs and keeps stirring. "Tastes all right to me," he says, smacking his lips.

"Back to Smoke," I say when I'm not about to die via red pepper flake poisoning.

"Smoke's a lone wolf, but that don't mean others ain't got his back. Who knows, he's probably just still messed up with all that shit from Rage," Nine says. His eyes go wide, and I see his regret. He's revealed too much.

"Uh, forget I said anything." he turns his back to me to stir his nuclear sauce. "Why do you want my laptop anyway?" he asks, changing the subject.

"I just want to look something up. A name. It will only take a minute, and you can watch the entire time," I assure him, knowing there's no way he'll actually let me use it. I wait for the idea to form, watching his face as he's deep in thought.

Nine puts down the spoon and scratches the back of his neck. I flash him yet another hopeful grin.

"Okay, here's the deal." He points to me and then to himself. "You tell me the name, and I'll look it up for you and tell you what I find."

Bingo.

"Deal," I say, holding out my hand.

Nine comes over and shakes my hand. He doesn't let go. He smiles and talks between his bright teeth. "I'm going to regret this, aren't I?"

I don't stop smiling either, talking through my own teeth. "Probably."

Nine fires up his laptop. It's top of the line and covered in stickers of rock bands and pot leafs. His desktop image is a pair of naked breasts.

"Classy," I sing.

"Who doesn't like tits?" Nine asks, keying in his passcode. "Everyone likes tits. Even women."

"Is this some sort of lead into a conversation about how all women are hiding an inner lesbian?"

"That would be cool, but no. You know all those popular women's magazines? You won't find too many pictures of men. Why? Because women like to look at women. Women are beautiful. Their bodies are beautiful. Even most porn catering to women don't have gigantic dongs swinging about. They're useful, but they ain't shit to look at. Unless, it's mine, of course.

"Uh, huh."

He cracks his knuckles. "All right, Frankie girl. What's the name?"

I tell him the name from the ultrasound I found in Smoke's cut. Nine begins his search.

A few minutes later, we both realize that Morgan Faith Clark is an enigma. She disappeared off the face of the planet last year. Nine can't find anything else about her. "That's odd. No missing person's report. No nothing. As of last year, she just...vanished."

"What about her address? Do we know where she lived?" I ask, leaning over Nine's shoulder.

Nine hits a few keys, and within seconds we're looking at the google street view of a small blue house with white trim and a flowery front walkway. "Who is this person, anyway? Someone important?"

"Honestly, I'm not sure yet," I say looking over the information on the screen. "She could be."

"How very vague of you," Nine says. "I'm pulling up the public records for the house. There's a bunch of city citations for overgrown grass and things like that which leads me to believe the house is abandoned."

"Can you see when it was abandoned?"

"I can get close. Yeah. Here. The last utility bill was paid for last June so anytime in July I would assume. Wait, look at this." Nine points to the screen. "Morgan Faith Clark was reported missing by an aunt in Sarasota."

Nine's fingers fly across the keyboard and I find myself missing the feeling. The sound of the keys sings to me like a favorite song I know all the words to.

"The aunt reported her missing on the 10th of July after Morgan didn't show up at her house in Sarasota the prior morning. The police opened an investigation." He clicks a few more keys. "But it's never been closed."

The screens change and flip as Nine flies through sites and codes, unearthing everything the internet wants to keep hidden like an archeologist of the web. Window after window appears then disappears as I follow along.

"Pull up the police report. Use the back way and use 911 at the end of the code if you're going in via their webhost. That usually works."

Nine scoffs, ash falling onto the keys. "Like I've never broken into a police department before. What do you think this is, amateur hour?" Nine's cigarette dangles from his lips. "And you really are a tech geek aren't you?"

I nod. "I am. Or, at least, I *was*."

"Okay, here. Police report states that they went to the house, and there was no sign of foul play. Morgan's purse and belongings were gone as well as her car, leaving them to believe she might have skipped town, but they note that there was no activity on her bank account or credit cards after July 9th."

"Does the house have a security camera?" I ask.

"Already on it." Nine reads down the report to the bottom

in a flash. "The police report indicates the house has a Aestro Pro 7688 security system, but when they tried to access the feed, it was blank."

I shake my head. "No such thing as blank feed unless a camera's broken." I say. "Aestro is high end security. Even if it's not on the mainframe, it can be recovered through their servers."

"How the hell do you know that?" Nine asks, looking at me with over his shoulder with an eyebrow raised. He stubs out his cigarette into a coffee mug and lights another joint. I pluck it from his hand before he has a chance to lift it to his lips, and I take a long slow drag, dramatically blowing the smoke at the computer screen.

"Maybe one of these days. If things work out for me. We'll meet again, and I'll tell you my story," I say.

Nine smiles and takes back his joint, turning back to the laptop. "It's a date," he says. "But, not that kind of date. I don't think Smoke would appreciate if it was."

"Why would he care?"

"Uh, I saw the way he stormed out of here. A man doesn't leave like that unless he's frustrated as all hell and needs to clear his head. Plus, I saw the way he looked at you."

"Bullshit," I say.

"I'm hacking into Aestro now. Entering her address and the dates she went missing and cross reference that with the connected motion detectors in a few seconds we should be able to pull the feed." Nine says. "And it's not bullshit. He looks at you like you like he wants to..."

"Like he wants to kill me," I finish for him.

"Yeah, that too." Nine says.

"Doesn't matter. He's got some deal with a guy named Griff. Smoke's keeping me while this Griff person tries to get my father to surface using pictures of me. If my father doesn't show his face in a few days, and he won't, Smoke's going to take me to this Griff person so he can get take his pound of flesh my father owes him out on me."

"Something sounds a bit screwy with your story," Nine says.

"What do you mean? It's the truth."

"I'm not saying it isn't. I'm just saying that if Smoke was hired to kidnap you for this Griff person don't you think he'd hand you over to him right away? There's got to be a reason why he hasn't. Something more personal to the story."

"Like what?"

"Beats the fuck out of me, Frankie girl."

Nine hits enter and a screen pops up. A black and white video. He fast forwards through the feed and finds the day in question. He pauses and hits play again. A woman, who I assume is Morgan is there. She's a little older than me with shorter wavier dark hair. She's alone and obviously very pregnant. She's just walking around the house packing for the most part. There's an open suitcase on the kitchen island. The video doesn't have sound, but she appears to be whistling.

That is, until she's no longer alone. "Shit," Nine whispers.

Morgan jumps back in surprise, but whoever she's surprised to see it off camera.

Nine tries to pick up another angle, but the feed suddenly goes blank.

"Where did it go?" I ask, needing to know and see more.

"Shit. It's not there. Someone must have washed it out," Nine says, slamming a few keys. "I'll try and recover."

After prying open a few internet doors that were never meant to be opened, the screen flashes with an image but it's hard to see what's on it because it's flickering on and off like a light bulb that's about to die.

"There, that's all that's left of it," Nine says. "Whoever

cleaned house knew what they were doing, that's for fucking sure." He takes another drag of his joint and passes it to me. I do the same.

"Can you freeze it?" I ask, leaning over his shoulder.

Nine presses a few more keys, and the image freezes and expands.

My stomach flips, and I cover my mouth.

"Holy fucking shit," Nine whispers, his eyes as wide as the computer screen.

I'm glad it's in black and white because I can't imagine how it would look in color if it's making me want to vomit now.

"I can't look at this anymore," I say, as Nine's sauce threatens to burn its way back up my throat. "Do you think Smoke could have..."

"I don't know." Nine shakes his head. "I know some sick fuckers, but this..." He leans into the screen and squints. "Wait! Look."

He expands the image again. In the corner of the frame, walking away from the bloody scene is a man. "I'm going to zoom in more." The face of the man is blurry, but he's too small to be Smoke.

I let out a breath I didn't know I was holding.

"So, all we can make out is that the man is wearing an old fashioned white hat with some sort of black ribbon or stripe around it above the brim," I say.

"And that it's not Smoke."

"And that it's not Smoke," I repeat.

I was hoping this would give me some insight into what Smoke's hiding from me, but all it's done is make me ask more questions than ever.

"Fuck me. Do you see that?" Nine says, pointing to what the man's carrying in his hands.

"Holy shit," I say, covering my mouth with my hand. Nine's right. There *is* more.

So. Much. Fucking. More.

CHAPTER THIRTY-FIVE

FRANKIE

Nine puts his laptop back in the van.

When he comes back he stands at the counter, eating his pasta slathered in his 'world famous' sauce. I pass because one more taste will surely set fire to my stomach and I'll turn into a dragon.

Nine cleans up while I go change.

I need to go outside. To breathe fresh air.

To think.

The weather is beyond beautiful. Eighty-five degrees and cloudless blue sky. The world around me is obviously unaware that it's not supposed to be so lovely under the circumstances.

It's odd to think that despite if I'm here or not, everything will still go on without me. Good weather. Bad. Droughts. Storms. Day and night will still take shifts

Just because I know what might happen to me doesn't mean I've given up hope.

Not yet, anyway.

I want to take advantage of the beautiful day so I rummage through the big storage container of clothes and pull out the only bathing suit I can find. Along with everything else in the box, it's new with the tags still attached.

It's a simple black string bikini that ties at my hips, behind my neck and around my back. It's a size too small so my ass cheeks hang out the bottom as do the bottom swell of my breasts, but it's all I got so I pull it on and tie my hair into a messy bun on the top of my head.

I grab a towel from the bathroom and one of the romance novels I found on a small bookcase in the corner of the living room. I need a distraction after seeing that gruesome scene on Nine's computer, and I decide that Mercy by Debra Anastasia, a romance I've read several times before, will be just what I need along with a little sun on my skin.

I let Nine know where I'm going, and he tells me he'll be out in just a sec. He's on his phone, talking in a hushed voice at the dining room table.

I lay my towel down in the middle of the small front yard, the only section for miles that isn't a tangled web of vines and weeds. I'm not two paragraphs into my book when The Warden appears, nudging my book with his wet nose.

"Okay, okay, boy" I laugh, taking the tennis ball from his mouth and tossing it across the yard.

After a few minutes of play, The Warden tires and lays down next to me, content to chew on his ball instead of chase it. I do the same and pat his head with one hand while lying on my stomach and holding up my book with the other.

"Mind if I join you?" Nine asks. I look up to find him shirtless. A big goofy grin on his face.

I sit up and put down my book. "You're the babysitter. I think if you left me alone that would kind of be beside the point."

"True. Although Smoke's on his way back. He just called so I'm gone soon. I just wanted to give you something first."

"What's that?"

Nine hands me a mini zip drive. "Hide it. I hope you can somehow use it to help your cause."

"Thank you," I say, taking the drive and tucking it into the pages of the book.

"And there's one other thing," he says. His hands come around from behind his back and before I know what's happening he's spraying me with cold water from a hose. The Warden barks, and I yelp in surprise, then spend the next ten minutes trying to take the hose from him to get him back.

When we're all out of breath, we collapse onto the towel, and I dry my hands, picking back up my now somewhat soggy book.

Nine is on his back with his hands behind his head and his eyes closed to the sky. I'm next to him on my stomach, again with my feet in the air.

"I hope things work out for you," Nine says, sitting up. "And just for the record. I would save you if I could."

"Thank you."

He lights a cigarette. "If nothing else. It was nice getting to know ya. I hope Smoke does the right thing as soon as he figures out what that is."

"Me, too," I say with a sigh.

The sound of a rumbling engine shakes the ground. We both turn our heads.

Smoke pulls into the pebble drive and kills the engine.

"I guess this is good-bye," Nine says. He takes me by surprise when he leans in.

"What are you doing?" I ask.

"Just go with it," he whispers. "Trust me."

I'm too shocked to pull away. His lips land on mine for a

kiss two seconds too long to be considered a peck. I feel Smoke's presence behind us.

"Who knows? Maybe, we'll run into one another one day," Nine says, standing. He looks to Smoke and smirks. "Good thing I parked in the back." With a wave to an approaching Smoke he turns to leave, but then pauses and kneels to quickly whisper. "The thing on your leg? It's not a bomb." He stands back up then disappears behind the house.

I don't even have time to process what he just said when a familiar shadow is cast over my entire body.

Smoke.

I look up and am met with his stone hard gaze.

"Shit," I swear.

His jaw ticks.

"What's going…" I'm lifted off the ground and tossed over Smoke's shoulder with ease. The leather of his cut is hot against my bare skin. "What are you doing?" I ask, kicking and yelling, pounding my fists against his back.

"I should break his fucking neck," he seethes.

"Whose neck?" I shriek.

Smoke doesn't answer. He doesn't even stop until we're back in the bedroom. He throws me down on the mattress and removes a set of cuffs from his wrist, cuffing my wrist to the headboard.

"What the hell!" I yelp.

"I should do a lot fucking more than cuff you." He looks as if he's trying to gain control over himself but he's losing. His breaths are rapid. His vein is pulsing in his neck. His knuckles are white.

"I don't understand. Why…" I don't get a chance to finish my question because he's already gone. The bedroom door is left partially open. I hear the front door slam shut and his bike engine roar to life.

I'm so wound up. I can't think straight. There's a sinking feeling pulling me down into its depths. I'm pissed the hell off. If I had any chance in hell I'd strangle Smoke with my bare hands. The pain and anger is crippling.

What the hell just happened?

All signs point to Smoke being jealous but is that even possible? He can't be mad that Nine kissed me. It was just a friendly kiss. But then I realize that's exactly what he is.

Smoke's *jealous*.

I scoff. He has no right to be. Not after the redhead. Not after he *kidnapped* me. I'm furious and hurt and feeling more alone than I ever did at home.

I'm also frustrated, annoyed, and yet again trapped — cuffed to the fucking bed.

But there's something empowering about having that effect on Smoke. Something satisfying about making him feel even a small dose of how he made me feel when he brought that girl here.

I scream out my frustrations into an empty house, kicking my feet against the mattress. I pull at the cuffs as if they will somehow magically release me.

They don't.

I'm wound up so tight I could burst. Maybe, I should show Smoke the drive when he comes back. Maybe, it will mean something to him, enough to set me free.

I remember the deep V in Smoke's forehead.

Or maybe, it will be my final undoing.

I try to calm my erratic heart and racing mind, but as I lay in the quiet room I find myself something beyond restless.

I stare at the ceiling, unmoving, heart beating wildly.

The empowerment over being able to make Smoke jealous turns into another kind of feeling that starts as a tingle between my thighs, growing and morphing into something more powerful until I'm pressing my thighs together to calm the growing ache.

I tell myself it's the romance novels that's ignited this need within me to feel more.

To feel *something*.

But I know, even as it's happening, that it's a lie.

With my one free hand, I try to untie the bathing suit top from around my back, but I can't reach. I pull up the top instead, freeing my breasts.

I've touched myself before but have never found it to be all that satisfying. Most of the time I can't bring myself to climax. But I needed to calm the storm in both my mind and body. Being tied to the bed limited my options.

I push off my bikini bottoms.

I close my eyes and rest my head against the pillow. My feet are flat on the mattress. Knees up. I squeeze my nipple, then run my flat palm lightly over the pebbled peak. A shot of desire pools in my lower stomach.

I bite my lower lip and move my hand to the other nipple. It feels better than I remember, although it's been a while. I pinch it lightly and my mouth drops open in a silent gasp.

I might even be able to come just from this. I'm wet, my thighs slippery. I move my hand down my body. I imagine that it's someone else's hand touching me.

Wanting me.

The first face that pops into my mind is Smoke's hoovering above me. I shake my head and decide on Duke instead. I remember his kisses. His good looks. It's working until my fingertips reach my clit, then the image switches from blonde curls and goofy grins to dark eyes and rough hands. Tattoos and frown lines. Handcuffs and scars. Lips that were made for sin. A perfect body with a corrupt mind.

I remember the way it felt to be on his lap. The way he

used my hips to rub me against his hard shaft through his jeans. I circle my clit with my fingers, using my own wetness to glide over and over it again and again. I lift my hips off the bed and imagine that it went further. That the phone or Zelda hadn't stopped us. I imagine the sound his jeans make hitting the floor. That he flipped me over with my back against the couch and sucked on my nipples while his fingers found my wet, aching folds.

I come before my imagination has a chance to get any further. It's hard. So hard. Shattering me and putting me back together with pleasure and pain and frustration. It's so wrong, but I don't care. I just care about this feeling running through me like a wild rapid-filled river. I'm screaming out into the otherwise quiet house. It's a wild cry, desperate, loud and unforgiving. I've never experienced an orgasm this strong before. This unpredictable.

My hand is still between my spread legs, my finger lazily flicking over my clit as I ride out the waves of pleasure. I shiver from the sensation of my hard nipples against the breeze coming through the window.

I'm coming down, my mouth still open in ecstasy, my fingers dipping inside me briefly to again trace lazy circles over my swollen clit with my own juices.

Smoke's name is still echoing through the house and through my ears. I roll my head to the side and open my eyes.

I freeze. My movements. My breathing. My thoughts.

Because, there, standing in the doorway, is Smoke.

CHAPTER THIRTY-SIX

SMOKE

I'd taken off after seeing Nine put his mouth on Frankie. I was pissed. She was mine. Not his. My job. My problem. My everything. I was pissed at myself for being so fucking pissed. It's a good thing Nine had parked in the other direction because I wanted to tear his arms off with my bare hands and beat him to death with his own useless limbs, and if he would have come close enough I probably would've.

I growl. I *know* I would've.

I'm on my bike not two miles down the road when I slam on the brakes and set my foot to the pavement, making a sharp U-turn. What the fuck am I doing? Why am I holding back? Frankie is mine to do with what I please.

An instrument of revenge.

Nothing more.

I shouldn't be running from her; *she* should be running from *me*.

I speed back to the cottage. I barely had the kickstand

down, before hopping off my bike and hurrying into the house with long determined strides.

Frankie doesn't understand the extent of my anger. She asked me why when I cuffed her to the bed.

Why? I'll show you why.

I'm about to step inside the bedroom when I stop like I've got a hand pressed to my chest.

This has got to be another one of her tricks.

My breath hitches at the sight before me. My cock hardens.

But what a fucking trick it is.

Frankie. Cuffed to the bed. That much I expected to find. It's what I didn't expect that has my throat dry and my fingers twitching by my side.

She's naked.

She's naked, and she's touching herself.

It's the most erotic thing I've ever seen. It's both pleasure and pain. Heaven and Hell. Disturbing and delightful and fucking luring me in like a siren from the deep.

Which sums up everything when it comes to how I feel about Frankie Helburn.

I can't look away. I can't fucking swallow.

Not now. Not fucking ever.

She screams my name as she comes.

MY. NAME.

I can't hold back.

Her eyes lock on mine.

Not *anymore.*

"You're back," she whispers, her cheeks are pink. Her eyes look like she's just shot up heroin. She's unfocused. High on lust. My cock throbs painfully behind my jeans, and I can't take it any longer.

"I'm back," I say. It sounds like a warning, and I meant it

to. I shrug off my cut and reach behind to pull my shirt up over my head, setting both my shirt and cut on the dresser.

I stalk over to the bed and place a hand on her knee. Her skin is soft and warm. I roughly push it down until it meets mattress, spreading her legs wide. She's glistening and dripping and perfect and pink.

"Fucking beautiful," I groan. Her thighs are slick. "You were thinking about me," I say, on a rasp, hearing the hunger in my own voice. I don't attempt to hide it. I'm past that now. So fucking far past it.

Frankie nods, her fingers trailing from her lips to her breasts where she lazily pinches her nipple, never taking her eyes from mine as her back arches slightly off the bed.

"Fuck, Frankie." I take off my boots, kicking them to the floor. "I can't stop this anymore," I say. I mean it. I'm powerless against this slight little thing. "No more fucking games. Just fucking. Just me and you."

She lifts her hips off the bed, silently begging. She whimpers, and the sound is like a stroke to my cock. My balls tighten.

"You left," she says on a breathy whisper, her eyes raking over my naked chest then dipping lower as I take off my jeans and kick them aside.

"I was pissed," I say growing angry all over again at the thought of Nine touching her.

Frankie doesn't react to my anger. Instead, she smiles and bites her bottom lip.

There's no way this was a show meant for me to walk in on. I parked my bike at Zelda's then walked back through the field. She couldn't have heard me coming, and there was no faking an orgasm like that.

"Why?" she asks.

Because I'm stupid. Because I'm losing sight of what's important.

Because I can't make decisions or think of anything else when you're walking around in that little black bikini that barely fits you. When someone else's hands are on you. Hands that ain't mine. When I'd take a bullet if it meant I could be inside you shortly after.

The same little black bikini Nine couldn't take his eyes off earlier is now pushed up over her tits, her nipples hard.

When she came with my name on her lips, I had to hold on to the fucking doorway for support. It was fucking beautiful.

She is fucking beautiful.

I want her. I've wanted her since the second I saw her face for the first time. But now, coming with my name screamed from her lips, I know she wants me. I'm not waiting. Not anymore. Fuck the consequences; I can't focus on anything else. Fuck everything and everyone.

Nothing is coming between us now except for Frankie, who WILL be coming.

Over and over again.

FRANKIE

Smoke's eyes are so heavily hooded with lust they're reduced to slits with his dark gleaming orbs shining underneath.

He places a knee on the bed and then the other, spreading my knees to the mattress as wide as they will go and covering my body with his, positioning himself between my legs. He pushes down his black boxer briefs over his perfectly rounded ass cheeks. They look like something from a sculpture. Tattoos cover his legs and continue all the way up to his neck but his ass is surprisingly tattoo free.

His cock is enormous. I've felt it against me, but I'd yet to see it. It's not just long enough to reach his belly button, but it's much thicker than I imagined. The tip glistening with need.

I blush. Heat rising in my neck and face as he places his hands on both sides of my head. I lift my hips again, and when my clit brushes up against his hardness covered in softer than soft skin, we both moan.

I was pretending to want him before. That my reaction to him was just nature. Biology. It was the biggest lie I've ever told even if it was only to myself. Because this thing between us, this electrical charge that sparks every time we're in the same room, there isn't anything usual about it.

There sure as shit isn't anything natural about it either.

I want Smoke. There's no denying it. Not when it's him I imagined touching me when I came. Not when I can't fucking breathe. Not when he possesses the ability to hurt me as badly as he did.

Not when I possess that same power.

If Smoke was holding back from me before, he isn't anymore.

The look in his eyes is downright wicked. His biceps and shoulders flex as he holds his arms on both sides of me, bracing himself, hovering just above me.

He's watching me as he swipes his thumb over my lip. I close my eyes and lean into his touch. He growls deep within his throat, then covers my lips and my body with his.

Smoke doesn't bother uncuffing me. There isn't time. The need between us sizzles in the air. Igniting the friction between us like a flint causing a spark. His kiss is hard and brutal, and I return it with all that I have. Our tongues aren't dancing. They're fighting a battle both of us know we are destined to lose yet neither of us will be the first to give up the fight.

His hand travels down between my legs while his tongue

strokes mine, he circles my already sensitive clit over and over again, bringing me right back to the brink then stopping. He does this again and again while never taking his lips from mine. I'm dizzy. My heart's slamming in my chest. My stomach is so tight it's about to burst at any moment.

Our kiss is passionately chaotic. "Please," I beg against his mouth between kisses and nips. I'm terrified and anxious but above all else is the pulsing need to have him inside of me.

His lips move to my neck, and he sucks and licks the skin behind my ear. I feel it everywhere. Wetness has pooled between my legs. The sheets underneath me are soaked. "I think you need to be taught a lesson," Smoke growls. "When I said you were mine, I meant it."

"Yes. Please," I beg again as he goes lower and sucks a nipple into his mouth. I cry out, loudly, not caring who hears or what happens. "I need to. I need to..." I trail off, not remembering anything I was saying when one long finger enters me, stroking my inner wall. I'm shaking. Trembling. I'm on the verge of full on convulsing when he stops.

"When you come again, it will be wrapped around my cock and when I say so. You may think you have some control here, hellion. But you don't."

I buck my hips in response, both in frustration and retaliation.

He chuckles against my skin. "That's it, hellion. Fight me. Just be warned," he grips my hips so tightly I see stars. "I fight back."

He releases my hips and rocks against me, rubbing his shaft over my clit again and again until I'm seeing stars. It's pure fucking amazing torture. A pleasurable agony.

I look down between us at his massive erection and a thought occurs to me.

"You're going to break me," I say, against his lips, feeling a sudden shock of panic take hold.

He smirks. "Yes, I am."

Smoke kisses me again. It's deeper, more frantic this time. Our tongues start the tortuous dance once more when his shaft leaves my clit long enough to line himself up with my entrance. He lifts my hips up off the mattress.

"I've never—" I begin to say.

"I know. That's about to change." Smoke surges into me with a strangled roar. His face tight. His neck chorded.

I grimace. The pain is like breaking glass and scratching. I'm breaking from the inside out. I'm being split in half.

"It's only fair that I break you," Smoke groans, seating himself fully inside me. He looks me in the eyes. "Since you've already broken me."

He reaches between us and rubs my clit while he thrusts into me again, ignoring my cries of pain until they slowly turn into cries of pleasure. He moves his lips from my neck to my ear back to my lips and down to my nipple. He uses his hands to guide my hips up to meet his thrusts allowing him to go deeper each time until I'm so full of Smoke he's all I can feel. All I can see. All I can smell. All I can think about.

I don't know if it's the room shaking or me when the eruption begins low within my stomach, spreading like fallout from a nuclear bomb. I'm screaming and crying, clawing at his back, tearing his skin.

This only urges him to thrust harder. Faster.

I want to hurt him. Mark him. I want his flesh under my nails and blood running down his back. I need to scar him. Remind him of me and this and us for as long as he lives.

Nothing outside the sound of the slapping of his skin against mine or the way he moans my name matters. Not now. Not while his lips are on my skin and he's deep inside my body.

The orgasm is so hard and rough and painful that I'm crying. Genuine tears are rolling down my face as Smoke's pace quickens and he slams into me. The thickening of his cock inside me causes another wave of pleasure crashing into this one like two hurricanes meeting in the ocean.

"Smoke!" I cry out.

"God damn this fucking tight pussy of yours," Smoke rasps sounding turned on and pissed off. "Open your fucking eyes," he demands.

His voice is a distant echo in my lust-riddled mind, but I hear him, and it calls me back. And because I'm all out of challenge when it comes to my body and Smoke's control over it.

I do as I'm told and open my fucking eyes.

Smoke holds my face, dropping his forehead to mine. He keeps his eyes on mine. His thrusts become wild. We breathe each other's air as Smoke's hips pound against mine over and over again.

It's rough and hard and everything I never knew I wanted it to be.

"Frankie. Oh Fuck. Frankie!" Smoke cries out. His muscles tensing, his cock twitching before releasing everything he has inside me. Warm spurts fill me, coating my insides, dripping out onto my thighs.

I'm still convulsing around him, tightening my internal grip like a vise until he sags against me. We're both panting for air. Smoke wraps an arm around me as he catches his breath.

My brain is muddled. I'm high on lust and Smoke.

"You were right," I say, unspilled tears in my eyes. I stare up at the ceiling.

Smoke answers wordlessly by gripping me tighter.

I lower my voice to a whisper. "You broke me."

CHAPTER THIRTY-SEVEN

FRANKIE

I wake up alone. Immediately, I feel three things.

Rejection, dread, and an aching soreness between my legs.

I throw on one of Smoke's t-shirts and my Converse, and when I'm sure Smoke isn't in the house, I go search outside.

I'm worried about him. The thought is laughable, but it's true nonetheless.

At first, I don't see anything until I spot a light in the far end of the yard up by the main prison. I walk toward it, and I find Smoke, staring down at the ground. He doesn't look up as I approach.

My eyes follow to where Smoke's staring blankly down at two large stones atop an overgrown mound of dirt on the otherwise flat land.

Those aren't rocks.

They're headstones.

"You can ask," Smoke says, reading my mind.

I think for a second it could be a trap of some sort, but I

ask anyway. My curiosity getting the better of me. "Who is buried here?"

"My parents."

"Who…who buried them here?" I ask, dreading the answer.

He looks up slowly. Our eyes meet.

"I did."

"MY PARENTS WERE REALLY YOUNG. TOO FUCKING YOUNG. Teenagers. Runaways. They were both stuck in the cycle of partying and drugs when I came along. We'd move around from couch to garage to abandoned building. We were homeless, for the most part. They were good parents when they weren't fucked up. From what I can remember, anyway."

"What happened to them?" I ask. I can't help myself. I feel for him. I reach out and place my hand on his arm.

He looks at our connection then up to my face like he's deciding if he'll approve of my touch. He nods and I leave my hand where it is.

"They always went to this house. It was one of the old outbuildings around the prison. I went to there to search for them after I woke up in a prison cell all alone. They weren't there. No one was. I hated that house. Hated what the things in there were doing to them. So I crawled on my hands and knees under the crawlspace. I cut the gas line and pushed it up into the main water pipe and lit a match. I almost didn't make it back out, my pants snagged on a nail and I had to tear away the fabric to get free. The force from the blast sent me sailing into a tree. I dislocated my shoulder. Broke my arm. But I barely felt the pain. All I felt walking back to the prison cell was happiness. But then they never came back."

"They were in the house, weren't they?" I asked.

He nods. "They were too fucked up to answer the door. I buried what was left of their belongings here. It wasn't much. Just some clothes and shit. The worst part was after the initial shock faded, I felt relieved. I no longer had to wonder if they were coming back. They weren't. I made the decisions from then on out. I was happier because they were dead."

"I'm so sorry."

"Why? Because I accidentally killed my parents? Don't. I'm not. Not anymore."

I'm thinking that the incident with his parents was the first step in the transformation from boy to the unhinged man standing before me.

"You were a child," I tell him. "You *shouldn't* feel bad. You were eight years old. You had no nurturing or supervision. It's not your fault. There's nothing to feel bad about."

"You don't know a thing about it," Smoke snaps.

I push against his arm. "Not about what you went through, but I know a thing or two about being alone! After my mother died, my father checked out on me. He worked in the basement and for years, I would only see him when he was giving me money for groceries. He didn't tell me what to do, but he also never told me what *not* to do. I was barely out of the toddler stage, but I was raising myself, so don't give me this 'how would you know' bullshit because I know plenty."

"Then how did you end up so..."

"Don't you dare say normal. I don't think that word has ever applied to me." A few moments of silence passes between us before I speak again. "This is going to sound ridiculous, but I used to pretend my mother was there. I used to pretend she was telling me what to do. I went to bed at 8 PM every night because I pretended she was giving me a bedtime. I took my baths, I ate my vegetables, all because I imagined I had a mother who wanted the best for me."

"What about when she was alive?"

"I don't know how she was when she was alive. I don't remember her. I tried and tried and tried to remember her; I'd stare at her picture in the hallway every day trying to remember one thing: a word, a look, even a yell or scold, but nothing. The only mother I know is the mother of my imagination. So you see, just like you, I raised myself."

"But, we still ended up very different people."

"Yes," I agree.

You're on one side of the gun, and I'm on the other.

Smoke looks back down at the grave. For a nano-second, I feel the heat of his palm on my lower back before he drops it, flexing his fingers and cracking the knuckles instead.

Is he trying to comfort me, or is he seeking comfort of his own? It feels almost like an apology for something horrible to come. Dread builds in my gut and jolts into my heart.

I'm not sure why the sudden confession from Smoke or why he's shared this part of his life with me, but I'm very aware now that there's much more to him than I've realized. There's only one reason why he's choosing to be personal with me now, and it's not a good one. "You're still taking me to him, aren't you?" I ask, already knowing the answer.

"I...I don't know." There's no emotion in his voice.

I take a step back and suck in a ragged breath. I hold my stomach like he's just kicked me in it.

"Well, thank you for your honesty, Smoke, but you can keep your stories to yourself. I didn't need you before. I don't need you now." I almost trip on a rock. Smoke looks like he's about to help steady me but stops himself as I quickly recover. "I've never been a big fan of consolation prizes."

My throat tightens as I turn and jog back to the house

with hot tears streaming down my face and disappointment burning in my heart.

"I told you nothing was going to change," he calls out.

His words stop me in my tracks. I turn back around.

The stars are twinkling overhead. A wolf howls in the distance. Crickets chirp all around us. Proof that horrible things can happen in the most magical of nights.

I march right up to him and stab my index finger into his chest. "But everything has already changed!"

"I told you I don't have a choice," he grates. I see the pain in his face and hear it in his words, but it's not enough, and it won't ever be enough.

"Why?" I ask, rethinking my question. "You know what. That doesn't matter. You *always* have a choice."

He shakes his head and lowers his voice to a whisper. "Not always. Not in this fucking case."

I push on his chest and walk away.

"Yes, you do. You just won't choose me."

CHAPTER THIRTY-EIGHT

SMOKE

"It may be hard to believe, since you think the world revolves around you, but as much as you want to make this all about you, it's not," I yell at Frankie, hot on her heels. She doesn't understand what this is all about. She doesn't understand what needs to be done in order to set things right. She has a right to be frustrated, but that doesn't make the guilt or anger I'm feeling any easier to choke down.

"Then, who is it about?" she asks, spinning around to face me. We're in the kitchen now. Her back is against the counter. "Because the last time I checked, I'm the only one here being held against her will. So, tell me, Smoke. Who the hell else could this all be about?"

I grab her by the shoulders. "It's about my kid!" I blurt.

Frankie's jaw drops open. She doesn't speak, just stares at me in disbelief. She's squinting at me as if she can't quite see me even though I'm right in front of her.

See me, Frankie. Please. See me.

"What?" she finally asks in a whisper.

It's the last shit in the world I want to tell anyone, never mind Frankie, but I can't keep it from her anymore. The hurt written on her face is strangling me from the inside. I'm twisted up. Telling her won't change anything, but maybe, it can change the look of betrayal in her eyes.

The look *I've* put there.

The world has stopped spinning. It's just me and this beautiful angry girl staring at one another like we're either about to fuck or claw each other's eyes out.

Maybe, both.

Who can blame us. We're supposed to be on opposite sides, but things have changed.

The only side I want to be on is *hers*

Mind. Soul. Body.

Her pain is my pain, and I'm fucking drowning in it.

"Your what?" she asks again, louder this time as if maybe she didn't hear me correctly. Although from the surprised look on her face and the way her eyebrows unfurrow, I know she has.

I lift her up by the waist, propping her up on the counter. I maneuver myself between her legs for two reasons. One, because I need to be touching her while I tell her what I'm about to tell her, and two, because I need to keep her in place so she won't run away on me again. I need her to stay and listen to every word I'm about to say.

It's that fucking important.

"Morgan," I start, feeling my throat tighten. "She was...a friend of mine. Well, I guess more than a friend. She was in the business, too, mostly tech stuff. Occasionally, she helped me out. She didn't love me. I didn't love her, but we trusted each other, and trust was better. At least, to us it was."

I cringe when I come to the part of the story I've never said out loud before.

"Keep going," Frankie urges me on. She lightly grabs hold of my bicep, and every time she does something to comfort me I feel like I'm both living for the first time and dying a slow motherfucking death.

I clear my throat. "I was away working clear across the country for several months. I go dark when I'm working certain jobs. No phone. No Internet. No communication with the outside world at all."

She nods against my chest, and I cradle the back of her head with my hand, threading my fingers through her hair.

"When I got back, I went to see Morgan, but she…" I feel my fingers tighten around Frankie's hair as the images of what I found in the house flash through my brain like a twisted picture show. "She was..."

"But she wasn't alive," Frankie finishes for me.

I nod slowly. "No, she wasn't. Far from it. There was nothing in her house but smeared blood. More blood than I'd ever seen, and I've seen my fair share. I had to look closer to realize what had really happened."

I nod and wrap my arms around her waist and pull her to the edge of the counter so I can press her soft body against me. I think she's going to fight me, but she sighs into my chest instead. I rest my chin on the top of her head and breathe her in.

"What really happened?" Frankie asks.

"Morgan. She was pregnant. I didn't know. We hadn't spoken in months. I was away. That's why there was so much blood. She was hacked to pieces. Every inch of her."

"Oh my God." Frankie gasps. "Why? Why on earth would someone do that?" She's sobbing against my chest. I'm now comforting her. Holding her.

I don't tell her it happened because the world is an evil place because I've committed my fair share of evil. I don't tell her it's my fault for getting close to Morgan when I shouldn't have. Her attachment to me was a risk I shouldn't have let her take. It made her a target.

"The baby…it was yours, wasn't it?"

I nod again, unable to say the words out loud. I reach into my wallet and hand Frankie the blood-soaked letter I found at Morgan's house under her body.

Frankie unfolds it slowly like it's something delicate that can be broken easily and not a creased piece of torn notebook paper. Her lips move as she reads it to herself. I don't even have to carry it with me anymore. I've read it a thousand times. I know exactly what it says, having memorized every word.

You,

I don't know why I'm writing this since I expect you back soon. I guess I'm writing it more to myself since I'll probably see you before I can give this to you. But just in case I can't find the words, this will be my backup.

You should know that I look like I've swallowed the entire Golden West buffet, but I love it. I love being pregnant. Truth is that I've always wanted to be a mum. For the first time in a long time, I'm excited about what the future will bring, and this child of ours is the best reason I could ever have to start a new life.

I'm leaving this life. I'm going someplace safe where I can raise this most beautiful and welcome mistake. I've got some money saved. I'm going to leave the state and buy a house somewhere in the suburbs on a tree lined street in a town with more than one stop-light. Who knows, maybe I'll be one of those suburban mums who wears tennis skirts every day but don't play a lick of tennis. You know, the kind who brag about the tech in their new mini vans and who complain about the misspelling of their names on their coffee cups at Starbucks. Of course, mine will be a teacup. I am British after all.

In all seriousness, I find myself very ready for this new adventure. A new challenge. You know me, I can do just fine on my own. I've been doing it my entire life. However, you can be a part of this is you want. I don't expect or want us to be an actual couple. You and I are far too realistic for something like that. But we can be good friends and attempt to be good parents. At the very least, better than either of us had. Although that bar has been set pretty low as it is.

Whatever you decide is fine with me. Just know that there's no halfway. Not with this. I won't risk it. I can't. You have to be out of the life to be in our lives.

I'll give you some time to think about it. It's only fair since I've had months to ponder all of this, and you're just now finding out. You're probably still doing that angry eyebrow thing you do when you're thinking over something. I'm quite sure of it. Don't give yourself wrinkles, old man. If you decide to come with us, I'm sure the two of us will give you our own fair share.

-Me

Frankie

"Holy shit," I say, piecing together the connection between the security video Nine and I found and the story Smoke is telling me. My heart breaks for him. For Morgan. I feel a depth of despair I've never felt before and an overwhelming need to take it away from his heavy eyes. I sniffle and get my tears under control.

"This right here," Smoke says, taking the letter from my hands and folding it back up. He tucks it into his back pocket. "It's why nothing changes."

"I still don't understand the connection. What does this letter have to do with me? With my father?"

Smoke walks over to his duffle bag and pulls out a photo which he pushes into my hands.

It's a black and white still image from the same bloody surveillance footage Nine and I found. Same date and time stamp in the upper right corner.

"Oh my fucking god," I gasp, holding my hand over my mouth. I don't have to pretend to be shocked even though I've seen it before. It's just as gruesome now as it was the first time.

"I think I'm going to be sick," I say, holding my churning stomach.

"Your old man didn't just steal from Griff. He stole from *me*," Smoke points to the corner of the image.

This picture is different than the one I found with Nine. The background is the same. The body is the same. The blood is the same. But the man in this image is a very different man than the one from the video. There's no hat with black stripe. It's a different man all together.

Someone had tampered with the image. One of them is fake.

And when I recognize the man in the image, I know immediately which one.

I begin to hyperventilate; my chest feels like someone's sitting on it. "No, no. It can't be." I start to say.

"Yes. It *can*," Smoke argues, slamming his hand down on the counter.

I understand now. Why Smoke is doing this. Why I'm here. What he wants out of all this.

Revenge.

Because the man in the photo isn't just vaguely familiar. He's *very* familiar.

He's my father.

CHAPTER THIRTY-NINE

SMOKE

Frankie looks up at me with tear-stained cheeks.

"Don't cry. That bastard doesn't deserve your tears," I say.

"I'm not crying for him," she sniffles. I see my reflection in her glassy eyes. "I'm crying for you."

I'm done. Dead. I'm been dealt a death blow. Something I can never recover from. My stomach lurches, and my breath leaves my body.

I'm crying for you.

I don't remember the last time someone has cried *for* me instead of *because* of me. I don't like the way it feels in my chest. Tight. Uncomfortable.

I'm suddenly feeling very claustrophobic in my own damn skin.

I don't give a second thought to wiping away Frankie's tears with my thumbs, resting my hands on either side of her face. I pause for a moment, enjoying the way my tattooed hands look against her creamy clear skin. The slope of her long slender neck. The feel of her quickening pulse against my palm.

"Ask me again," she says, drying her tears with her hand.

"Ask you what?"

"Ask me to tell you where my father is."

I'm frozen in shock, but she's serious.

"Frankie, where's your father?" I ask, cautiously.

Frankie is silent while my heart hammers in my chest. She looks to her hands then up to me. "Okay," she whispers.

"Okay what?"

She straightens her shoulders and looks me in the eyes. "Okay, I'll take you to him, I'll take you to my father."

CHAPTER FORTY

SMOKE

S*ilence.*

It used to be something I enjoyed. Something I craved. I'd sit alone in a room somewhere hours after the world had gone asleep and just breathe. For hours, I'd just *be.* It had always been enough for me.

Until now.

Until I find myself in the van with Frankie in the passenger seat. She's staring out the window. There hasn't been a word spoken between us in over two hours. Her plump lips are turned down in a frown. Her eyes shine with unshed tears.

I want to be mad at her for keeping this from me until now, but I'm struggling with staying angry at her when I've kept my fair share of shit to myself this past week.

I'm still processing it all. Her. Frank. Morgan. It all seems so different now and it's suddenly as if I'm looking at it all with a fresh pair of eyes.

I don't know what the fuck Frankie has to tell me, or why

she's decided now to take me to her old man, but I know she's wrestling with something big. I've waited this long to get to Frank Helburn. I can wait a few minutes longer.

Even so, the trip is taking forever. Every bump under the tires is jarring. Every beeping horn in the distance sounds like a freight train descending upon us.

We arrive at the townhouse under the cloak of night. The same house I watched Frankie go in and out of from afar for weeks.

I get out and slam the door. I stand in front of the van and wait. Frankie doesn't follow.

"You coming?" I ask, knocking on the passenger door. After a few seconds, it opens and Frankie slides down from the seat.

"Aren't you going to ask me why we're here?" she asks, straightening her shirt. She looks up at the dark townhouse. Her eyebrows crinkle like she's looking it over for the first time.

"No," I answer. "Because I know you're going to tell me. That's why we are here, right? It's truth time." I hold my hand out to her. Frankie pauses, looking between my face and my hand.

"Come on, hellion," I say, wiggling my fingers.

She puts her hand in mine.

It's truth time.

CHAPTER FORTY-ONE

FRANKIE

"Why now?" Smoke asks. I open the front door and flick on the light, but nothing happens. Probably because I didn't pay the power bill last month. "Why do you suddenly trust me to tell me whatever it is you've been hiding, now?"

"You'll see soon enough," I say.

Smoke darts back to the van and grabs a flashlight. He runs back, powering it on. He follows me into the dark house, lighting the way over to the door leading to the basement.

I reach around and feel the wall under the sloped ceiling until I find the dial for the generator. I turn it, and after a few seconds, a rumble sounds. The lights in the basement flicker and blink until they're fully on. The microwave button beeps with the reminder to set the clock and for once I don't jump out of my own skin.

Seems a little superfluous at this point.

We get to the bottom of the stairs. Smoke sets down the flashlight and takes in the sight before him.

The computers in the center of the room come alive. Several small fans underneath spin to keep it all from overheating in what sounds like a collective roar.

"I call it the monster," I explain as Smoke steps into the room. He stops to stare at the eight large monitors. Four on the long desk and four mounted above on pipes hanging from the ceiling.

"You mean your old man called it the monster," Smoke says, examining my life's work. He turns to me. "I thought you said you were taking me to him."

I take a deep breath and stand between him and my life's work. "I did take you to him."

"Explain," Smoke says, crossing his arms over his chest. His vein is pulsing again and I know it's a sign of his temper growing and his patience shortening. "Cause I don't see anyone here but us and a bunch of computers your old man used to steal money from Griff."

"That's where you're wrong." I sit down at my desk like a pianist at his instrument. I run my fingertips lovingly over the keys. I close my eyes and take a deep breath. My fingers play the keyboard will practiced efficiency. The monitors flash screen after screen.

Smoke stands behind me and watches. "Holy shit," he whispers.

"You already know my father was a hacker. Funny thing is he always told me he worked for the government. Later on, I found out it was all a lie. He was laundering money, but he wasn't JUST laundering money, he was transferring funds for human traffickers. Taking the money from the people buying sex slaves and sending it to the people selling sex slaves."

I find my rhythm and glance up at the screens at the visual music I'm creating.

"He spent his whole useless life helping those who buy

and sell people. Hiding their monetary transactions so they wouldn't get caught. HE was the real monster. THIS," I wave my hands at the computer system I spent years perfecting. "is *my* monster."

"What the fuck," Smoke says. I spin around in my chair and he looks from me to the screens, still flashing.

"Frankie, you said you were taking me to your old man," he growls.

"And I said I did," I argue.

Smoke looks around. "Then where the fuck is he?" He asks between gritted teeth. "Don't fucking toy with me."

"He's over there," I point to the darkened corner of the basement where only the bottom of a large blue rectangular freezer can be seen peeking out from under a blue roof tarp.

Smoke rips the tarp away.

He turns and storms over to me. His heavy feet thudding against the cement floor. He's furious and aggressive and fucking beautiful all at the same time. My heart and head are pounding. I'm afraid for both myself and for Smoke. He grabs my chair, hands on both of the arm rests and leans in, his face in mine. I see the anger burning in his dark eyes, but I also see hurt, so much hurt my chest pangs despite the position I'm in with my feet dangling above the floor. He thinks I've betrayed him.

"Where—" he snarls.

I don't take my eyes off his. "My father. Frank Helburn is there. He's IN the cooler."

Smoke pushes off the chair and stands. "What?"

I meet his eyes. "He's in the cooler. He's dead. My father's dead. He's *been* dead."

Smoke

My ears are fucking ringing. *Dead.* The motherfucker I'd been looking for all this time is DEAD.

I cross the room to the corner where the dusty blue cooler sits caddy corner underneath a section of dropped ceiling.

I pull on the padlock, but it doesn't budge. I look around and spot a pair of bolt cutters hanging from the wall. I grab them, snapping the lock off after several blood-vessel-bursting tries.

I need to see for myself that the bastard is dead. I can't decide if I'm happy or pissed off I didn't get a chance to do it myself, but I'll work that out later.

The lid of the cooler doesn't move when I try to raise it. I bend at the knees and use my back strength. It finally it gives. The ice lining the lid breaks off and shatters around the floor, bouncing around like tiny diamonds as they catch the light from Frankie's monitors.

Inside is yet another blue tarp which I hastily rip to the side revealing the frozen open-mouthed corpse of Frank Helburn.

Fuck.

Frankie stands beside me, looking down at her dead old man. I think she's emotionless when it comes to seeing his dead body but then I see it out of the corner of my eye. She's shaking. And not with despair either. I raise my eyes to hers and sure enough she's staring down at him with so much hatred burning in her eyes I'm surprised the ice doesn't melt. "For how long?" I ask.

She meets my eyes.

"Five years."

CHAPTER FORTY-TWO

SMOKE

"Five years. That's not possible," I say. "Morgan died a year ago and your old man killed her. So, you're wrong, or you're lying."

"Please sit," Frankie pleads, with a hurt on her face that makes me pause to take a breath.

I shake my head. "Truth first. What the fuck is going on here?" She's just told me that the man I want to take out my revenge on is fucking dead. There's no way I could be calm. Not now.

Maybe, not fucking ever.

"Okay." She sits back down on the chair, and her fingers move so fast over the keyboard they blur together. "I'll start at the beginning, if that's okay?" she asks without looking back at me.

It's so unlike her to ask me before she does something. I'm not sure if I love it or hate it.

She sees me nod in the reflection of one of the screens. She inhales a shaky breath. "I never saw my father much," she starts. "But you know that already."

"Keep going," I urge her on.

She's pulling up security feed for Aestro, and I recognize it as a company that does high-end systems for...well, people like me.

"I spent my time in the house, and my father spent his down here. He ate down here. He had a cot down here that he slept on most nights. I always thought he was just a really hard worker. He told me he designed websites for the government." She chuckles and looks up at the elaborate computer system. "I used to show my friends at school the White House website and brag that my father was the one who built it." She glances at me. "The only meaningful time we ever spent together was when he was showing me how to use computers. I could type before I could write with a pencil. I could write in code better than I could write my ABC's. Occasionally, he showed me a few tricks. I think he was showing off. It was the only thing he was ever really proud of. And it was all fucking bullshit."

"Like what kind of tricks?" I ask.

"Like how to hack into the school mainframe and set off the fire sprinklers on prank day," she says with a laugh. "Other tricks I picked up by watching him. I'd sneak down here and sit on the step that was covered the most by the shadows. He never heard me, but I watched him working. I can tell you I never saw a single picture of the White House on any of his screens."

Frankie was downright graceful. She barely blinked as she moved from one screen to the next, and the fact that she could talk to me while doing it made me realize she was on an entirely different level of smart then the rest of the population.

"And then one day," she continued. "I'd learned enough from watching him and doing my own research that I realized what he was really doing."

"Hacking?"

"Not just hacking. Trafficking. People. Women," she grates, the anger in her words floods into me, and I can feel my blood boiling for her, which makes sense, because she's a part of me.

The sounds of the keyboard clicks grow louder as she pounds on them with a lot more pressure than needed.

Frankie shakes her head. "He was a facilitator, a closer. He was responsible for the deaths of thousands of women around the world. I was so disgusted when I first found out that I didn't eat for weeks."

Frankie's fingers slow. "I was going to call the cops, but I wanted to confront him about it. So one day, I gathered all my courage and all my evidence against him. I stormed down here ready to be jury and judge only to find him slumped over his keyboard, dead."

"How did he die?" I ask, curious as to all the details surrounding the death of the man I missed the opportunity to kill.

Frankie shook her head. "He was always really unhealthy. Never slept. Ate all the wrong things. Chain smoked sixteen hours a day. I think his heart just finally gave out."

"And you didn't call anyone?" I ask, wondering why a girl her age wouldn't reach out and call for help.

"There was no one to call. I don't have any other family, and I would've called the police or coroner or whoever, but then I wouldn't have been able to stay here on my own and do all this." She waved her hand at the monitors. Her eyes glassy. She sniffled. "So, I made a pulley with some chains, hung it from the ceiling, and shoved him in the freezer so that no one would know of his death, and I could live here and pretend to be him. Online anyway. That's when I started my work."

"Which is what exactly?" I ask hesitantly.

She smiles, beaming with pride. "When I realized I could hack my way into the dark web and continue his work, but in a different kind of way…I did. I knew the drop off points. The method of transport. It was all at my fingertips. I saved them, Smoke. I stole money from the assholes trading people like stocks on the Nasdaq, and I hired mercenaries to rescue them. Hundreds of them. Hundreds of women are now back with their families because I stopped it all."

"Holy shit," I say, not expecting what has just come out of her mouth. I take a moment to process what she's just told me. SHE'S been Frank. For YEARS, she's been pretending to be Frank. She's the one who stole from Griff.

"Say something else. Something besides holy shit," Frankie says.

"I'm blown away here. I'm pissed you didn't tell me. I'm surprised…and I'm fucking amazed. I'm kind of…proud," I say, cupping her face in my hands.

"No one's ever told me they were proud of me before." Her eyes light up.

"Assholes. All of them," I say. I mean it. Someone should have told this amazing girl every fucking day of her life how amazing she is.

"I thought when you took me that day that it was about the money I stole. I didn't tell you where Frank was and that he was dead because…"

"You lied to me," I accuse, sounding madder than I actually am. I understood her reasons for lying but the barbarian in me was still pissed.

"Yes, because if I told you the truth you would've known it was me who stole the money, and—"

"And you would be dead anyway," I finish for her.

She nods. "Because you thought you were looking for Frank Helburn, but you never were. You didn't know it, but this whole time, you were looking for me."

CHAPTER FORTY-THREE

FRANKIE

"You manipulated me," Smoke says. His proud is turning to pissed off again.

"Yes, and I'd do it again," I tell him, sticking up my chin.

"Fuck," Smoke curses, standing from the chair with such force it falls forward onto the ground. "You pissed off the wrong people, Frankie."

"But hopefully I saved the right ones," I defend. "I couldn't stand by and NOT do anything." I stand and face him. "Anyone in my position would have done the same."

Smoke scoffs. "No, they wouldn't. The people you pissed off wouldn't. *I* wouldn't."

"Any DECENT person in my position would have done the same," I say, staring him down.

"Decent?" Smoke asks with a laugh.

I feel the corners of my mouth turning upward as Smoke walks up to me and cages me against the wall. He looks me in the eyes. I meet his gaze. Challenging him.

Always challenging him.

"My little hellion," he murmurs. "But tell me something, Frankie." He brushes his lips over mine then pulls back, teasing me. He lowers his voice to a whisper. "Do all decent people bend their dead father's corpses like a pretzel before shoving it in the motherfucking freezer?"

"That's unfair," I say, talking through my teeth, barely moving my lips.

"That's what you don't understand," Smoke explains. "In this dangerous game, the one you've decided to play alongside some of the most dangerous people in the world, there are no rules. There is no fair and unfair. There is only dead and alive. Black and white. That's it."

"Exactly, and a lot of women would be dead if I didn't do what I did. Now, they're alive."

I push against his chest and make a move toward the stairs, but he pulls me back. A million emotions are running through my mind along with a million worst-case scenarios.

"What else you got?" Smoke asks against my neck. My pulse begins to race.

"What do you mean?" I ask, sounding breathless.

"Tell me what other secrets you're keeping from me." Smoke nips at my earlobe, and I can't help the full-body shudder that erupts from within. I unwrap myself from his hold and turn to face him. "I can see there's more."

Smoke watches as I go back to the desk. I lean over and hit a few keys. I've already cued up the surveillance video. I press play, and Smoke watches as Morgan is surprised by someone before it all goes blank.

"My father was a lot of things," I continue, reaching in my pocket I pull out the USB drive Nine gave me and plug it into the port. "But a cold-blooded murderer wasn't one of them. At least, not in this case." I point up to the screen at the still image that shows a very different picture than the one Smoke had showing my father walking away. I keep my cursor over the lower right-hand corner, blocking the full view of the photo. "Someone wiped the feed, then altered the photo. Do you know this man?"

"Fuck, that's Griff," Smoke's face reddens as his knuckles whiten. "Are you sure it's real? That this one isn't the fake one?"

"I'm sure." I say. "As I said, my father died five years ago. That I'm sure of. It couldn't be him who killed Morgan. It wasn't. It was Griff."

"How sure?" Smoke yells.

I stand tall and refuse to recoil. "I'm positive."

Smoke exhales.

"The white tux my father was wearing in your version of the picture? It was a rental that he wore once, to his own wedding to my mother *years* before I was born. It also happens to be the only photo that even the best hacker would ever be able to find of him."

Smoke turns and punches his fist through the drywall. I jump at the sound, my heart breaking for him over and over again. I'm in tears as I watch him crumble before me. My chest swells with both love and despair. "All this time. All this motherfucking time! I'm gonna rip his goddamned head off!"

"Smoke!" I yell, frantically trying to get his attention.

He looks at me, but he's not seeing me. He punches the concrete wall over and over again. His knuckles are bloodied. His arms drip with red. The skin torn but he keeps going and going.

"Stop!" I yell.

"Why?" he grinds.

"Because we need a plan," I say, not backing down. "What happens now?"

Smoke closes his eyes for a moment, and when he opens

them again, he's refocused. He smirks and lights a cigarette. "Now?" he chuckles wickedly. "Now, Griff and everyone he's ever known and loved dies."

"Smoke look at me, look at me!" I yell, getting in his face. Needing him to see me. To hear me.

He looks over my head, but I pull his face down and press my nose to his. "Smoke, calm down."

"There's nothing anyone can do or say to get me to calm down now."

I step back, rip off my shirt and shove my shorts to my feet.

"That's not a fucking good idea right now, Frankie," Smoke warns.

"I'm a big girl. I can take it." I step closer, pressing my body to his. He needs to feel our connection. I know sex won't make the anger go away, but it could take it down a notch.

"Frankie," he warns. His pupils dilate. His nostrils flare.

All I know is that I feel an overwhelming need to lift off some of the rage weighing on him so heavily, and I'll gladly use my body to do it. I need to ground him to me. "Well, someone once told me I was dumb. Seems fitting don't you think?"

Smoke

My bellion. My ballsy fucking bellion.

Frankie has taken away my revenge then handed it back to me all in a matter of minutes. I'm a disaster. A swirling fucking hurricane about to unleash on everyone in my path and right now it's Frankie who's foolishly standing in the way.

There's no turning back. No going back to pretending that I don't want this girl more than my next fucking breath. I don't want to be careful with her. She's not going to break although the thought of breaking her, breaking her IN, makes me salivate.

"I'm not going to be gentle. I don't think I can be," I rasp, pulling her slender body to mine. I place my hand at the delicate curve of her hip and splay my fingers out on the pert top of her high round ass. I dig my fingers into her flesh, and her mouth opens and her eyes close. "Not now. Not after what you just showed me.

Frankie doesn't say anything. Instead, she presses her lips to my neck.

My little fucking manipulator.

"Look at me," I demand, needing to see her face.

Frankie opens her eyes and blinks rapidly. She looks deeply into my eyes and shakes her head from side to side. "I don't want gentle. I just want you," she whispers. "All of you."

I growl, and then my lips are on her. She wants all of me, so I give myself to her. All six foot three of barren soul and misguided morals. All of my broken, black heart.

All of the nothing I am is now hers.

She's my victim, and I'm her tormentor.

She's my prey, and I'm the predator.

She is mine to do with as I please.

And what I please right now is to make her come. Make her scream my name. Make her feel every inch of my desire for her and show her she's always belonged to me.

I want to see her tears of pleasure. I want to hear her screams of pain. I want her moaning my name.

I want it all.

I have it all, and right now there's no going back. I'm going to take it. Take HER.

Because she's *mine*.

THERE'S A TUG OF WAR GOING ON BETWEEN US, AND I'M losing my grip on the rope.

I've been at the wrong end of a gun, but this? This...whatever it is between us? That's new for me and far more frightening than a bullet to the fucking head.

But what's even more terrifying?

Not acting on it.

Not feeling her skin on mine.

Not plundering her body like the half-starved man I am. Starving for her. All of her.

It's like my body is no longer my own when I take her hand and pull her to me. When I press my lips to hers. When I peel off her clothes, lay her down like she's more precious than a ten-pound diamond. She's the sky, and I'm the wind. We're a matching set.

We fucking belong together.

I'm tired of fighting it. Tired of being alone. Tired of not getting the revenge I crave. Tired of not being inside of her again.

I'm. Just. Fucking. Tired.

Yet looking at her beneath me on the cement floor of the basement with her father's frozen corpse only a few feet away, I feel a new energy coursing through my veins, and I know that energy is courtesy of Frankie.

I fuck her hard. With my entire being, I fuck her. The pleasure is enormous, and it's not just in my cock; it's everywhere. It's not knowing where I end and she begins. It's some otherworld shit I never thought could exist.

Everything with Frankie is new.

Fucking is new. Kissing is new. This feeling in my gut like I could break her in half and break me along with her is new.

It's because I fucking love her.

The very thing I thought I was incapable of has been given to me by this girl. A gift I won't ever be able to repay.

I thank her for it. Not with my words, but with my body. I thank her in every way I can. Fast. Pounding hard. I make sure she understands the depth of my gratitude before sending her soaring into an orgasm that has her digging her heels into my lower back and screaming my goddamned name.

In the end, I'll have both Frankie and my revenge.

CHAPTER FORTY-FOUR

FRANKIE

Before I shut down 'the monster' I send an untraceable message to Nine and hope he understands what I'm asking him for.

"Aren't you going to send the text to Griff?" I ask Smoke as we ascend the stairs. It's already light out. We've been in the basement all night.

Smoke tucks the phone in his pocket. "Not just yet. We've got a little time. I'll send it later. Griff can wait to find out Frank's dead while I decide how to go about killing him."

"I don't suppose you're hungry," I say.

Neither of us has eaten since the day before.

"Fucking ravenous," Smoke rubs his stomach, his abs flexing under the thin material of his t-shirt.

I lead him to the kitchen and find dried pasta and a jar of marinara in the pantry. I take some ground sausage from the freezer, which thankfully was still frozen even with the power off, which means it must not have been off that long. I defrost it in the microwave.

Smoke watches me as I brown the meat and add it to the sauce to simmer. When I'm done and set the plate in front of him, he leans in and smells the food like it's something to be savored. "It's not much, but it's all I could manage with what's here," I explain.

Smoke digs in like it's the best thing he's ever tasted, and something about that makes my heart flutter. He moans in pleasure while he chews, and I lean forward on the counter to hide my hardened nipples.

"By far, the best I've ever fucking had." Smoke says, but he's not looking at the food.

He's looking at me.

I blush, then feeling uncomfortable under his unyielding gaze, I go back to my own food and change the subject. "I'm sure there are plenty of other women out there who've made you better food than this." I stab at a rigatoni and pop it into my mouth.

It is good. But as I suspected, it's not great by any means.

Smoke's answer surprises me. "I've never had anyone cook for me before, besides Zelda."

There are wounds peppered in his voice. A vulnerability in his eyes. It makes me want to take care of him. Cook for him something better than dried pasta and canned sauce.

"I've never had anyone cook for me either," I confess. "At least, I don't think. I don't remember much about my mom. I was too young when she passed so I'm not sure how she was in the kitchen. And well, my Dad, you know that story now."

Smoke's hand slides across the table and briefly covers mine. He squeezes my hand then slides it back and returns his concentration to his food as if nothing had happened.

As if he hadn't just wrecked my entire world with one fucking touch.

CHAPTER FORTY-FIVE

FRANKIE

Smoke's upstairs in the shower.

I'm in the kitchen having stayed behind to wash the couple of dishes and throw away anything in the fridge that could be rotting. I open the refrigerator and realize my concern was pointless.

"Can beer go bad?" I mutter to myself, grabbing a bottle from the six-pack, popping the top off against the edge of the counter. I take a sip. It's not super fresh, but it's not completely skunked either. I shrug and take another sip before setting the bottle down next to the sink.

I turn the radio on and grab a sponge to scrub out the dried marinara sauce from the bottom of the pot. I'm singing along to "Stupid Girl" by Garbage when a hand covers my mouth from behind, muffling my scream. I drop the pot into the sink, water spills over the edge onto my feet.

"Shhhhhh, Sarah, it's me. It's Duke. Don't scream." Duke releases my mouth and spins me around.

I'm breathing hard. I lower the ladle poised above my

head in strike position. "What are you doing here?" I whisper, glancing up the stairs. I can still hear the water running from the bathroom.

"I was delivering groceries next door, and I saw you through the curtains. I just wanted to make sure that you're okay. I haven't seen you in school. Not since the day the cop dragged you out. What was that all about, anyway?"

"This isn't the time or the place for that story," I say, "You've gotta go." I shove him toward the door then stop. "How did you get in here, anyway?"

Duke smirks, puffing out his chest with pride. "I broke in through the basement window when you didn't come back to school. I half-expected to find your decaying corpse somewhere in the house, but I found nothing. No sign of you, but all your shit was still here. Where the hell have you been, Sarah? You disappeared off the face of the fucking planet."

I can't help but smile at the concern in his voice. "I promise I'll tell you everything, but I can't tell you now. You've really got to go." I push him toward the door and unlock all the locks. Before I can open it and give him the gentlest of shoves over the threshold, he puts his hand on the door to prevent me from opening it. He takes my hand in his. "Duke," I whisper yell.

Duke looks down like he can't believe he's holding my hand again, rubbing his thumb over my fingers. "I missed you, is all. I'll go. I'll go. Just…just tell me that you're okay. That you're going to be okay. That whatever is going on with you isn't a life or death thing."

"I'll be okay," I tell him. "I promise."

Duke flashes his winning smile. "Good, then I'll see you back at school?" he asks, removing his hand from the door.

I exhale. "I'm not sure," I say, dropping my shoulders. I reach for the door.

"Oh," Duke stops me from opening the door again.

I'm not expecting Duke to wrap his arms around me and press his lips to mine. They are still as soft and skilled as ever but even though they are warm, his lips feel cold. Wrong. I don't want this. I don't want him. He doesn't smell like oil and cigars and soap.

I push on his chest and disconnect my lips from his just as a deep voice cuts through the space between us. "Get the fuck away from her."

Smoke's standing less than ten feet away wearing only his opened jeans. His hair is wet and slicked back. Beads of water fall down his chest as he moves. His feet are planted wide. Dark eyes are cold, flinty. I can see his quickening pulse through the throbbing vein under the pocket watch tattoo on his neck. He raises his gun and aims it at Duke.

"Fuck," Duke swears. He pales, blinking rapidly as if he can't believe what he's seeing. He shuffles backward and forgets the door is still closed, hitting his back of his head against it.

"Smoke. Don't."

"He laid his hands on you," Smoke seethes. "The only reason I haven't already fired is you're standing too fucking close to him so step away, hellion." Smoke cocks the gun.

I step in front of Duke. "No, Duke is my friend."

"You let all your friends stick their tongues down your throat?" Smoke says with a snarl.

"I knew you weren't okay," I hear Duke whisper from behind me.

"I am okay! I'm fine, but you aren't going to be if you don't leave," I say to Duke. "Now go and don't say shit about this to anyone. I mean it. It's important. I promise I'll explain all this later but please. I need your word, Duke."

Duke glances wide-eyed over my shoulder to Smoke and

then back to me. I don't need to look over my shoulder. "You...you've got it," he says on a shaky voice. He feels for the door at his back, and when his hand finds the handle, he turns it quickly and stumbles out.

Smoke steps in front of me. "Before you ever think about touching her again, think about this. Any part of you that comes in contact with her I'm going to rip off your fucking body with my bare hands."

Duke scrambles backward and runs for the GrubTrain car. Smoke steps back and closes the door. I take a step back from the fuming volcano before me.

"You fuck him?"

"No!" I toss back. Now, it's my turn to be mad. I cross my arms over my chest and jut out my hip. "He's my friend. Or, he *was* my friend."

"A friend, who you let kiss you?" Smoke closes the distance between us. His nostrils flare.

"Sometimes," I admit, swallowing hard. I remain defiant, pushing out my chest. "And sometimes more."

"More?" Smoke questions, the word is a rumble in his throat and touches me right between my thighs. I press them together. He's so close now. Water drips from his hair onto my t-shirt. "I swear to fucking Christ, Frankie, I need one good reason why I shouldn't chase after that motherfucker and paint that ugly ass green car of his red with his own fucking blood."

"Smoke, he was my sort of friend. When I had to stay away from the world, he was the only person I let in because he was nice and he was safe. He dated all the girls in my school so I knew he wasn't looking for anything serious so yes, from time to time he came over, brought me groceries, and kissed me. Sometimes a little more. Never more than what I've given you. Ever."

Smoke's shoulder muscles seemed to relax, even if just a fraction. His knuckles, on the other hand, are still white. "My little hellion." He brushes my hair from my eyes.

My shield is down along with all the other defenses I've tried and failed to keep him from getting to a place he can really hurt me, and I don't mean physically. Physical hurt is nothing compared to what Smoke can inflict on me now. Because he's broken through. He's inside.

And there's no turning back.

I'm terrified. More so than in that prison cell as his captive.

I try to remain defiant. I stick out my chest and straighten my shoulders, holding my chin up high. "And don't you expect me to apologize for it, either. I won't. Duke kept me company. He made me laugh. He was my friend. My *only* friend."

I press my flat hands against Smoke's warm wet chest and a current runs through me, zapping my arm hairs to attention. My breath catches, and I glance up at Smoke. He's looking at my arms, and I know he felt it, too. I lean into him. He smells like fresh soap and toothpaste.

I remember I'm trying to make a point, so I don't inhale deeply as much as I want to.

"Duke was there for me. I had nobody," I say, then pause, rethinking my choice of words. "I *have* nobody."

Smoke tilts my chin up. Our eyes meet. The anger is still written all over his face from his furrowed brows to his tight jaw but there's something else there that looks a lot like concern.

"You have me," Smoke whispers so low I think I might be imagining it.

"Do I?" I regret the words as they leave my mouth.

Smoke's answer is pressing his lips to mine in a slow and

tender kiss that shakes me to my very foundation. He tells me everything I need to know with his lips. His tongue.

The uncontrollable man is showing me control. I'm lost. To him. To this.

To *us*.

Forever has passed when we finally come up for air. My skin is flushed. Lips swollen. Pussy throbbing with unrelenting need.

My heart stops.

"I *do* have you." I say, running my hand through his wet hair, keeping my fingers tangled within it.

"Yes, you do have me," Smoke nods. His forehead falls to mine and my heart starts beating again. His pupils are dilated, his dark eyes are glossy. His words lick their way across my skin. He lifts me into his arms, my legs instinctively wrapping around his waist. "Now, I'm going to *have* you."

CHAPTER FORTY-SIX

SMOKE

We're lying in bed. Frankie's bed. Some tiny frilly thing that smells like her. Frankie is curled up around me, her leg hiked up over my thigh.

I send the text to Griff.

FRANK HELBURN IS DEAD.

It's done.

Not even three minutes pass. My phone rings.

"You found him and killed him without permission? Where's my fucking money?" Griff snaps. "That asshole is the only one who knows where my money is, and he better have told you before you ended him."

"I didn't kill him," I snap back. "The fucker was slumped over when I got here. And Griff? I'd watch my tone if I were you. I'm not one of your boys, and I ain't a 'yes man'. I wasn't the one who killed him. I think his ticker just gave out. So remember who you're fucking talking to."

There is a moment of silence before Griff speaks again. "I'll send a team for his computers tomorrow. Maybe, they can track down my fucking money."

"Send mine while you're at it," I say, "What the fuck do you want me to do with the girl?" I don't have to pretend to sound annoyed because this fucker is grating on my every nerve. More than usual. I look over at Frankie, the sheet draped haphazardly over her tits, her shiny dark hair splayed all around the white pillow.

She wakes with a flutter of eye lashes. Her golden eyes meet mine.

I'm done for.

I can't imagine a world without her in it. I can't kill her. Don't think I ever really could've. Not when she's already killed me, or at least the person I used to be.

"Whatever the fuck you want," Griff snorts. "Dispose of the girl. But before you go, move Frank's body off the desk so my team has complete access to his computers when they get there tomorrow. Maybe, second time is a charm, and they can track down my fucking money. I'll transfer your funds now." The line goes dead, and I stare at the phone. Griff wasn't his usual self. There was no small talk. No questions about my future plans. No comment about my one-man team. Something is off. Not to mention this was the first time he'd hung up on me and not the other way around.

"Is everything okay?" Frankie asks sleepily.

I click the burner phone shut and set it on the nightstand. As much as I want to wrap my arms around her and sink into her again for a much needed repeat of last night, something isn't sitting right with me about that call.

About Griff's demeanor.

"Did he buy it?"

"Yeah," I say softly, but I'm going over the conversation in my mind for the hundredth time in the last few seconds, searching for the knife in the needles.

"What is it?" Frankie asks, sitting up and wrapping the sheet around her chest.

It hits me like a bullet to the back. "Shit," I leap out of bed. "Get dressed. We gotta go, and we gotta go NOW."

For once Frankie listens and pulls on her clothes, I do the same "What happened?" she asks, shoving her feet into her shoes and pulling her t-shirt over her head.

"He told me to remove your old man from the desk to give his team better access to the computers when they get here," I tell her.

"So?" she asked, hopping up and down to pull up her shorts.

I grab my cut and shrug it on. "So, the problem is My text said that I found your old man slumped over dead. Didn't say shit that he was at the computer or at a desk."

Frankie's eyes went wide with understanding and fear. "Cameras?"

I nod. "Fucker saw and heard everything."

"Shit," she says, pushing her feet into her shoes.

"He knows it was you and not your old man. He'll be coming for us soon. I bet his men are almost here already."

"I have to tell you something," she says.

"Not now, right now we have to get the fuck out of here." I take her by the arm and lead her from the room just as the window of her bedroom shatters. Glass shards pierce my back. A bullet whizzes right by my ear before exploding into the wall a few inches over Frankie's head.

Over the unending, unyielding barrage of gun fire, the urge to protect Frankie is downright overwhelming. It's my only goal. My only mission. The most important fucking job I've ever had. While the house explodes around us, a realization hits me harder than any bullet.

I'm not just in love with Frankie.

I'm prepared to die for her.

CHAPTER FORTY-SEVEN

FRANKIE

There's so much gunfire. I barely have my shirt on over my head when the walls explode all around us like they're made of paper. Smoke's grip on my hand is so tight it's almost crippling as he yanks me down the stairs, but I don't tell him to let up. I won't. I need to be connected to him.

We race down the stairs and out the back door through the woods.

The gunfire follows.

The pace is lung-burning and never-ending. I'm in good shape, but I'm falling behind.

Smoke stops, tugs on my arm and lowers me to the ground on my hands and knees. He pushes me toward a large tree with a hole no larger than a couple of feet hollowed out at the bottom of the trunk.

"Hide in here," Smoke orders. Voices shout to one another in the not too far off distance. "I'm a huge moving target. They'll spot me a lot faster than you, but I can outrun them. Stay here. Stay quiet. I'll lead them away from you."

"No! Don't go!" My words are a whispered yell followed by a choked-out sob.

I'm hurting. My feet. My muscles, my heart. I can barely see him through the blur of my own tears like I'm looking up at him from under water. I'm drowning in the depths of my own misery, every breath I suck in is killing me. My heart is hammering out a frantic SOS to the rest of my body and it's crushing me from the inside out.

"Meet me here in the morning," Smoke says, reaching into the inside pocket of his cut and producing a black sharpie. "If I'm not there. If I don't make it—"

"No!" I shake my head and close my eyes, not able to bear the thought.

Smoke's grip on me tightens. He tilts my chin up so our eyes meet. His voice isn't louder, but it's sharper, more precise, like he wants to tattoo his words into my memory.

"Listen, Hellion, and listen real good. First light, I want you to head to this address. It's the Lawless MC compound. You'll be protected there."

I hold out my hand thinking he's going to write on my palm, but he surprises me by pushing the fabric of my shorts up my leg, writing directly on the skin of my upper thigh.

"Less obvious," he mutters. "Take this," he says, unclasping a pair of the cuffs from his wrist and clasping them around mine. "Show it to them. They'll know I sent you. Just get there and wait for me. Can you do that?"

"Yes. But you better be there, Smoke. I mean it." I'm trembling. My lip quivers. "Is this good-bye or just good-bye for now?"

Smoke brushes his thumb over my cheek. "Always with the questions," he says, a sad smile on his beautifully scarred face. "I'll do everything I can to meet you there."

"I'll come with you," I try to argue once more.

The sound of gunfire and shouting in the distance is all the argument Smoke needs.

"It's the only way to keep you safe," he says, softly. He tenderly brushes his rough thumb over my cheek, and I can't help but to lean into his touch. I close my eyes briefly then look up at him through my wet lashes.

More gunshots. This time they're closer. Smoke looks over his shoulder and then back to me. "First light," he repeats with a much too brief searing kiss to my lips. "You wanted me to choose you, Hellion. Well, this is me...choosing you."

My. Fucking. Heart. Breaks.

I can't find the words to protest as he places branches over the cutout in the trunk to conceal my hiding space. I hear him jog off, and I silently cry into the dark space. I pull my knees to my chest and crawl as far back into the hollowed-out stump that I can.

Every gunshot I hear feels like it's a direct hit to my heart because with each one, there's a possibility that come morning light, Smoke won't be there.

This is me…choosing you.

CHAPTER FORTY-EIGHT

SMOKE

I move through the woods like a wild animal because I *am* a fucking wild animal. It's dark, but I use instinct to creep up behind Griff's men. I slit one's throat; the blood sprays in my face. It's warm and wet, and I don't bother wiping it off as I drop his body quietly to the ground.

I move without making a sound. My boots don't even crunch against the fallen leaves. I lay another man out, knife to the base of his spine. And then another, stab and twist to the neck.

I feel like a kid again. These woods are my home. I breathe in and use the smell of pine to fuel me.

My hands are covered in blood. Not an inch of my skin can be seen through the thick red.

I just killed for her. I've killed a thousand times before. But this was different. This meant more.

I down another and another man until all that's left is me and the sins I've committed.

I sheathe my knife. It's daylight. I know I told Frankie I'd meet her at the club, but I go back for her anyway.

She's not there, but the cuffs are.

And the cuffs are covered in blood.

"No!" I roar, racing through the woods. I race back to the townhouse where, thankfully, the van is intact.

I speed the entire way to the Lawless MC clubhouse with my foot slammed to the floor. I run it right up to the gates and scare the shit out of Nine, who's talking to the prospect standing guard.

"Is she here?" I ask, pushing him to the side and running through the gates.

"What the fuck happened to you?" The prospect asks. I pull my gun and aim it at his skull. "Is. She. Here?"

"I...I...uh," he stutters.

"I'm here," a voice says, and I spin around to see Frankie. Leaves in her hair. Clothes torn. In one motherfucking piece, Frankie.

"Oh, thank fuck."

CHAPTER FORTY-NINE

SMOKE

"Guest room is two doors down on the right!" Nine calls out as I race to Frankie and scoop her in my arms. I carry her into the room and slam the door shut, pushing her back up against it.

I've heard love described as clean or pure. I've heard it a million times in a million different ways, but it's always been like this big mythical unreachable shining white ball of fuckin' glitter. It wasn't real.

Until now.

Which makes me think that even though what I'm feeling for Frankie is strong, there's no way it can be love because there isn't a damn thing clean or pure about the thoughts I have involving her. Nothing angelic about the things I dream day and night about doing to her. In fact, my feelings toward her are sending me more into the darkness than the light. More toward Hell than Heaven.

She's not an angel here to guide me toward a better path;

she's a demon like me, here on Earth to do God only knows what. What she has done is make me feel like I've lost my fucking mind because around her I don't feel…wrong.

The things I've done to her. The things I've done WITH her. If each person is only given a certain amount of feelings, of love, then there's no way she could feel the same because there's no way I'd let her waste it on me.

All thoughts about how we don't fit together are put on pause because Frankie's eyes are wide as she looks me over.

"The blood," I realize. I turn to head toward the bathroom to grab a towel, but she reaches out a hand, stopping me.

The energy in the room shifts like someone's left a torn wire in an open puddle. Frankie gives me a look, silently asking if I can feel it, too. I give her a small nod because it's all I can manage.

My words have left me along with the air in my lungs. Frankie's hair is tangled. Her long lashes touching her cheeks.

She shakes her head. "Don't go clean up. Not yet."

I'm rock fucking hard for her. Throbbing. Aching. Not just my cock. My mouth waters at the thought of tasting her again. My fingers twitch at the anticipation of touching the nakedness beneath her t-shirt.

"Are you sure?" I ask.

"I want you. Just as you are. Bloody, beautiful, Smoke."

"My little hellion," I growl.

We crash into one another in the center of the room. I feel pressure at my back as if we're being pushed together by a force bigger than ourselves. Just two pawns in a game that's no longer about life and death. It's bigger and more complicated and more…everything.

Frankie pulls back as if she can read my thoughts and stares up at me for a beat before closing her eyes. She sucks in a breath, and I'm lost. To us. To her. Those eyes. That shiny black hair. Those soft fuckable lips. Her mouth is calling to me once again, and Lord fucking help anyone who tries to get in the way of me answering.

She doesn't want me clean. Frankie wants me dirty. Real.

And I want her.

Any way I can fucking have her.

She belongs to me.

Frankie Helburn is *mine.*

She isn't under my skin. She's fucking torched it. My flesh burns for her. She's the flame and the balm, both painful and soothing. I want more of her.

All of her.

She owns me. Body. Soul. Bloody hands, along with whatever the fuck is left of my heart. It's hers. All of it.

I'm not just obsessed or consumed by Frankie Helburn.

I lift her into my arms. Her legs wrap around my waist and our lips crash together.

She's part of me.

Frankie

Our teeth clank together as he lifts me in his arms and tosses me down on the bed. He rids himself of his clothes and mine, revealing his thick, swollen cock that bobs against his belly button as he pulls me to the edge of the mattress and devours my lips and neck with his tongue, nipping at my earlobe with his teeth. He trails down my jaw, and I can't help but lift my hips and rock into the air. I need to feel him. In me, around me. I need him to show me that I'm his, now more than ever because Smoke doesn't know that tomorrow, everything is going to change, and I selfishly need this. Need him. I need to be his tonight because by the time the sun's first rays hit the ground, I'll be gone.

I've already arranged everything with Rage and Nine. Griff won't stop until he gets to me, and he'll kill anyone and everyone in the process.

I'm going to give Griff what he wants.

Me.

And in the process I hope to give Smoke back a piece of himself. A piece he doesn't even know he's missing yet.

But right now, it's just me and the bloodied, beautiful man before me.

Smoke bites the inside of my thigh, then crawls up my body, lacing his fingers through my hair and yanking to expose my neck to him. He kisses and sucks on the sensitive skin behind my ear, and I feel a buzzing in my nipples and pussy. Awareness. Pleasure. Anticipation. His hard heat brushes up against my wet folds, and I buck up off the bed. My core painfully empty and clenching.

"Please," I beg.

Smoke growls against my skin then pulls back for a moment to look me in the eyes and press a hard kiss to my mouth. A deep kiss. A kiss that both apologizes and makes no apologies. A kiss that makes me feel alive. Special.

I am loved by him in a way that no one else on the planet could ever love me.

He pulls back to hover over me, bracing himself on both sides of my head on the bed. His biceps and forearms flex with his every movement. His tattoos dance as he lowers himself down my body, lines his cock up with my already painfully ready pussy and pushes in with a groan that sounds like the love-child of love and lust.

I meet him stroke for hard stroke. Lifting my hips, pulling

him closer. For a long time, we just stare in each other's eyes until Smoke tries to speak.

"I... I want you to know," he says, before growing frustrated and stopping.

"I know," I tell him, feeling a tear fall down my cheek. "I know."

Smoke picks up his pace, pounding into me harder and harder. Faster and faster. He's giving me everything he's got, and although he thinks it's not much to me, it's everything. He's everything.

Smoke's powerful. And I don't just mean in his sculpted muscles. I mean powerful in mind. Spirit.

He may be a monster, but he's *my* monster.

I feel the pressure mounting in my core and see the chords of Smoke's neck pull tight. He's close, and so am I.

So very close.

"You're *mine.*" His nostrils flare as he picks up his pace, hammering hard into me until I see stars. "You're mine," he says louder, pushing even faster and harder, and I realize he's trying to fuck those words into me.

"Yes," I pant as my orgasm takes over and pushes through my body like a cannon shot. I'm writhing underneath him as pulse after pulse of pleasure like I've never felt explodes from my every nerve ending until I can see only white behind my eyes.

Smoke grunts, holding my hips in place while he pounds into me a few more times before roughly grabbing my face and forcing me to look him in the eye.

"Mine." His voice falls to a whisper, and he closes his eyes. "Always mine."

The orgasm continues to tear me apart limb from limb. I welcome it. Never in my life have I ever wanted so badly to be in pieces. I want to be scattered on the wind like ashes, so small and so many I can't ever be put back together.

Smoke has both broken and healed me. I'm shattered, and I'm complete. I'm so in love, and I'm scared out of my fucking mind, but that won't change what I must do.

It feels so good it hurts. I come with tears seeping from the corners of my eyes. I love him. The good, the bad, the violent, the brutal, and the bloody.

I love all of him.

Smoke's face twists as I feel him explode inside of me in long wet hot spurts that fill me to the brim. I come again, squeezing around him until my vision is blurry, and all I see are stars and blood and smoke.

A FEW HOURS LATER, I WAKE TO A KNOCK AT THE DOOR. Smoke doesn't bother covering himself when he walks to the door, tight muscles of his ass and his huge half-hard cock on full display, much to Nine's obvious displeasure.

"Cover your junk, and head upstairs. The boys want to have a talk," Nine says.

Smoke snorts and stares him down.

"Fine, PLEASE Smoke will you come up the fucking stairs?"

Smoke shuts the door in his face. "I'll be back, hellion," he says with a quick kiss. He pauses, then ads, "I choose you."

I'm smiling both on the inside and out. "And I choose you."

He grins.

I sit up in bed and watch as he dresses quickly and heads out the door.

I wait only a few minutes, until I'm sure he's upstairs, to get out of bed and throw on my clothes.

I place the USB drive Nine gave me on the pillow.

I ignore the crushing pain and agony taking over my body and mind. I feel like I'm dying, but what I must do is more important than how I feel.

I take a deep breath and sneak out the door.

I don't look back.

CHAPTER FIFTY

SMOKE

"Where's Rage?" I ask after explaining how Griff framed Frankie's old man as Morgan's killer to the other's in Bear's office on the second story of the MC.

"Skinning the neighborhood cats?" Preppy jokes, popping his suspenders with his thumbs.

"She was with Nolan in St. Augustine. They're back now. She's around here somewhere," Bear, the President of the club, says.

We've got a lot of history between us and a shit ton of mutual respect, but I didn't realize I had his loyalty until he just offered to help me go after Griff.

I feel unworthy and grateful, the same way I do about Frankie's love.

"I'm still in shock you let her convince you to join your club," I say, lighting a smoke.

Bear shrugs and looks me in the eye, man-to-man. "Would you have done any differently?"

I shake my head. "Fuck, no. I know better than anyone

that it's always better to have Rage with you than against you."

"You two still got unresolved business," King says.

It's a statement, not a question. King, otherwise known as King of the Causeway, rounds out the trio in the room. These cats couldn't be more different, but they're tighter than a nun's vagina. They run Logan's Beach and everyone in it like the white trash mafia. Nothing happens in this town without them knowing.

Guns, drugs, even the fucking Twinkie truck.

"Sort of," I say. "We talked a bit. I think we might get there though." For the first time I'm feeling hopeful about the future.

After I kill Griff, of course. The need for retribution and vengeance has only grown with the knowledge of who really killed Morgan. I feel it spreading inside me like a welcome disease.

"You know, you say no connections, no relationships, but you're one shit-talking motherfucker if I've ever met one," Preppy says, cocking his eyebrow at me. "Cause I saw you almost take out half this fucking MC just to find her when she was standing like ten feet from you earlier."

"If you stand in between me and her, I'll take you out, too," I warn, feeling myself heat and readying myself for a fight.

"Preppy's right," King says.

"I am?" Preppy's eyes widen in shock.

King lights a cigarette and continues. "It's not just the girl either. You say you ain't on no one's side, yet you saved Preppy in the hospital. He wasn't one of your jobs. He wasn't your business."

I think about his words and reply with a half-truth. "No, but I had another job at that hospital. Didn't need any shit going down while I was trying to move bodies from the morgue."

"Oh, shut the fuck up, Smokey," Preppy says.

I don't have time to warn him about his upcoming death if he calls me Smokey again because the kid talks without taking a breath between sentences. Rapid fire. A tongue like a Gatling gun.

"You didn't have to do shit to help me, and you know it. You could have done your job without getting involved in our shit. You did it because you wanted to."

Fucker was right, I could have, but that didn't mean I was going to admit it.

"Trust me. This will go so much easier if you just admit it," King says. "Also, it will get him to shut the fuck up faster."

"Admit what?" I ask, wondering exactly what this fucker is getting at.

Preppy places his hand on my shoulder, and I glare at it like he's just stabbed my grandma, but he ignores my unease.

"That you *loooove* us," he sings.

"Can't we just do this the old-fashioned way and stab each other? Or maybe a rousing game of Russian Roulette?" I ask. "That could be fun." I down the glass of whiskey Bear hands me. "I thought you three were ruthless sons-of-bitches. Can't we just have a shoot-out like the good old days?"

King chuckles and shakes his head. He's got a smile on his face that tells me he's been there before, but there is still no way I'm admitting to anything. He adjusts the thick black studded belts he wears wrapped around his forearms. They aren't for decoration. They're weapons and I've seen a motherfucker or two meet their end with one of King's belts wrapped around their fucking necks.

"How about a compromise?" I ask, flicking Preppy's hand off my shoulder.

"What kind of compromise you thinking, darlin'?" Bear cocks his head, and much to my dismay, he seems amused rather than annoyed.

"I'll admit that…there are a lot of other people I'd rather kill than you three," I offer. "It's the best I've got."

"Sounds like Rage's club pledge," Preppy mutters. He straightens his bow tie and claps his hands together. He bows his head then glances back up with a huge smile on his face that seems off for someone whose been through all he has. "You dooooo love us!" he exclaims, bouncing on his heels. "I could just kiss you. Come here, you big, burly bitch."

Bear and King laugh as Preppy leaps into the air, heading straight for me. I sidestep, and he goes crashing onto the couch. Rebounding without missing a beat, he rolls onto his back. Smile still in place.

"You're way too happy for someone who's been tortured the way you have," I point out, taking a drag of my smoke. Bear pours out another whiskey and hands it to me. I down it in one burning gulp and hold it out for a refill which Bear obliges, this time filling it almost to the brim.

"I know, sickening, isn't it?" Preppy asks. He winks at me and sits up, lighting a joint. "Sometimes all you need is a smidge of torture to put shit in perspective."

What was really sickening was what had happened to him. Preppy should be dead. For a long time, everyone, including his friends, thought he was dead, but he survived and rejoined the land of the living. If Preppy is still smiling after all that happened to him, I should be able to smile, too. To let Frankie in. To make this shit with her more…permanent.

"I recognize that look," King says. I hadn't realized I'd been staring into my whiskey.

"What look might that be?" I ask, staring out the window

into the courtyard below at the closed door of the room Frankie's in.

"The look that says she's gotten to you," Bear says, downing his own whiskey. His grin is of the shit-eating variety.

"Some people say that a good woman can tame a man. Train him. Make him less violent," King says. He chuckles. "It ain't true. It makes you more violent. It makes you more everything."

"Ain't that the fucking truth," I say, taking a drag from my smoke. "Something I've recently learned."

"Says the man covered from head to toe in what I assume is someone else's blood," Preppy says.

I look down. "Kind of forgot about that."

"Been there," Bear says.

"We all have," King adds.

"Ditto or trippilo, or some shit like that. Me, too, is what I'm trying to say," Preppy chimes in.

The three of them laugh, and as hard as I try not to, I can't help the slow tremor growing in my chest and shoulders until I'm laughing right along with Bear, Preppy, and King.

And damnit it feels good.

Motherfuckers.

When the laughter dies down Bear's expression turns serious. "We'll get this son of a bitch, Smoke. We'll plan our attack on the compound. You'll get your revenge, brother, and we'll help you," Bear says.

I nod because I don't know what else to say. Shit feels overwhelming. I cough into my hand.

"We're working on a way to get on the inside. Got our tech people examining the blueprints. We'll burn that motherfucker down and everyone in it," King pipes in.

"Shit, haven't killed anyone in a while," Preppy purses his

lips and shrugs then begins to stretch like he's preparing to run a marathon, running in place. "Sounds like a fucking good time to me."

"We got you," Bear says. "We all do."

The thought of finally getting my revenge and getting to keep Frankie makes me smile.

I down another whiskey then Bear walks with me back down to the room where Frankie's asleep. I push open the door and the smile on my face dies a quick death. My heart falls from my body.

Frankie's gone.

CHAPTER FIFTY-ONE

FRANKIE

"Okay, let's do this," Rage says, pulling out a long knife. She's standing behind me in her room at the club. I'm sitting down, facing the mirror above the dresser. She turns the knife over, inspecting it. After a few seconds, she seems lost in the glint shining back at her as she rotates it again and again.

I clear my throat, and she glances up at my reflection.

"So how do we do this?" I ask. "Should we do a count to three? I think that's the best waa—ouch!"

"Or I can just do it now," Rage sings, having already made the thin slice into my skin below my ear.

"That works, too," I mutter, trying not to wince in fear she'll take the whole ear off for shits and giggles.

Rage twists her lips while she works to shove the small device just below the skin under my ear. When she's done, she covers the wound with a flesh colored patch that matches my skin. "That should do it."

"Any words of advice?" I ask, feeling terrified. I don't

want to think about the look on Smoke's face when he realizes I'm gone. I don't want think about anything other than the plan and what lies ahead.

Think now.

Feel later.

Nothing else matters.

Rage lifts her large blue duffle bag that says LEE COUNTY HIGH SCHOOL on the side and throws it over her shoulders. She shrugs. "Don't die?"

Rage opens the door, and I follow her out into the darkness of night. We reach the back gate, and she crouches down, tossing her bag through a hole in the fence before crawling through herself. "Don't die," I repeat to myself on a whisper. I get on my hands and knees and follow her through. "I'll try to remember that one."

As we move through the dark, I focus on why we're doing this.

The entire reason for me leaving Smoke without telling him.

The surveillance video image. More specifically, the corner of it I didn't show Smoke. The part where you can see that Griff didn't leave Morgan's house empty handed. He was holding a wrapped bundle of towels in his arms, but it isn't the towels that's fueled this mission, it's what was peeking out from underneath them.

A tiny pair of pink feet.

CHAPTER FIFTY-TWO

FRANKIE

"You're Rage?" Griff asks, adjusting his glasses as if it would make her morph from a girl to a guy. "I pictured someone different."

He's wearing the hat. The one from the surveillance video. White with a black stripe above the brim. He's much shorter than I imagined, but he's got this look in his red-rimmed beady eyes. He's unhinged. Disturbed.

The dread moving up my stomach into my throat threatens to strangle me but I swallow it down.

"Someone with a little more penis perhaps? I get that a lot," Rage says, pursing her lips, giving the impression that she's bored. She looks so unruffled. So composed. I wish I could feel that way or at least fake it better because I'm quaking from the inside out. My stomach is twisting as if it decided to take up gymnastics. But even with this level of fear coursing through me, I can't help but notice that Rage and I make a good team.

Griff looks amused. He sucks his top teeth and steeples his fingers. "That's exactly what I was expecting."

"If a dick is what you want, I can cut one off one of your guys and give it to you. Would that make you feel better?" She pulls her blade from the sheath.

Griff smiles. His overly tanned skin is in contrast with his too-white teeth.

Rage, growing impatient, shoves me forward, and I fall onto the ground on my knees. My chin bounces off the concrete since my hands are bound behind my back.

"What's this? A gift? For me?" Griff asks, looking down at me like I'm a species of goat he's never seen before. He places his fingers under my chin, and I jerk my head from his touch. This buys me a backhand to my cheek. I see stars.

"Frankie Helburn," Rage says. "Word is she stole from you. Consider her an offering to prevent the war and the deaths of my brothers that would happen if this bitch keeps hiding behind the walls of my club like a scared bird instead of taking her punishment like a woman. Now say 'thank you' like a good boy so I can get the fuck out of here. It's cold and dark and dusty in this fucking place. You're like Batman without the cool car." She gives Griff a once over. "Or the good looks."

Griff ignores her insult and glances down to me. "You don't care that I'm gonna kill her?" he asks, straightening his jacket as if it will make him better looking.

Rage rolls her eyes and tightens her hair tie around her long blonde ponytail. "We all die, Griff. Don't act like that's a surprise to you. We're all just biding our time until we meet the dirt again. I'm just buying us a little more time is all. One in exchange for many. I hear that's how morals work. I'm giving it a shot. Do we have an agreement? The bitch for laying off my club?"

Griff places his hand under his chin and pauses for a moment. "We have a deal."

Another man comes up and yanks me off the floor, roughly pushing me across the room and tethering me to a small metal chair.

Rage doesn't look in my direction when I yelp as he tightens the knot on my wrists, cutting off my circulation.

"You don't care that Smoke won't be happy with this revelation?" Griff asks curiously. His voice is high-pitched for a man's. He sounds like a grandmother from Queens.

"I don't know what you've heard, but there's bad blood between me and Smoke," Rage says. "I know people think I abandoned him. Just packed up and left, but he's the one who broke up the team. He left me so he didn't have to split the paycheck two ways anymore. So, you see? There's no love lost between us. I'm looking forward to seeing his face when I tell him I'm the one who brought his bitch back to the kennel. But Smoke's mine. To kill, to let live. He's mine. That's part of this deal."

"Search her," Griff orders suddenly.

I'm hoisted out of my chair and patted down. There are hands and fingers everywhere, and I mean *everywhere*. My eyes water from the painful intrusions.

Rage still looks bored, buffing her nails on her pink t-shirt that reads WHITE GIRL WASTED until they toss me back down onto the chair with such force my tailbone stings.

"We done here?" Rage smooths down her ponytail and taps her foot impatiently.

"We're done here," Griff says after his men give him a nod that assures him I've got nothing hidden on my person. "It was a pleasure."

"It was creepy as fuck for me," Rage turns, her blondness swaying back and forth as she makes her way out the same way she brought me in until I hear the roll of the heavy door.

Griff kneels before me and runs a fat finger across my throat. My skin crawls, and bile rises in my throat as I flinch away, but he holds me still by grabbing my throat and squeezing until I can't pull in air.

"You and I are going to have so much fun," he grinds out.

My last thought is of Smoke on the porch of the house in the prison, puffing on a cigar, strangling the neck of a whiskey bottle. I focus on his laugh as everything around me turns fuzzy and gray at the edges.

"You don't know a lot about me, do you?" Griff asks, he pulls out a switch blade. He lets up on my throat so I can answer. I pull in a deep breath.

"I know that you buy and trade human beings like baseball cards," I say.

Griff smiles proudly. "True, but there's more to me than that, my dear. Did you know my mother was a midwife? For many years, she delivered babies, and I was her little helper. That's how I was able to cut the child from Morgan's womb. That's how I was able to keep it alive.

"You're a fucking monster," I say. I'm vibrating with rage.

"I have no interest in being the hero of the story. Quite the opposite. I am only interested in being the one with the most money in the end. Morgan was asking Smoke to leave the business. I couldn't let that happen, could I? He's too valuable to me. But now, you've ruined everything. You've stolen my money, and I've lost my best man. You, you little bitch, have thrown out the anchor and you're making this ship drag. I don't like to drag."

Griff runs the blade across my cheek, blood drips to my chin. "Where the fuck is my money?" he growls.

"I used it to pay mercenaries to stop your trading of lives."

Griff raises the blade above my head.

"But not all of it. I've hidden a big chunk where no one but me can find it. It's not in one place. I've spread it around. I can get it back, though" I say with shaky words.

Griff rolls his eyes. "Like I'd allow you near a fucking computer after all the damage you've done. I'm not that fucking stupid. Besides, I don't fucking believe you."

"I'm telling you the truth. I've got nothing to lose," I say. "Not anymore anyway. Kill me if I'm lying."

Griff thinks. "No, you won't do it." My hope sinks. "Leo, my nephew. He'll do it. You'll just tell him where to look. Leo!"

I'm looking at the floor at bright white sneakers. I lift my head. Khaki pants. I look higher. Bright green polo. Higher still. Bright white smile. Curly blonde hair.

"Duke?"

CHAPTER FIFTY-THREE

SMOKE

I push my bike to its limit. The engine growls at me as I lean forward, willing it to go faster. The wind stings against my skin, but it won't slow me down.

Nothing will slow me down.

Not now, not *ever*.

Revenge has fueled me for so long. The thought of taking the life from the person who'd taken lives from me. Revenge is the ultimate decision maker. The one thing I thought that could turn a rational man into the devil himself. I was a step closer to the devil than most men already, but I know now it's not revenge that makes the sane insane.

It's love.

For love, I'm willing to burn down the world and everyone in it.

For Frankie, I'll destroy, maim, and avenge until I'm swimming laps in the blood of those who dared to lay hands on her.

The landscape passes me by in a blur. I can't see it even if I slow down. I can only see one thing right now and one thing only.

Frankie.

It's fueling me to go faster, push harder, and fight the wind to get to her.

The thought of her smile, her laugh, her heart, her body. Her everything I didn't deserve but can't imagine ever living without.

Please be alive, Frankie. Please be FUCKING alive!

CHAPTER FIFTY-FOUR

FRANKIE

"It's gonna take some time, Uncle Griff," Duke says, but he's not really Duke. Griff had called him Leo.

I'm in a state of shock when I'm pulled up and dragged to another room. One lined with a wall of computers and another with a server just as large. Fans blow on them from the ceiling.

The ties at my feet have been cut, but my hands are still bound.

"But can you do it?" Griff asks, his jaw ticking impatiently.

Duke looks from me to Griff. "Of course."

"Good, you have two hours." Griff turns his back and leaves the room. "Or you're both dead."

Duke lifts me up by my elbow and pushes me into a chair. "Shocked?" Duke asks, firing up the center computer and taking the seat next to me.

"Why?" is all I can ask.

"Coincidence if you can believe it. I didn't realize you were my Uncle's enemy number one until he asked me to break into your house and install the cameras in the basement after you were taken from school that day by that cop."

"He's not a cop."

"I know that now," he says.

"Since when are you good at computers?" I ask. "Didn't you fail your computer course last semester."

"I guess I'm like you in that way," Duke says, flashing me a sad smile. "Hiding in plain sight."

He turns back to the computer, and for a second, I feel bad for Duke. I don't know all the details, but from where I stand, he might be just as much a victim as I am.

"Where do I begin?"

Duke wipes his palms on his khakis, his fingers poised over the keys.

"You'll want to start with..." I fire off the most intricate exaggerated knowledge of the inner workings of the web. It's a test to see what Duke really knows.

He fails.

Duke's eyes go wide. "Fuck," he swears, dropping his head to his hands.

"I'll do it," I tell him. "I promise, I'll get your uncle's money back. I just want him to leave my friends alone. Please." I beg, even going so far as to push out my lower lip.

Duke growls. He's going to give in. I haven't given him a lot of choice. "Fine, but don't fuck it up, or we're both dead," Duke says.

I'm sorry Duke.

He cuts the restraints from my wrists and slides the keyboard over to me. He looks over my shoulder, and I don't bother to cover my tracks as I pull up the codes I need. Something tells me Duke's biggest hacking boast is stealing someone's Facebook password.

My fingers fly across the screen as I tap into the in-house server and empty every single account Griff has. Then I do exactly what I came here to do. Why I had to come here alone. Why I couldn't risk Smoke and his friends storming in here for revenge and possibly destroying the information before I got my hands on it. When it's done I send a backup of every file on the server to Nine, including what I hope will be enough information to allow him to locate Smoke's baby.

I'm the conductor again, leading my orchestra to the grandest of finales. The entire time Duke is watching me and nodding like the poor fucker knows anything about what I'm doing.

"One more thing and it's all done," I say.

"No funny business," Duke warns.

I turn to face Duke and smile sweetly. "Oh, I guarantee, there isn't anything funny about it." I press enter. The power to the building shuts down.

The room goes black.

"You little bitch!" Duke shrieks, pounding on the keys of the now dead and useless computer.

I smile. "Oops?"

The door swings open. Griff appears flanked by two men dressed all in black with guns at the ready. The three men are aglow in red from the emergency lights lining the ceiling.

Duke stands and points accusingly at me. "She…I…" he stammers.

Griff nods to the man next to him who raises his gun and fires a single bullet into Duke's chest. Duke stammers back with a shocked look on his face and blood seeping from his mouth. He collapses backward onto the table, breaking it in half and taking it down with him.

I'm oddly calm as Griff enters the room, storming up to

me. His fist connects with my jaw, and for a moment, I see stars. The room is spinning around me as I fall off the chair.

"What. Did. You. Do?" He breathes his question as he stands over me. His angry, red face made even redder by the lights.

"I took away your power," I say, laughing maniacally at my pun.

"How much did you take?" he asks.

I smile in response.

"How the fuck much?" he bellows, holding out his hand for his lackey to place a gun in it.

"All of it," I say. "I took all of it."

"Fuck!!!!!" Griff yells, tearing at his hair and yelling to the walls. "Fuuuuuuuucccckkkk!"

"You think you took my power?" he chuckles and kicks me square in the gut. I feel my ribs crack on impact. I fold in on myself trying to breathe through the pain, but it's impossible because it's too much. It's all too fucking much.

"You're not smiling now, are ya?" Griff says, aiming the gun at me. "We'll see who has the power when I'm through with you."

Whatever is heading my way has been a long time coming. I'm as prepared as I can be as he cocks the gun. At least it's only me dying in this scenario. I brace myself and close my eyes. For the first time in my life, I have a happy place to escape to. Or rather, a happy person. I immerse myself in thoughts of Smoke. Of our time together.

Of the love I feel for him stronger than any bullet.

Griff pulls the trigger.

CHAPTER FIFTY-FIVE

SMOKE

I park my bike at the top of the hill. The van stops behind me, and Nine and Preppy get out while King and Bear pull their bikes up beside me. Below us is Griff's three-story building. An old library from the sixties turned warehouse is tucked into a quiet valley that's about to be anything but quiet.

"Two on top, two on left, and three guarding the door," Bear says quietly, peeling the binoculars away from his eyes.

"And one blonde holding what looks like a detonator," Preppy chimes in. My head turns to him, and I quickly spot what he's staring at.

There's Rage, lying on her stomach in the tall grass, holding a very recognizable detonator in her hand because it's one I'd taught her how to make. Realization hits me, and I sprint toward her, not caring who hears me.

"Rage! No!" I scream.

"Keep your voice down!" King shouts, but it's too late. They've already heard me. The dirt all around me begins to explode when bullets being shot from the roof of the building connect with the ground.

"Rage, don't!" I scream, but she has her earbuds in. Her foot tapping from side to side with the beat of whatever she's listening to.

She turns and sees me, glancing back up at the building like she's confirming that I'm being shot at. I'm almost to her, I can almost grab the detonator from her hand, but with one last glance, Rage offers me something I've never seen on her face before. An apology.

Her finger squeezes the trigger and the building explodes in spectacular fashion, vibrating through the ground like an earthquake, crumbling down like a sandcastle being trampled over.

"Nooooooo!" I scream, as half the building falls and my heart along with it. "Nooooo!" I haven't lost any of my forward momentum. I roll into Rage, toss her on her back and press my gun into her forehead. She doesn't react, just stares up at my face like she's trying hard to understand something. She won't be looking like that long. She'll be looking like she's missing her brain in a minute because I'm about to put a fucking bullet in it.

"Can't let you do that," Bear says, producing his own gun and holding it to the back of my head.

"Then do it!" Another explosion shakes the ground. "What the fuck did you do?" I ask, only able to get out every other syllable. My voice shakes and cracks. "What the fuck did you do?"

Bear presses his gun against my head again as if to remind me he's still there.

"I don't want to do this, man," Bear growls.

I see King slowly walk to one side and Preppy the other as

if they could somehow tackle me off her before I pull the trigger. They're not that fast.

"Tell me why!" I demand again.

Rage looks up at me expressionless. There is no fear in her eyes. "Because she loves you," she says softly, placing her palm against my cheek. The act of kindness and the softness of her tone throws me off balance. "Because you love her. Because I love YOU." Her face twists in pain, not from me on top of her but at her own words.

It doesn't make any fucking sense. Has Rage finally lost her shit completely?

"Wow," Preppy says. "Should you two get a room?"

"Not like that, dumb-ass," Rage says, rolling her eyes like I'm not about to murder her. She glances up to me. "Frankie asked me to, but I couldn't do it." She shrugs.

"Couldn't what?" I ask, slamming my fist on the ground beside her head.

"She asked me to bring her to Griff then wait a half hour. If she didn't come out by then she wanted me to blow the building. I couldn't do it. Not with her inside. So I set the explosives on the exterior and only one inside. I've only blown the exterior ones. It won't bring the place down until I blow the final one, but it will shake the place up a bit. Hopefully cause enough of a distraction for her to get the fuck out."

I'm still trying to wrap my brain around it, but there's no time. I have to get to Frankie.

"It's true, man," Nine chimes in. "How did you think I knew where this place was? Why do you think you're here?"

"Why the fuck would she do this?"

"She went in so you wouldn't. She didn't want anyone to die when…"

Holy fuck. Frankie sacrificed herself….for me.

I get off Rage who sits up and passes me a tablet. "I inserted one of those thingies into her skin behind her ear before she went in. She's in the far east side of the building. "Here," Rage says, pointing to a blinking red light on the screen.

"Come on, then. You two can talk this out later," Bear says. "We need to figure out how we're…"

I make a run for my bike.

"What are you doing?" Preppy shouts above my revving engine.

I look out at the warehouse below. "I'm going in!"

"We'll cover you!" he shouts, his words lost to the wind as I take off down the hill.

King was right. I'll shed the blood of every fucking man who gets in the way of my saving Frankie. There's no one I won't kill.

I'll burn the fucking world down for her and bask in the motherfucking flames.

CHAPTER FIFTY-SIX

FRANKIE

I'm in so much pain. My shirt is stained red as blood seeps from the bullet wound in my stomach. I clutch my hands over it, but there's no keeping it in; it pours through my fingers and drips onto the concrete floor.

I'm light-headed. Everything around me seems to slow down.

An explosion sounds in the distance like far off cannon fire. The walls shake and dust falls from the rafters to the floor.

Wood and concrete is falling all around me. Griff's men are running, but I can't run with them. I can't even move.

Griff is shouting orders. A large metal panel falls on top of the man he's shouting at so he turns to the next one. I throw away paint brushes that have lost most of their bristles less flippantly.

The wall explodes, the garage door caves in. A huge black motorcycle appears from nowhere, airborne, its tires spinning against the air, crashing down onto the ground.

Smoke.

Tears of relief spring to my eyes followed by a pit of horror burning a hole in my stomach. He can't put himself at risk like this. Not for me. He has too much on the line now, and there's too many of them.

"No! Go back!" I shout, but there's no way he can hear me over the roar of the engine echoing through the large open space.

The bike lurches onto its side, but Smoke stays upright, stepping out from the spinning pile of metal like he's stepping over a puddle in the street. He heads straight for the two men guarding me. There's a look in his eyes.

Determination.

He's hyper-focused. I realize it didn't matter if he heard me tell him to go back or not. He's beyond hearing right now. Beyond thought. He's somewhere I can't reach him.

No one can.

Smoke's movements are fluid. Downright graceful. He's wearing black fingerless gloves and his cut, with nothing on underneath except his colorful tattooed skin and lean ripped muscle.

The bike careens into the wall in an explosion of fire yet Smoke doesn't so much as flinch as he's backlit in flames.

Griff's two men stare, slack-jawed, for a beat too long when the realization hits. They both raise their guns at Smoke. I want to scream I want to jump in front of the bullets, but sharp pain meets my every move, rendering me useless.

Smoke's fingers flex at his side. His nostrils flare. He stares down the men holding their guns on him like he has all the time in the world. The men fire, but Smoke continues to advance on them, side-stepping the bullets.

"Shit," the shorter of the two men curses while reloading

his gun with trembling hands. The other does the same, but it's too late for them. Much too fucking late.

Smoke crisscrosses his arms over his torso, reaching under his cut, each hand emerges holding a large metal gun boasting long wide barrels. He's eerily calm as he stretches out his arms in front of him and fires a single bullet from each gun into their heads. Just as they fall lifeless to the ground, more men appear on opposite sides of the room. Smoke lifts his arms out to his sides and fires. When a bullet misses his head by only a few inches, he turns his gun behind him and fires, hitting the man without so much as a glance in his direction.

This isn't Smoke the kidnapper or Smoke the killer or even Smoke the lover. No, this is Smoke, the man. The rescuer. This was Smoke with someone and something to live for.

It was both terrifying and thrilling all at once.

Despite what has transpired between us, this beautifully brutal man came here and put his life on the line to save me.

A bullet pierces Smoke's shoulder. Streams of bright red drip down his arm to his wrist, seeping into my shirt as he bends to gather me into his arms. He places a heavy gun between my bound hands

"Can you shoot?" he asks.

I nod even though the gun feels heavy. So does my own head. I can barely lift it.

"Listen to me, and pull the trigger when I say so." He sets up the gun so it's mostly resting on his arm, and it's no longer heavy in my grip. "Can you do that?"

"Yes," I say on a feeble whisper.

Smoke lifts me into his strong arms, his blood both wets and warms my skin.

There's movement to the side. A shuffling of feet.

"Fire," Smoke orders, turning us around.

I do as I'm told and fire along with Smoke. I hear a deep grunt followed by a crash as his body hit something on its way down to the ground.

Smoke's on the move, heading back out from the hole he created with his bike.

"Fire," he says again, and I do as I'm told.

"Good girl," he says, and I smile, or at least I think I do. It's hard to tell with all the spinning going on above me. I lock eyes on his jaw, the slope of his nose, the scar above his eye. I think of how beautiful this man is. How angry and horrible and violent and beautiful.

I'm tired. Oh so very tired. My wrist goes limp. The gun falls from my hand. I focus on Smoke. On the lines of his face and neck. I look out to the field around us. Construction matter, bodies.

Blood.

I am having the nightmare again. The one where I'm in Smoke's arms being carried across a bloody battlefield. Only this time it's not a nightmare. There's no fear, only comfort. I now know that the feeling of safety that envelops me in the dream as he wraps me in his arms isn't wrong.

He's protecting me. Loving me in his own way. So, I let him love me. Protect me. And I close my eyes, letting the darkness take me under. I'm lost to the dream. I'm safe.

I just need to rest now. Just for a moment. The feeling is overpowering. I give in, closing my eyes, because I have to. I have no other choice. I'm just so tired.

Oh, so very tired.

CHAPTER FIFTY-SEVEN

SMOKE

"No!" I scream as Frankie's eyes flutter then close. She's covered with blood oozing from her stomach. I give her a shake while the dirt continues to explode all around me. I'm running up the hill. King, Preppy, and Bear follow me, covering me, shooting anyone who comes near.

Nine is waiting with the van when we get to the top.

"I thought you said you planted three bombs?" Preppy asks.

"I did," Rage says.

"I only heard two," Preppy crosses his arms over his chest.

Rage flashes him a wink and another explosion sounds, taking the last bit of the building with it to the ground. "As I was saying," Rage smiles victoriously. "Three bombs."

"You two conspire to take out an entire criminal organization by yourselves and fail to include me?" Preppy asks, feigning hurt, with his jaw open and his hand on his chest.

"Next time we need a court jester for a job, I'll let you know," Rage says, tucking her earbuds into her pocket.

"Listen here, Rambo Barbie," Preppy says, taking a step toward her as we reach the van.

"Children," King warns.

Nine opens the door, and I place Frankie gently across the seat. She's fading fast. Everyone heads further into the woods to retrieve their bikes, and Rage her Vespa. Preppy hops in with us, and Nine backs us out and speeds down the road.

"Why did you do this?" I ask Frankie as I haul her across my lap and look down at her beautiful face.

My chest is hurting. My throat burns every time she gasps for air. She winces with every rattling breath.

"You risked your life," I tell her, and I want to yell at her, throttle her, punish her for putting herself in danger like that. But my need to punish her dies a quick death when her eyes close and her chest shakes. "Why?"

Frankie's eyes open slightly. She stares up at me. "For you. For the flash drive," she coughs out. Her head falls to the side. Her eyes close.

This time they stay closed.

CHAPTER FIFTY-EIGHT

SMOKE

"I'll love you with everything I have and all that I am. It ain't much, but it's yours if you'll let me give it to you. If you'll wake up. Please fuckin' wake up, baby. Wake the fuck up!" I beg Frankie as I carry her in the front door of the club.

I set her down on the pool table in the main office area. I'm gentle for the first time in my memory, careful not to bump her head. I feel like a meteor struck the earth, splitting it in two because my world has been split in two. With the sudden possibility that Frankie may no longer be in that world, it all might as well crumble to dust.

Rage is watching me. I can feel her eyes at my back.

"If you're going to stand there staring, you might as well fucking help," I bark.

Frankie let's out a strangled breath, and for a moment, I think she's waking up until the sound fades, and nothing is left in its place.

I've been shot before. I've been stabbed. But nothing, nothing I've ever experienced could compare to the pain of possibly watching the only woman I'd ever truly loved take her very last breath.

"Smoke, I'm not a damn paramedic, I can't put her back together," she says, her calm voice grates on me like sandpaper across my knuckles.

"Neither can I," I whisper.

Frankie was the one who had gathered up all the scattered pieces, all the jagged shards of me and painstakingly, piece by piece, put me back together.

My despair turns to anger as my throat closes.

I can't do the same for her.

"Why is that little shit taking so long!" I roar.

I look back to Rage, she's eyeing me cautiously. She's not frantic, but that's not her style. Never was. She twirls the end of her long blonde ponytail between her fingers.

"He's coming. I called him. He knows better than to stand me up."

There is no doubt in my mind that that's true. Any man, ship, or person would be insane to skip out on Rage. And although I know she's changed in so many ways, I'm glad that she still can command the kind of fear that has men bending to her will.

That fear may very well save Frankie's life. After all the shit that's gone down with this crew inside of hospitals, they aren't trusted. Plus, they've got the best of the best medics and surgeons on their fucking payroll, so hospitals be damned.

My insides hurt like someone has flayed me open from neck to dick. I'm dying. I know I am. I'm dying right along with her because there is no way I can live if Frankie isn't gonna make it.

I lean down and place my ear against her chest to listen for a heartbeat, and my own seizes when I can't hear hers over the blood rushing through my ears.

"Here, let me." Rage says, kneeling beside me. She presses the side of her head to Frankie's chest. When she lifts her head, she places her index finger under Frankie's nose. "It's shallow, but it's there."

I take a breath, and suddenly, I can feel the pounding of my heart in my chest, like just knowing Frankie was breathing was also bringing me back to life.

The medic runs in and pushes us aside. He works on Frankie quickly, tearing at her clothes and stabbing her with an IV. It's all over in a flash. I'm looking over his shoulder because one wrong move and this fucker will be the one needing a coroner.

"Now, we wait. We'll know more if she wakes up in the next few hours." He runs out just as quickly as he came.

I rest my forehead on Frankie's shoulder. She stirs, and I watch without breathing for so long I cough because my heart skips a beat.

I don't know how long I sit there with her, but it's a long time.

I assume Rage has been long gone until she speaks.

"You love her?" she points to Frankie who stirs again.

This time Frankie's eyes flutter open. I'm greeted with a beautiful but strained smile that I can't help but return. Crouching down, I take her hands in mine and press them to my lips. I don't take my eyes off her while I answer Rage's question.

"Yeah, I do. I fucking love her." I kiss her hand. "So very fucking much."

CHAPTER FIFTY-NINE

SMOKE

"You got a second to talk?" Nolan asks, knocking on the open door. I knew this was coming eventually, and it might as well be while Frankie's asleep. I pocket the flash drive and remind myself to ask Frankie about it later.

"I think I've had enough talking for a fucking lifetime, but sure, why the fuck not." I slap my hands on my thighs and stand. I follow him from the room into the courtyard and shut the door quietly behind me so Frankie doesn't wake up.

I stand in front of Nolan and cross my arms over my chest. I may be bigger than him but our fight isn't about size. If the fucker wanted to kill me, I'd get it. Fuck, there was a time I'd have handed him the fucking gun.

The man was tied up and beaten and was forced to watch with one non-swollen eye open while I was made to fuck his girl at gunpoint.

"Rage told me about earlier. What her and Frankie did." He shakes his head. "Those girls. Sometimes, I think Rage's got bigger balls than me."

"I KNOW her balls are bigger than yours," I say.

Nolan adjusts his Wolf Warriors cut. I remind myself to ask Rage later why the fuck she didn't join up with her man's MC and joined The Lawless instead.

"I know you've kept your distance. I just wanted to let you know I appreciate that. I also wanted to let you know that I appreciate you saving my life. You didn't owe me shit, but you did it anyway," Nolan says.

"I did it for Rage," I correct him.

"I know. And that's why you don't have a fucking bullet in your head right now," he says with a smile.

"Fuck," I say, taking a step closer. "You're even starting to act like her," I can't help the laugh that escapes me. "You're doing that thing she does where she says something really fucked up but with a smile on her face like she told you she's running out for fucking frozen yogurt."

Nolan glances at the mirror then back to me, dropping the smile. "Fuck, I am doing it," he says.

We both laugh.

"What happened out there that night? That wasn't your fault. None of it was," Nolan says.

"I know that," I say. "Now."

"I wanted to kill you," Nolan cracks his knuckles.

"I would have killed you," I say. "You're a better man than me."

"But I came here for a reason. I got something to say. Something important."

I sigh. "What?"

"You don't gotta leave again. You can stick around without worry. In fact, after talking to Rage, she brought something up, but she didn't want to ask you so I'm gonna, and just so you know, the answer is yes because I'm not going to be the one to tell her otherwise."

"What is it?"

"It's for her."

"Just fucking spit it out already!" I groan.

"We're getting married," Nolan says.

"Holy shit," I say, a smile spreading across my face.

Nolan returns my smile looking downright proud of himself. "And I only had to ask her about sixty times before she said yes."

"I'm impressed," I say, because I am impressed. Rage of all people. Married?

"What do you want from me?"

"I ain't gonna ask your permission or nothin' because she's my girl, and I don't need your fucking permission, just let me say that first."

I nod.

"But, I do want to ask you if you'll give her away."

"What about her dad?" Rage is the only killer I know who's in tight with her mom and pop.

"We're doing a little backyard ceremony for them. Just the four of us. She doesn't want to bring them around this world, and I don't blame her. But we're gonna do something here right after. At the club. And in that part of it she wants you to give her away."

I'm so stunned by the request that I don't speak for a while.

"And?" Nolan waves his hand in the air, waiting for me to answer.

"And I'm really surprised there aren't bullet holes in the wall right now, and that we're really talking about this," I say, making Nolan laugh.

"Me, too, motherfucker. Me, too," Nolan says. "So, you'll do it?"

I look across the courtyard and catch Rage watching us.

She turns around and pretends to be picking something up off the floor like she wasn't listening and watching us the entire time.

"Yeah, man. I'll do it."

Nolan nods. "Good." He turns to leave but stops again. "There's one more thing. The Wolf Warriors are merging with Lawless. I'm going to be Bear's new second in command. I talked it over with Bear, and this is yours if you want it." He kicks a bag at his feet that I didn't even notice he'd brought in, then leaves.

I get up and empty the bag onto the bed. A new smelling leather cut falls out.

The back has The Lawless MC with their logo and on the front, is my name and a new patch underneath. LIFE MEMBER.

I sit.

They want me to be a part of something. Something bigger than myself. I shrug off the worn leather cut from my shoulders. The blank one that tells no stories and no lies. And I shrug on the new one. I pause in the mirror as I turn around and inspect the new logo on my back. I expect to feel overwhelmed. Suffocated.

But I don't. I feel warm. Comfortable. I can breathe again; the same way Frankie makes me feel I can breathe again.

I feel like I belong. To these people. To the club.

To Frankie.

After thirty some odd years adrift, I've found my place in the world.

Who'd a fucking thought.

CHAPTER SIXTY

THREE WEEKS LATER

FRANKIE

"Sit," he demands, and I'm too tired to fight so I take a seat at the edge of the mattress.

Recovering is exhausting.

Smoke hands me a manila file. "I have something for you."

"What's this?" I ask.

Smoke takes off his cut and hangs it over the back of a nearby chair. "Something didn't add up to me about your father, who was an accountant and a money launderer, suddenly taking up something like human trafficking. One doesn't exactly lead to the other. So, I had Nine look into it for me."

I open the file and gasp because at first, I think it's a picture of me I'm staring at, but it's not me. It's my mother. "What is this?" I ask scanning my eyes down the page. It's like an HR file, but it's not about her work, it's a resume about her life. Smoke points to the bottom of the page where it says in big red bold letters. DECEASED May 13th, 2012 in Mumbai India.

May 13th was two days before I found my father's body in the basement.

"That's wrong." I say shaking my head. "She didn't die in India. She was here. And the date's wrong. She died when I was a toddler."

Smoke shook his head. "No, she died in India three weeks after being kidnapped coming home from work at the dentist's office…by Griff's men."

Panic hits me in the chest like I'd been struck with an arrow. Sharp and deep. I look to Smoke, but he doesn't say anything. He's looking down at me cautiously like he's waiting for whatever it is he's trying to tell me to sink in. Finally, it does. But sinking isn't just the feeling I get when the information hits my brain, it's my heart and soul shriveling up, pitting in the bottom of my stomach.

"She was sold into human trafficking," I say on a whisper as the bile rises in my throat, and I can actually feel the tearing of my heart as it pulls apart. I sink down, but Smoke catches me before I hit the floor, pulling me onto his lap.

"Look at me," he demands, turning me to face him.

I look up at him. The file falls from my hand to the floor and papers flutter all around the carpet as my arms fall limply to my sides. I search Smoke's eyes, but I don't feel anything but a sickening awareness of what had been done to my mother.

"Why are you telling me this now?" I ask, my voice a weak rasp.

I search for anything in his expression that will tell me that he's trying to intentionally hurt me, but there's nothing but stern calmness. A well-built ship navigating stormy seas.

"Yes, your mother was sold into slavery. We don't know

the details of what or who killed her, but we know her body was found off a road connecting two towns."

"I don't..." I start, but Smoke isn't finished.

"Frankie, your father knew. He found out she'd been taken and the reasons why."

"I still don't understand."

"Frankie, your old man still did all the bad shit. He transferred all the money for Griff. He contributed to a lot of deaths and his share of despair. That much is true. But the reason why he did it wasn't greed," Smoke says. "He was trying to find her. Your mom."

"Oh my god," I say as his words sink it. I press my face into Smoke's chest and my tears are absorbed into his shirt. "He was looking for her. But he still hurt so many others."

Smoke nods again. "He did," he admits, holding my face in his large rough hands. "He hurt a lot of people. People died because of him. Women. Men." The sinking feeling returns. "But you can't blame him. He was willing to turn Heaven and Hell over searching for your mom. He was willing to kill everyone standing between him and her." He leaned in close and brushed his lips lightly over mine. "I know the feeling, hellion."

My chilled blood warms. Smoke had just given me the greatest gift I'd ever received. He'd given me my family back. My father.

Who didn't die of a heart attack, but of a broken heart.

The door creaks open. "Got a minute?" Nine asks.

I look up from Smoke to Nine who gives me a thumbs up.

"I...I have something for you, too," I say with a sniffle.

Smoke's eyes grow wide. He turns around slowly as the most beautiful sound in the world floats through the open door from the courtyard.

Toddler giggles.

the [illegible] or [illegible] who killed h[illegible] [illegible] had [illegible] took [illegible] ever [illegible].

"[illegible] than [illegible] Smoke and Rosalie."

[illegible]

"[illegible] understand."

"[illegible] went [illegible] killed [illegible] all his money for [illegible] the condition [illegible] and his [illegible] he did [illegible] Smoke [illegible] The [illegible].

"[illegible] good," [illegible] Smoke [illegible] into [illegible] [illegible].

[illegible]

My [illegible] gave [illegible] my father.

[illegible] broken heart. The [illegible] "[illegible] a [illegible]?" [illegible]

I [illegible] Smoke [illegible] up.

"I have something for you," [illegible]

Smoke's eyes grow wide. He turns around slowly as the most beautiful sound in the world floats through the open [illegible] from the [illegible].

[illegible] toddler giggles.

EPILOGUE

THREE MONTHS LATER

FRANKIE

We've taken up permanent residence in The Warden's cottage. After working day and night for months, I finally have a set-up with an internet speed measured in a unit faster than the time it takes an ox to plow a field, and the room with all the storage is now a princess room for Smoke's daughter who Nine found using the files from Griff's server I'd sent him before Griff put a bullet in my gut.

Her name is Morgan, and she is Smoke. Dark hair. Dark eyes and a total brute. I'm completely in love with the both of them.

We're a team now. The three of us.

I continue saving lives, but with Nine's help, I've become completely untraceable. Smoke's been spending more time with King, Bear, and Preppy, but he's bonded with Nine most of all.

Smoke has yet to put on the cut, officially that is. Even though I know he wants to. Bear said it's his decision, and he can take his time. I'll know when he's ready because the cut will no longer be hanging off the chair in the corner of the living room.

He won't let me hang it up. I think he likes to know it's there. Not just the cut. The option. The club. The people. Bear, King, Preppy, Rage, Nine. They all stuck their necks out for him.

For me.

I don't think he can put on the cut until he gets used to the idea that once he does, people are going to be sticking their necks out for him all the time. No questions asked.

"That should do it," I say to myself, climbing down from the ladder.

"Wow," Smoke says behind me. I join him in the center of the room. Together, we admire the place above the mantel where I've chosen to display my most favorite painting. My very FIRST painting.

"I'm not sure that's the place for it," Smoke says. His forehead is wrinkled in thought.

"Why? I thought it was perfect. Don't you like it?" I ask.

"It's fucking beautiful, but it's too... I don't know. I'm not really sure what to think of it," Smoke says.

"It's from a dream I had," I tell him.

"You don't think it's too morbid for above the mantle?" Smoke asks, wrapping his arms around me from behind.

"YOU of all people think it might be too morbid?" I tease.

"I don't know. Maybe, it hits too close to home is all."

"Art is all about perception. What it makes you feel. Everyone sees art differently," I say, and that's when I smell it.

Leather. *New* leather.

I glance out of the corner of my eye to the chair.

The *empty* chair.

I can't help the smile spreading across my face.

"What I see is me carrying you into Hell," Smoke says. There's a sadness in his voice that makes my heart hurt.

I turn and stand on my tip-toes, wrapping my arms around his neck. "No, you're not carrying me through Hell." I press a soft kiss to his lips and look deeply into his dark eyes. "You're carrying me out of it."

THE END

Keep reading for a special bonus scene!

BONUS SCENE

SMOKE

This scene is also included in
All The Rage from Rage's perspective

I'm in the middle of the fucking woods, and I don't want to be here. All I want to do is kill the piece of shit I came out here to kill and fucking leave. I'm tired. More tired than I've ever been, and I feel it weaving its way through my muscle and bones.

I'm standing across from Mugs, a member of the Beach Bastards MC, and I wish to fuck I wasn't. I work alone. Always have. But there's a reason why Mugs is there, and I aim to get the fucking job done and get the fuck out of there.

Mugs is a fucking mess. Greasy blond hair flat on his head and a crooked smile on his face as he chews on yet another fucking toothpick, which is about as thick as his twig legs. He's holding a shovel casually across his shoulders, having just finished digging the hole I ordered him to dig.

One of the reasons why we are even in the woods to begin with is because of the other man in front of me. Jerry. The one with his mouth duct taped shut and his wrists tied behind his back. He pissed himself. I smell the urine before I see it. The motherfucker lived like a coward, and now he's gonna die like one.

I aim my gun at his head. "You thought you could fuck with us and get away with it, Jerry?" Jerry can't answer, but I don't fucking care. I cock the gun. Jerry was a job assigned to me by Bear, the VP of the Beach Bastards MC, after Jerry raped and practically disfigured the daughter of one of his brothers.

"No…no, Smoke. Don't do this. I promise, I didn't mean to hurt her," Jerry whines. There's nothin' I hate more than a fucking whiner. Especially someone who whines while begging for his life.

I chuckle. "You didn't mean to hurt her? She was a kid, motherfucker. You raped her, sliced up her virgin cunt, and gave her a fucking concussion. So, don't fucking tell me you didn't mean to fucking hurt her just so you can spare your own life, you weak piece of shit! It's too late for that now."

Tired of Jerry's bullshit, I raise my gun and bring it down against the side of his head. He falls sideways into the dirt. "Mugs, pick this shit-bag off the fucking floor. I want him upright when I blow his fucking brains out," I order.

Together, we drag Jerry over to the fresh hole and kick him inside.

Jerry's eyes are on something over my head. Mugs and I turn at the same time. Mugs drops his shovel, grabbing his gun instead. I raise mine, too, but only because I'm in shock at what's in front of me.

A girl. And a young one at that. My guess is barely a teenager.

Blonde hair pulled in a tight ponytail. A curious look on her eyes as she looks past me and the guns being aimed at her to the hole where Jerry is about to be reunited with the dirt.

"Who the fuck are you?" I demand, closing the gap between us in two strides. She's got big blue eyes and she's wearing cut off shorts and a tight pink t-shirt with the words Princesses Suck scrolled across her chest. Most girls would take a step back. Most girls would shake with fear. Most grown men too.

Not this girl. Not a tremor or quivering lip to be seen. Just pupils the size of Frisbees and a look of vacant wonderment in her eyes.

Her gaze flits quickly from Jerry, to Mugs, then to the gun in my hand…which I redirect to her head in warning.

Then, she does something I can't wrap my fucking brain around. The bitch SMILES. Not only does she smile, but she points to my gun and claps her hands together like a little kid asking to play with her parent's keys.

She clears her throat and asks in a whisper, "Can I? Please?"

"Can you what?" I bark, still not believing what I'm seeing. "What exactly are you asking, girl?"

And that's when I see it. The pain in her eyes. The need. I recognize it because I see it in myself, but this girl, this girl is just so much MORE of all of that than I've ever been. She's a monster. A killer. I know it as well as I know the sky's blue and the dirt's brown.

"Why the fuck are you smiling, girl?" Mugs asks. The fucker doesn't see what I see. He wouldn't.

If stupidity is a terminal disease, Mugs is stage four.

She turns to me, ignoring Mugs, like she's asking me for help. She points to Jerry and bites her bottom lip.

I look at her again and something between us just makes sense. It's a connection. Something strong working its way between us like a maze of invisible vines tethering us together in some out of this world way.

I scratch my head with the barrel of my gun. "How old are you, girl?"

"Fifteen," she answers eagerly. She corrects herself. "No, sixteen. Today's my birthday." I stare at her without speaking as the understanding continues to pass between us.

"Well happy fucking birthday, girl. Smoke, what the fuck are you doing?" Mugs whines, grating on my last fucking nerve. "Let's take this fucker out and then take her out. She's a witness now. We can't let her just walk." He walks toward us, but I hold up a hand to stop him, waving him back before he can take another step.

"Hurry the fuck up, man. And just know that you're not getting out of helping me dig another fucking hole."

The girl looks past me. "I won't be a witness if…I'm the one who does it," she offers, bouncing on the balls of her feet.

"You're not afraid are you?" I ask, just verifying that what I see in her is really there because I still can't really believe it.

She's little and cute and a kid, but she's the fucking devil himself, and if I were Mugs, I'd shut the fuck up before the ground opened up and swallows him whole. I wait for hesitation on her part. Any sign that this really isn't what she wants but I get nothing

She bites her lips again and rocks on her feet.

"You high or something?" I ask, quirking an eyebrow and ignoring another call from Mugs to hurry up and kill her. One last attempt to make sure what I'm seeing is real.

"No," she whispers, and for some reason I believe her.

I raise my gun, again aiming it at her head. I take another step toward her, closing the gap between us and roughly pressing the barrel of the gun against her forehead.

She doesn't move. She also doesn't stop smiling.

I holster my gun and begin to laugh. I look her in the eyes. "I recognize that look," I say, scratching at my forearm. "Never seen it in a chick before, though. Especially not one so fucking young. Only ever seen it in guys. Guys like me."

"Guys like you?" she asks, scrunching her forehead.

"Yeah, guys like me. The bad guys." I crack my knuckles.

"Please," she begs, "Bad, good..." She shakes her head. "I just have to."

I keep my eyes on her and call back to Mugs, "The girl's right. She ain't a witness if she does it herself." I say, moving around to her side.

We both look to Mugs who rolls his eyes and lights a smoke.

"Wow, I knew you liked some fucked up shit, Smoke, but a sixteen-year-old who begs strangers to let her kill mother-fuckers?" He scoffs. "I hope you two deviants will be really fucking happy together."

"No, that's not what..." the girl starts to argue.

"You don't gotta explain shit to him," I tell her. I lower my voice to a whisper and my head to her ear. "Mugs is a fucking moron. He doesn't get it."

He doesn't see what I see.

"I heard that," Mugs says. "And what I get is that the longer we're out here, the higher the chances are of getting caught. I mean, I hate to kill and run, but we gotta fucking go." Mugs turns his gun on Jerry. Without warning he pulls the trigger, sending a spray of dirt raining down into the hole.

"What the fuck?" I roar.

The girl falls to the ground and wraps her arms around her knees, not out of fear, but disappointment, as if she's devastated and can't even stay upright.

I kneel beside her. "You okay, kid?" I tip her chin up to

meet mine. She gazes up at me with a wild look before the tears began to spill.

I pull her against my chest. "I'll take care of you," I whisper into her hair. I feel possessive over her. Like she was always meant to find me. Not in a sexual way, but in a way that makes her feel like instant family. She's blood to me, now. There's no turning back.

I want to show her that she isn't alone. That she isn't the only one who feels or doesn't feel the way others do. There wasn't anyone like that around for me growing up and I'm determined to be that person for her.

"I'll help you. Would you like that?" I ask.

Through her tears she nods, accepting my offer although not completely understanding what it was she was agreeing to.

"Just kidding," Mugs says suddenly. He stabs his shovel down. He walks over to where we're crouched on the ground. "Look for yourself. He's still alive. Just had to know you were serious."

"You're a fucking prick, Mugs," I spit.

"Yeah, I know. Now let's hurry the fuck up and get out of here. I got shit to do."

"What's your name, kid?" I ask, keeping her against me.

She doesn't answer right away. "Rage." She finally says with an audible swallow. "My name is Rage."

"Rage. I like it." I say, offering her my gun. "Ever shoot one of these before?" I pull her off the ground.

"No," she admits.

"Stand here," I direct her in front of me. I place the gun in her hand. "Take this, hold it just how I'm holding it now."

She does what I say and her hand drops like the gun is a lot heavier than she expected it to be.

I push her forward, walking her toward where Jerry's

crouched figure is huddled in the hole. "Aim like this, and then squeeze the trigger," I say softly. "You sure you want to do this?"

"Yes," she answers. No hesitation.

I have no doubt she's telling the truth, but I feel like I gotta warn her once last time. "'Cause this is life-changing shit right here. You do this and things won't be the same ever again. This is the kind of shit that haunts grown men at night." I pause. "The kind of shit that has them begging Jesus for forgiveness."

"I don't need forgiveness," she whispers, squeezing the trigger.

Jerry's one eye stays open. The life that had been there seconds before, now gone. His stare completely blank. The dirt underneath him darkens as his blood seeps out from the fresh wound on the side of his head.

She stays stone still, breathing hard, staring at what's left of Jerry's head with wild excitement.

"Oh, yeah?" I ask. "Everyone seeks forgiveness sooner or later, Princess. Why not you?" I hold out my hand for my gun, she hands it over. It's still warm.

She turns to face me and shrugs. "Because, I'm not sorry."

"Good, that's the first lesson," I say, suddenly turning my gun on Mugs and pulling the trigger in quick succession. Three bullets explode into his chest, sending him teetering back over the hole's edge until he falls backward into it, his body joining Jerry's.

What I forgot to tell the now very dead Mugs was that Bear knew he'd raped the girl first before Jerry had taken his turn. My job wasn't to return one body to the dirt tonight, but two.

"What's the second lesson?" Rage asks, staring at the gun as I change the clip.

"The second lesson, is that in order to survive you are loyal to no one. You are on nobody's side except your own." I holster the gun and look her in the eye to make sure she understands exactly what I'm getting at. "You got that?"

Rage nods. "Yes, loyal to no one," she says, adding, "What about you?"

I laugh. This fucking kid.

"No one, kid." I look over to the bodies in the dirt then back to her. "*Especially* not me."

ACKNOWLEDGMENTS

This part is always really hard for me. There is so much that goes into creating a book. So many days of feeling like a complete failure in every aspect of life. Then you guys read my words and open the flood gates of love and by the time I get to writing these things I'm a blubbering mess.

But I'll give it a try. Here we go. *wipes tears*

Thank you first and foremost to my husband and daughter. There is so much you both sacrifice for this crazy dream. I can never thank you or apologize to you enough. You two are my everything.

Baby Frazier, you can do anything and everything you set out to accomplish in life. Your mama isn't the brightest bulb on the tree and she's shit at laundry and dishes, but if I can put a lasso around my dreams then so can you, my bright little love.

Logan, you have taken this dream of mine and turned it into a dream of ours. That means the world to me. Your endless support is the only reason I can do this some days. Your strength makes me stronger and I am forever grateful we found each other exactly when we were meant to. Who would have thought twelve years ago as crazy twenty-something's that we'd be where we are now? And not a single stint in rehab between us! HAHA. But, seriously, look at us go, babe! I love you more than words. Forever I am yours. To the moon and beyond. Always.

Thank you to my readers. You are such a huge part of my soul. Your enthusiasm for my stories still FLOORS me. I am so grateful you love my words. Thank you for allowing me to continue writing them. I promise I'll give you all the stories I have, with everything I have, for as long as you'll let me.

To all the women reading this, thank you for being such strong complicated beautiful creatures who inspire me every day. Do not doubt what you are capable of. I sure don't. So go! DO IT ALL. Try and fail at your dreams then try again because that's when you will truly shine. Because you CAN. Because you are LOVED. Because you're WORTHY of everything this life has to offer. And if all else fails, because I *motherfucking* said so.

To the classiest bitches in the trailer park, my girls (and like two guys) in Frazierland, LOVE ALL YOUR FACES AND THEN SOME. Thank you for hanging out with me. Talking to me. And being there for me. YOU are my safe place.

To all those who laughed both behind my back and in my face when I said I wanted to write books for a living, THANK YOU FOR THAT PUSH.

Thank you to my agent Kimberly Brower of Brower Literary & Management for opening doors for me I didn't even know were there. I can't wait to see what the future holds.

To AudiOMG, and to all my foreign publishers, Thank

you for taking a chance on me and my work. I promise I'll try not to let you down and I'm so excited to discover what's next.

Thank you to Karla Nellenbach *DOUBLE MIDDLES*, Evident Ink, and Love-N-Books for the edits. Thank you for helping me tell my story and for making sense of my madness.

Thank you to my author friends who inspire me and offer encouragement and words of wisdom daily. You help me both professionally and mentally. You guys are the SHIZNIT. (You know who you are S.T.-ers)

Thank you to Jenn Watson and the team at Social Butterfly for helping birth my book babies into the world with gusto. And just like birth, sometimes launching one of my books can be a bloody mess, but in the end it's so worth it. I'm grateful for all you do.

Thank you to Wander Photography (Wander and Andrey) for the amazing cover image and for giving life to Smoke. I love your work and the both of you. Margaritas on Mr. Frazier very soon!

Thank you to Jessica, Rea, Pavlina, Lydia, Lizette, Kath, and Kris for reading through the ARCS so quickly for me. You are life savers. Special thanks to Lydia and Rea for all the amazing detail and hard work. You are all very much appreciated and I'm a thousand percent less frazzled because of your help.

Thank you to Julie Vaden for being my friend and for being the most excellent admin of Frazierland. Wait, that's not good enough of a title. PRESIDENT of Frazierland! I'm unworthy of your help or your friendship, but I'm a greedy bitch, so I'll take 'em both.

Thank you to all the AMAZING bloggers and Goodreads reviewers who continue to sign up for my blog tours and ARCS. Thank you for continuing to support me and spread the word about my books to the masses. Your role is VITAL to what we do and I appreciate each and every one of you more than you can ever know.

I meant to keep this short. SHIT. Oh well, I'm just VERY thankful. *DROPS MIC*

Word to your mother,

T.M.

ALSO BY T.M. FRAZIER

COMING SOON:

THE PERVERSION TRILOGY

PERVERSION (Book 1)

POSSESSION (Book 2)

PERMISSION (Book 3)

NINE (King Series #9)

AVAILABLE NOW:

THE OUTSKIRTS DUET

Finn & Sawyers Story

THE OUTSKIRTS

THE OUTLIERS

KING SERIES

King & Doe's Story (Duet)

KING

TYRANT

Bear & Thia's Story (Duet)

LAWLESS

SOULLESS

Preppy & Dre's Story (Triplet)

PREPPY PART ONE

PREPPY PART TWO

PREPPY PART THREE

Up In Smoke (Standalone)

STANDALONES

Jake & Abby's Story

THE DARK LIGHT OF DAY, A KING SERIES PREQUEL

Rage & Nolan's Story

ALL THE RAGE, A KING SERIES SPIN OFF

KEEP IN TOUCH WITH ME!

Facebook Group: www.facebook.com/groups/tmfrazierland

Newsletter:
https://www.subscribepage.com/tmfraziernewslettersignup

Instagram: www.instagram.com/t.m.frazier

Twitter: www.twitter.com/tm_frazier

Facebook: www.facebook.com/tmfrazierbooks